A BAG FOR LIFE

Nick Yapp

Cover Design by Michelle Abadie
www.abadie.co.uk

ISBN 978-1-909122-89-5

Acorn Independent Press

THE CREATIVE TEAM

This book was created by the author and the creative team from Llandrindod High School, who are:

Lauren Bradford	**Toby Colley**	**Meg Dingle**	**Alex Griffiths**
Jack Hughson	**Rhodri Jones**	**Alyssa Lewis-Davies**	
Lucy Mason	**Nathan Millington**	**Leroy Morris**	**Alex Parry**
Tomos Powell	**Imogen Roberts**	**Kathryn Wilson**	

ACKNOWLEDGEMENTS

A Bag for Life would never have been reached completion without the time, help and encouragement of Anwen Nicholls, Head of English at LHS, and without the expertise and commitment of the book's editor Ruby Lescott.

OTHER BOOKS

BY NICK YAPP

Children's Fiction
A Dog's Life
The Shack by the Sea
The Broken Tambourine
Adult Fiction
Tales from the Festival Hall
Non Fiction
My Problem Child
Memoirs of a Maladjusted Teacher
The Bluffer's Guides: Cricket
Teaching
Poetry
The Xenophobe's Guide to the French
Decades (10 volumes) – a photographic history of the 20th
Century

INTRODUCTION

It turned out to be one of those days. Sam never caught up with the clock. Late for school, and from then on everything got out of hand, culminating in a late exit from the school for his lift home from Martin, a lift that he hadn't been looking forward to.

His own bad mood matched Martin's.

The car was parked at the side of the road outside the school. Martin pressed the button to lower his window.

"Get in."

Sam opened the rear passenger door and flung his bag on the back seat.

"Get in!"

Sam hated taking orders from Martin. He had no right to give orders. He wasn't Sam's dad. He wasn't Sam's step-father. He was Mum's boyfriend, that was all. Sam waited until Nessie and Charlie were close enough to exchange high-fives with him.

"See you guys tomorrow," he said.

And they both replied 'Oh, my God, yes' except that Charlie ran the first three words together into a single 'Omygod' and followed it with a long drawn-out 'yesssssssssssss!'

Sam opened the passenger door.

"Tomorrow! Yeah!"

Martin shoved the BMW into gear and the car began to move before Sam was properly in.

"Wait!"

"Shut the door and shut up."

Sam slammed the door as hard as he could.

Martin braked sharply. "Don't you treat my car like that. You're a damn lucky brat, getting a chauffeur-driven ride home."

A car behind sounded its horn and pulled out to pass the BMW. The driver shouted something at Martin. Sam opened the passenger door.

"I'd be happy to walk," he said.

"For Christ's sake!"

Sam slammed the door shut.

"I've told you." Martin began to accelerate.

"Hadn't you better wait till I've got my seat belt fastened?" said Sam, in what he hoped was a smugly annoying voice.

The car was speeding now.

Sam pulled the belt harness over his shoulder. The last thing he remembered afterwards was that there was a smell of liquor in the car... whisky, perhaps... And then there was a crumpling noise and he was thrown forward and back, almost in a single move. The airbag inflated. His knees cracked down on the floor of the car and his left arm smacked into the passenger door.

He felt searing pain and then passed out.

TUESDAY

Morning

Azim woke up as he did every morning now, hoping this was all a bad dream. But no, this was real. He was still in this bad place they called 'The Farm', and still a slave to these bad men.

It was dark. It was cold. He pulled the rough blanket tight up under his chin. He was frightened. The whole Farm was run on fear. Yesterday, one of the boys had been badly beaten for trying to run away, and all the other boys had been made to watch.

How long had he been here? He reached out from the grimy mattress and counted the deep scratches he'd made in the wall with a small knife he'd stolen from the kitchen. One scratch for each day. Fifteen days. How long was it since he had left his home in Afghanistan? He had no idea. It was Uncle's idea. The idea had been to protect Azim, because of what had happened to Azim's brother. One day, more than a year ago, while Azim and his brother had been tending their Uncle's goats on the mountainside, an open truck had approached. Azim's brother had told him to hide behind the rocks, as quick as he could. A cloud of dust had been thrown up as the truck swerved to a stop. Peeping out from behind the rocks, Azim had seen armed men sitting and standing in the back of the truck. They were warriors who had come to take young men away, to train them to kill and fight for the Taliban. It had been quick and terrible. The men had grabbed Azim's brother, and loaded him on to the back of the truck. Then they'd shot three of the goats, slung the carcases on board, and driven off. Azim had run screaming back to the village.

His father and his uncle had talked long into the night. Next day, it had all been decided. Uncle said he would pay for Azim to leave Afghanistan and go to somewhere called UK. Once Azim reached UK, he would have to work hard. There would be a debt that had to be paid off. Moneylenders charged a lot of money for fake passports and the cost of journeys across half the world – in Azim's case, a journey that had started in a mule cart and ended in the back of a big truck.

"Work hard," Uncle had ordered him. "Then the English will be pleased, and they will send money to pay off the debt. And once that is finished, you will grow rich."

The journey had taken months. Sometimes Azim had to remain hidden in a town, in some sort of cheap and grubby hostel, waiting for another truck to take him on the next stage. He had crossed the Middle East, Turkey and the whole of Europe, living for much of the time on biscuits and bad bread. For the last stage, Azim, three other boys, and six men had climbed into the back of a large truck somewhere in France. The three other boys had died; Azim and four men had survived to reach the Farm. And, as soon as they arrived, the men had been taken away to work in the fields, and Azim had been set to work in the kitchens.

He had no idea how many hours a day he'd been working: scrubbing floors, wiping work surfaces, sweeping rooms, cleaning things called 'WCs', and fetching and carrying anything from laundry to things in little boxes called Blue Rays. The work started long before it was light in the morning and ended long after it was dark at night. He was regularly kicked and cuffed, and shouted at in a language he didn't understand. All he'd received in return were two poor meals a day. The man in charge of the Farm, the man they called 'Chief', had made it clear to Azim that this was all he would get until the debt was paid off. That was the deal, but Azim was beginning to have doubts about the whole thing. The boy who had been beaten had told him that, far from borrowing money to get Azim to the UK, the likelihood was that Azim's Uncle had sold him outright into slavery. It happened to girls, it happened to boys. In which case, Azim reckoned that he would work as a slave for the rest of his life and the debt still wouldn't have been paid off.

A kick on the back of one of his legs signalled that it was time for Azim to get to work. He pushed the blanket aside and pulled on his worn brown sweater and threadbare black jeans, then hurried down to the kitchen.

The cook shouted at him. Azim was beginning to recognise a few of the words and guess what they meant – a threat is a threat in any language. He collected a broom, brush and dustpan from a cupboard and started sweeping the floor, making the same promise that he'd made to himself every day for a week now. He would try to escape as soon as he had a chance. If they found him and beat him, he'd wait till he'd recovered from the beating, and then try to escape again. If he did get away, he would hide. Azim had learnt a lot about hiding in the last year.

Night

Twelve hours later, a chance came.

Azim's last chore of the day was to sweep, dust and clean the Farm Office on the ground floor of the main building. Tonight the man they called 'Chief' was working late. He was sitting at his desk, counting what looked like piles of paper money. Each time he reached a certain number of banknotes, he put them in a plastic wallet, then placed the wallet in a bag on the floor at the side of the desk. The bag was like a sports bag, with a zip at the top and two handles. It was made of black and grey canvas. It was not particularly big – as long as Azim's arm and as wide as his young chest.

The counting came to an end. The bag was now full. The Chief zipped it shut and fitted a padlock so that it couldn't be unzipped. Azim kept his head well down, but his eyes and ears were open. He was excited by the thought that he could escape and take the bag with him. There must be enough money in that bag for him to get back to Afghanistan and pay off all Uncle's debts.

The Chief was searching for something, patting his pockets, rummaging through the drawers of his desk. Whatever it was, he didn't find it. He got up, went to the door, and shouted down the corridor, as though he was calling someone.

No one came. There was no answer.

The Chief called again. No answer. No sound of footsteps hurrying to the Office.

Azim risked looking up. Through the Office window he could see one of the Farm trucks backed up to the loading bays. A heavily overweight man, whom Azim guessed might be the driver of the truck, was closing the rear doors. Azim guessed the truck would be pulling out any minute now.

The Chief called a third time.

Azim studied the window. If it could be opened, he could squeeze through it, taking the bag with him. Once outside, he might be able to reach the truck without being seen. It was dark outside, with only a single lamp lighting one corner of the yard.

The fat truck driver had finished closing the doors. He was now locking them. There was no chance of hiding in the back of the truck. That was a pity, but there were other ways. The driver was now out of sight, behind the truck.

The Chief shouted once more, and then stamped out of the Office. This was the moment.

Azim dropped his broom. He grabbed the bag and rushed to the window. It was opened by pulling a catch back and then sliding one half to the side. But the catch was stiff. It wouldn't give. Azim broke his fingernail tearing at the catch. Still it wouldn't open. He picked up the broom and used the handle as a lever to force the catch, then slid the window open.

Azim threw the bag out ahead of him. He made his body as thin as possible and squeezed through the narrow opening, then closed the window behind him, in the hope that it wouldn't be immediately obvious how he had escaped. He picked up the bag. There was still no sign of the truck driver outside, and no sight or sound of the Chief inside.

He knew what to do. One of the other boys had told him of a terrifying ride he'd had, clinging to the underside of a truck to avoid Immigration Control. There was a tiny platform above the wheel arch of these big trucks, where the spare wheel was kept. You rolled yourself up into a ball and jammed your body in the space between the toolkit and the fuel tank. Azim raced across the yard. Was there enough space on the platform for a boy and a bag? There was only one way to find out.

Azim heard the door on the driver's side of the truck slam shut. He shoved the bag onto the ledge by the tank.

He heard the engine start up.

He swung his body up onto the ledge. The bag was safe now. In the next few seconds he'd know if he could be safe, too.

The truck slowly moved off.

Azim stretched out his body as far as it would go, with his feet pressing on the toolkit and his back painfully tight against the fuel tank.

The truck accelerated, and then braked sharply, jolting Azim's body so that he was almost thrown on to the yard. He reached out with both hands and grabbed part of the chassis frame.

The truck accelerated again.

Azim shut his eyes. He told himself to think of nothing else but holding on. The driver couldn't possibly see him. They had left the yard and were now travelling along the road from the Farm in complete darkness. The only light was that shining ahead, from the truck's headlights. Danger would come when they drove through some brightly lit town. Azim thanked Allah for the gift of a worn brown sweater and black threadbare jeans. Only if someone shone a light directly at the side of the truck would he be seen.

The truck roared on into the darkness.

It was dark and cold and frightening under the truck. The roads were wet, and the spray thrown up by the wheels was soaking Azim's clothes. He had kept his body wedged as tight as he could in the space between the fuel tank and the toolkit, but since they'd left the motorway, the road had turned into one long series of sharp bends, each of which threatened to sling him out of his hiding place and chuck him on to the road. If that happened, there was the danger that the rear sets of wheels of the truck's trailer would crush the life out of him. He had no idea how far he'd come, how far he needed to go. The road was bad here, and the truck was bumping up and down like an unbroken pony. The muscles in Azim's arms were aching, his back was sore, his hands were cold, his fingers were stiff, and he knew that he couldn't hold on much longer.

What mattered was the bag clamped between his legs. He risked reaching out a hand to feel it. Good. It was still there. It was safe.

The truck slowed. The brakes screeched. Azim instinctively wanted to put his hands to his ears to shield them from the noise, but the truck was juddering to a halt and he needed both hands to hang on to the chassis. The truck stopped.

Azim now had a choice. Stay on the truck for another two or three hours and risk falling from it while it was belting along, or… or take a chance, get off now, wherever he was, and make a run for it.

Go, he told himself. Now… Go, go, go…

He tumbled on to the road and staggered to his feet. The bag! Where was the bag? There on the road. It had fallen with him. He grabbed it. He had to get out of sight, and the only way to do that was to dodge behind the truck. He prayed to Allah that the driver was looking ahead and not in his wing mirror.

Azim looked about him. He was on a narrow street in some sort of town. There were a few lights in the street, giving a glimpse of how heavily it was raining. The truck had come to a halt at a crossroads, and now began to move slowly forward. As it did so, Azim nipped into a dark alley, away from the street lamps. The truck accelerated. Azim breathed a sigh of relief but his heart didn't stop pounding until he was sure that the truck had driven away. He came out of his hiding place in the dark alley. He had no idea where he was. All he knew was that it was raining, that he was wet and cold, and that he must find somewhere to shelter for the night.

There was no traffic on the roads and no lights in any of the buildings. The only light came from one or two shop windows and the few street lamps that were reflected in the puddles. He was at a crossroads, where a small clock tower would have told him what time it was if he could have read that sort of clock. It was late. He knew that. Any shops or cafés wouldn't be open for hours, which meant there was no chance of food.

The truck had gone straight on. Azim decided not to follow the same route. Nor did he want to turn back to where he'd come from. He'd had enough of what lay behind him. That left him with the choice of turning either left or right. He chose left because it was downhill, which would make walking easier for his cramped and bruised legs. It wasn't long before he heard the sound of rushing water, a sound that reminded him of home in the Afghan Kush during the rainy season.

He came to a bridge where old and empty buildings clustered by a river. There was a rough cinder track leading from the road down towards the buildings. Moving with great care, and listening hard for any sound other than that of the tumbling water, Azim approached the dark buildings.

No one could possibly be living in any of them – no one who wasn't desperate. The headlights of a vehicle heading for the bridge shone through the rain. Had the truck driver turned back? Azim threw himself on the sopping ground. The headlights swept over the bridge and up the hill. Azim got slowly to his feet. He was soaked to the skin, his worn trainers were full of water, and the ragged clothes he stood in were the only ones he had. But the bag was safe.

He looked about him. To his right, less than a stone's throw from the river, was a large brick building. The windows were boarded up and there was a coating of corrugated iron covering one entire wall. He felt his way along that wall, turning at the corner so that he was at the back of the building and hidden from the road. Here, a low wall enclosed a small back yard. Holding the bag tightly, he hauled himself up and over this wall into the yard. Facing him, on the back of the building, there was a door. Azim listened. There was only the sound of the river. He slowly approached the building. The door was padlocked, but looked fragile enough for him to try forcing it.

He heard the sound of another truck approaching. Headlights again gleamed through the darkness. Azim looked about him. There was nowhere to hide. He froze. Was *this* the fat driver's truck? Had he come back to search for the kid with the bag? Would there be other men with him? But the truck crossed the bridge and drove away. Azim tried to reassure himself that he was safe – alone and frightened, but safe.

He dropped the bag and put his shoulder to the door, but he wasn't strong enough to break it. Could he risk trying to kick the door down? He had to. If he didn't find shelter soon, cold and hunger and exhaustion threatened to put an end to his misery. He kicked. The rusty hinges gave way and the door swung back, leaning at an angle, hanging by the padlock. Azim waited to make sure no one had been disturbed by the noise he'd made. Everything was quiet, save for the river rolling on and on. He picked up the bag and went into the building.

There was the smell of dust and dirt and damp. Underfoot, he could feel grit, broken glass and crumbling bits of brick. He moved forward and almost tripped on some rough planks that littered the floor, but his eyes gradually grew used to the dark, and he saw that he was in a small room, empty save for rubbish and litter. There was a doorway to another room, a corridor, and the remains of a staircase leading up. Testing each stair to make sure it would bear his weight, Azim climbed to the upstairs floor. This was drier, less cluttered. There would be rats and spiders in the building, of course, but Azim was used to rats, and he had yet to come across any spider in this little country to match the camel spiders at home… as big as your hand and strong enough to carry away your shoe.

He wondered if he could shelter in this place. Not for long, but for a day or two, while he found some way of stealing food and clothes and, above all, another pair of trainers. Then he remembered that, in the bag there was plenty of money, enough to buy anything he wanted. Like a bicycle. If he had a bicycle, he could ride to the coast, to the sea. And once he got to the sea, he could find a boat and pay the captain to take him on board as a passenger. Almost certainly, the boat wouldn't be headed for home, but at least it might be heading for somewhere nearer home than this awful place. Back home, two of his cousins had bikes, and one of his uncles had a motor scooter. Azim had learnt how to ride it. If he could steal a scooter... No, that was a stupid idea. Stealing something like that would be risky. There would be problems with permits and police and maybe soldiers. A bike would be safer – easier to steal, and with no registration number to be traced.

He found a corner in one of the upstairs rooms where most of the floor was sound, with no missing boards. It would have been better if he'd had the grimy mattress with him, the one he'd slept on back at the Farm, but at least he was free – for the moment.

The chill of the room hit him. He shook violently and then began to shiver. He needed to take off his wet clothes. He needed to find some sort of covering, it didn't matter what – rags, an old blanket, dust sheets, sandbags, anything to wrap round him and keep his body off the floor. He made a quick search of all the rooms in the house. All he could find were some grimy plastic sacks and a piece of mouldy carpet. He had no idea what the sacks had once contained – sand, grain, fertiliser, maybe poisonous chemicals. But the sacks were better than nothing. He arranged some of them in a pile on the floor of the safe corner upstairs.

He undressed, and wrung as much water as possible from his clothes. He spread them out on the floor, hoping they would dry at least a little in what was left of the night. He wrapped the bit of carpet round his shaking body and lay down on the pile of plastic sacks, pulling more sacks on top of him. He hooked one arm through the handles of the bag so that no one could take it from him without waking him up. There was money there, lots of it, and tomorrow he would see if it was possible to spend some of it safely. There was trouble ahead, lots of it. There would be trouble for his family back home, for Uncle especially. But it was Uncle who had sent him here, had borrowed money to sell him into virtual slavery. For that, Uncle deserved trouble, but Azim knew that, most of all, trouble would be headed his way. The Chief at the Farm would send people to look for the bag. By now, there might be Hunters everywhere, searching for him, looking for the bag. But they wouldn't be looking here. Nobody knew he was here. Surely? Nobody.

He was exhausted, but not ready to collapse. He wanted to sleep but neither his body nor his mind would let him. His body was painfully uncomfortable – cold, damp, lying on hard boards and wrapped in rough materials. His mind had not yet come to terms with the events of the last forty-eight hours. It wanted to relive the scenes of the brutal beating of the boy who'd tried to run away. It demanded replays of the risk he had run in snatching the bag and fleeing from the Farm. It insisted on showing him the worst moments on the terrible journey in the underbelly of the truck: the spray from the road stinging his face; the braking, the accelerating, and the cornering of the truck pressing his body against bone-crunching metal or, more frighteningly, against nothing at all, so that time and again Azim feared he would be hurled into oblivion, and then under the wheels of traffic heading in the opposite direction.

If only he had someone to talk to, to offer him sympathy, understanding, anything to bring mental relief. If only there had been something to bring bodily comfort. But there was nothing… nothing but the cold, wet, smelly room with its bare hardness and its atmosphere of emptiness and ruin.

*

The truck that had brought Azim to Rhayader had reached its destination. From a warehouse on the edge of Aberystwyth, the driver was making a call to the Farm on his mobile. He was reporting something odd that had happened on his journey.

"… a kid dropped out from under my truck… came from nowhere… must have been one of your kids… small, thin, wiry… carrying a bag… like a sports bag… I've no idea what colour, it was too dark… no, I don't know exactly where it happened… one of those little Welsh towns… Llan-something or other I expect. Might have been a place called Ryder, or something… Of course I didn't bloody turn the truck round and go back for him. It would take half an hour to do that on these bloody Welsh roads… What do you expect me to do? Run after him? I'm not built for that… You told me the stuff had to be in Aberystwyth before midnight… If you want the kid back, you'll have to send someone to look for him… Anywhere on the A 470 or the A44… I know it's a bloody big area, but if you want that bag back…"

WEDNESDAY

Morning

Azim woke several times in the night. Each time, he woke
to fear. More than once, he woke in an attempt to escape
from the same bad dream; that he was being pursued by
the Truck Driver and other hunters, and they were gaining
on him. Twice he woke because he felt he was freezing to
death. And, each time he woke, it was ages before his mind
relaxed enough for exhaustion to send him back to sleep.
Hunger finally woke him and made him decide not to try
going back to sleep. He had had nothing to eat for twenty-
four hours. Only his courage had enabled him to survive
the last dreadful weeks. It did not fail him now, but helped
him to see that, though he was cold and hungry here in this
ruin of a house, he was at least free to move about. It was
time to explore his new surroundings and find something
to eat. Whatever the danger, he had to find a shop or a store
or a café, somewhere that would sell him food, before his
body collapsed. He had seen people die from hunger back
home, and when the end came, it came quickly, suddenly,
silently, relentlessly.

Wrapped in the bit of carpet, he staggered to his feet, his body stiff with cold. He felt his clothes. They were still damp. He'd need to light a fire to dry them, but a fire would attract attention, and that was dangerous. It would be better to put his clothes on and hope the warmth of his body would eventually make them dry.

He picked up the canvas bag. He tugged at the zip. It didn't move. The strong padlock fastening it meant he would have to cut his way into the bag. Not easy. The canvas was thick, and he had left the little knife he had stolen back at the Farm. He looked about him. No sharp piece of metal, but plenty of broken glass, on the floor by a boarded-up window. He selected the biggest shard and attacked the bag, stabbing it repeatedly. That was useless. All he did was cut his hand. He tore the bottom off his T-shirt and wrapped it round the cut.

Maybe he should use the shard like a knife. He began slicing along one of the seams of the bag. It was hard work, but after a few minutes he had cut a small slit in the bag. He pushed the tip of the shard through the slit. That was better. Half sawing and half slashing, he made an opening big enough to push his hand through.

He could feel the plastic wallets. He pulled out a couple. The first was full of what looked like banknotes with '20' on them; the second wallet had notes with '50' on them. He cut open the 50 package, and counted the notes… five… ten… fifteen… thirty… fifty…   There must have been a hundred of 50 notes in this wallet. And there were lots of wallets in the bag.

He guessed he had plenty of money to buy food. Should he take a 50 note or a 20 note? A 20 note might not be enough for breakfast. It would be safer to take a 50. People in shops and stores might be suspicious of a young foreigner who spoke almost no English trying to buy a sandwich with only a 20 note. They'd send for the police or the soldiers, and they would arrest him because he had no papers and no passport. His passport – the fake one that had cost Uncle so much money – was locked in the safe back in the Farm Office. He'd never see that again. His only hope was to keep moving, to make his way to the sea. Other boys at the Farm had told him the only possible way to escape from the UK was by boat. Airports had many armed men to check documents and tickets and luggage. It was impossible to get away by plane. But if you could find a port with a big ship, it was always possible to find some way of getting on board. If rats could do it, so could a smart boy. Azim didn't feel smart, but he was desperate. Sooner or later, he must get to the sea and stowaway on a big ship, to get to a country where the men sent to hunt him down would never find him.

But he had no idea where the sea was. He'd never seen a map of this country that they called UK. He had no idea what shape it was. He knew it was a small country, obviously much smaller than his homeland, because he'd noticed on last night's terrifying ride how close everything was packed together – the houses, the roads, the trees, even the filling stations.

But whereabouts was he in this small country? Was he anywhere near the sea? The river that rushed past the empty house where he was hiding must lead to the sea. But here it was only little, not much wider than a mountain stream. Where it flowed into the sea might be hundreds of miles away. He couldn't walk hundreds of miles without help, advice, friends, and food. Especially food. He had to get food now, before he starved to death.

The weather was better today. The rain had stopped. There was blue sky, but he couldn't risk drying his clothes outside. He'd have to keep wearing them while they were still damp. Maybe he could risk going to one of the shops he'd passed the night he arrived, when he had crept through the town after dropping from the truck. Maybe he'd find a shop that sold bread, biscuits, cans of food with rings on their lids that you could pull open… and matches, to light a fire. He thought again. No, that was a stupid idea. People would see the smoke and the flames, and they'd come looking to see where the fire was. He'd better stick to buying only ready-cooked food, and water. He needed water most of all. He'd tried drinking a little of the river water last night, but it tasted bad. When Azim had been a very small boy, his father had taught him how to recognise the taste and the smell of bad water. No… he wouldn't take any risks. Instead, he would buy water in bottles… and food already cooked.

Azim shivered again. He must get his heart pumping and the blood flowing through his veins. He did some running on the spot and some arm exercises. That was better. What he needed was lots of exercise. There was a path that ran alongside the river, away from the town. That should be safe. It didn't look much used. Hopefully, it would mean that he could approach the town from a different angle. And on the way back, he'd make sure that no one was following him, that no one could discover where he was living. To survive he had to think like an animal. He had to hide his tracks. He had to double back, like a hunted fox. He had to use water like a deer, so that dogs couldn't track him. He had to keep his scent downwind from any of the Hunters.

Food, water, and a pair of trainers. With a new pair of trainers, life would be really good. And some sort of coat or a sheepskin. That would be best of all, because he could wear it and sleep beneath it. He would buy a sheepskin like the ones all his cousins had at home. And a knife. He would need a knife to cut up food, maybe to kill for food... and maybe for his own protection. He still hoped that he was in no danger in this town, but he'd learned in his short life that with a weapon, you were strong; without one you were weak.

All the things he needed would cost money. He must take great care of the bag. It should be safe to hide it under the floor of this room. Many of the boards were rotten. It took little time to stamp a few into pieces. When he had made a big enough hole in the floor, he lay down and stretched his arm under the boards that remained. That would do. That was big enough. The bag should be safe there. He put all the wallets back in the bag, keeping only two 50 notes for his shopping. He was about to cram the bag in the space under the floorboards, when he saw the shard of glass he'd used to open the bag. He might need that. Until he bought a knife it was the only weapon available. He had no sheath to keep it in, but there was a side pocket to the bag. When the time came to leave, he would put the shard in there. For the moment, the bag and the money were safe. It was time to go.

Azim left the old empty building, crossed the little yard, climbed over the low wall, and half-walked, half-limped up the gentle climb into the town. Running had warmed him, but he was still nervous. As he walked, he looked about him. More than enough time had passed since he had dropped from the truck for the Hunters to pick up his trail. He saw danger as most likely to come from the street. There were many cars travelling through this town and, what scared him most, a whole lot of trucks – many of them frighteningly like the one that had brought him here from the Farm. The town itself seemed peaceful enough. There was no one firing a gun, no bombs going off, and no robberies in progress. And the town offered many good places where a young lad on the run could hide. There were narrow alleys leading off each street, low walls to duck behind, and many more empty buildings.

He still had to be on his guard. Have courage, he told himself. The escape from the Farm had been hours and hours ago. Like the money in the bag under the floor at his hideout, he was safe now, and it was time to concentrate on what really mattered – getting hold of the things he needed.

It had been weeks since he had tasted fresh fruit and vegetables. At the Farm, the two meals a day had come from boxes and packets and plastic bags – burgers or chicken pieces or sausages, but always chips. His mother would have been so angry if she had known what rubbish he had been eating since he came to UK. But in this town there was food that looked good. He saw oranges and grapes, tomatoes and peppers in a shop window. He was tempted to walk in and buy some, but there were no prices on the oranges or the grapes, and perhaps that meant they cost enormous sums of money.

He moved on to the next shop. It was a café. He knew that because people were sitting at little tables, drinking from white cups and eating from white plates. And, in the window, there were little cakes with what looked like honey and pistachios on the top. He would start here. Maybe it was not a dangerous place, because most of the people in it looked very old. He plucked up his courage, and pushed the door open. He could smell coffee, real coffee, not the powdered coffee that he and the other boys had to make for the workers at the Farm. He went up to the counter. A man and woman were giving money to a grey-haired woman behind the counter.

Azim watched what they did, so that he would know what to do when his turn came to buy something, and he wouldn't make a fool of himself. The man gave the grey-haired woman a piece of paper money. She gave him coins in return. The man put most of the coins in his pocket but dropped one into a glass jar on the counter.

It was Azim's turn. He pointed to the little cakes in the glass cabinet and raised four fingers.

The grey-haired woman smiled, but shook her head. She said something to him. Azim couldn't understand a word. He held up his four fingers and pointed again.

"Please," he said.

The woman looked puzzled. Again she spoke to him. He shook his head. She pointed to the cakes, and then pointed to the tables, raising her eyebrows as though she was asking a question. Azim frowned.

The woman pointed to the little cakes, and then pointed outside.

Azim nodded. "Please, yes," he said. He understood. She wanted to know if he wanted to eat his cakes inside or outside. He pointed outside. "Please, yes, for me," he said.

The woman nodded. She put four sugar coated cakes in a paper bag and said something else to him. He assumed she was asking for money. He handed her one of his 50 notes. She looked very surprised, held the note up to the light, then called into the room behind her.

A man appeared. He was clearly important, for he had a grey beard and fine-looking spectacles with golden rims. Azim took him to be one of the town elders. The woman passed the note to the elder and said something. The elder looked closely, but not unkindly at Azim. He said something. Azim shook his head and showed his empty hands. The elder said something to the woman.

Azim realised that everyone in the café had stopped eating and stopped talking, and that all eyes were on him.

He wanted to run, but knew that would make matters worse. The police or the soldiers would be called, with everyone suspecting that he was a common thief. He had to stay and see this through.

The elder and the grey-haired woman spoke to each other some more. Then the village elder shrugged his shoulders, turned to Azim and smiled. "OK," he said, and he nodded.

It was going to be all right. The woman placed the 50 note in the same drawer that she'd used for the other man's money. She took coins and notes out of the drawer, and offered them to Azim, together with the paper bag of cakes. He took the cakes in his good hand, and held out the hand wrapped in the bit of his T-shirt for the notes and coins.

The woman gasped and said something. Azim shook his head. She spoke again.

"OK. OK... OK," he said, and put the change in his pocket. Perhaps she was frightened by the bloodstain on the bit of T-shirt.

She said something else. He nodded and tried to smile. It was time to get out, quickly. He was about to leave the café, when he remembered that he must do as the other man had done. He took all the coins he had just been given, and dropped them in the glass jar on the counter. He had nowhere else to put them. There were holes in every pocket of his threadbare jeans. He held the notes tightly in his fist.

There... he was out of the café. He had done his first piece of shopping, successfully, for he hadn't been arrested. After walking a few steps, he turned round. No, there was no one following him. He crammed one of the little cakes into his mouth. It tasted good. He gobbled two more of the cakes. Now he must buy the other things he needed. There was a shop that sold many things, on the other side of the street. He took great care crossing the road, making sure there were no trucks in sight. He would go into the shop and say 'yes, please, for me' again, and point, to get all he needed.

But before he reached the shop that sold everything, he saw an impressive double-fronted shop with big windows. In the windows were pictures of food – pizzas and kebabs, and brown curly, crusty looking things with chips beside them. He was unable to read any of the signs, price lists, and menus posted in the windows. But through them, he could see the gleaming black-and-white tiles on the walls, and the magnificently clean speckled white tiles on the floor. At the back of the room was a high counter. Azim could see a man bending down, as though he was scrubbing the floor. Azim went inside. It was deliciously warm, and there was a smell of cooking oil.

The man stood up and turned round. His skin was the same colour as Azim's. They both stared at each other, as though neither of them had ever seen anyone with skin that colour before. Azim was the first to recover from the shock. It seemed good that the man looked as though he came from Azim's part of the world. That didn't mean that the man would be a friend, but there might be a chance that he spoke Azim's language.

"*Subha-ba-khair.*"

"*Se-pehar bakhair.*" The man pointed to his watch.

Azim felt stupid. Of course, it was afternoon.

There was a long silence. It looked to Azim as though the man was not pleased to see him. He was scared by the man's reaction. He looked anxiously around him, until his eyes fixed on the food counter.

"You want food?" said the man. "I am not ready for customers."

Azim shook his head. "*Pani*, please, for me," he said.

The man took a glass from the shelf behind him, filled it from the tap at the sink, and handed it to Azim. He drank the water quickly, then held out the empty glass and asked for more. "*Khush kama*," he said.

The man smiled nervously, nodded, and refilled the glass. While Azim drank the second glass, the man leaned on the counter, studying him closely. Azim sensed there was a problem. His clothes were filthy, his T-shirt was torn, and his shoes were falling to bits. On top of that, there was the rough bandage on his hand, as though he'd been in some knife fight.

Azim finished drinking the second glass, and got ready to run from the Shop of Chips before the man called the police, or grabbed hold of him and took him prisoner.

Instead, the man pointed to himself. "Saqui," he said.

Azim gave a little sigh of relief, and pointed at himself. "Azim," he said.

They shook hands. It was Azim's turn to smile nervously. As far as he could remember, it was the first time he'd smiled since he'd come to this land. It was far too soon to be sure, but perhaps he had found a friend. Perhaps he would be safe. Perhaps he would not have to keep running and hiding… just for a little while. He felt in his pocket and pulled out some of the notes he had got from the cake shop lady. A 20 note should be enough to pay for the two glasses of water. He placed one on the counter and pushed it towards the man called Saqui.

The man looked surprised, and that look scared Azim. He pushed the note nearer the man.

"Yes, please, for me," he said.

"No, no, no," said the man. "No!"

Azim became more frightened. It sounded as though he had made the man angry. But the man was smiling.

"You are my guest," he said.

That was all right. Azim knew about hospitality, and how you would never take money from someone who was a guest in your house.

"You live here?"

The Saqui man said no, he didn't live in the shop that sold pizzas and burgers and chips. He lived nearby.

"Where do you live?" said the Saqui man.

Azim began to feel more fear. If he told the Saqui man that he lived in the derelict house, perhaps the Saqui man would have to tell the police. Azim was conscious that he had no right to live even in a derelict house.

Saqui looked at the state of Azim's clothes. The lad clearly had no one looking after him. He must be living on his own. It was possible he had nowhere to live.

"Do you have somewhere to live? Yes? No?"

The man took a step towards him. Azim backed away.

"... Don't be frightened..."

Azim backed further away.

"I won't hurt you..."

Azim backed further away.

"I won't hurt you..."

Azim fled from the Shop of Chips, and didn't stop running until he reached the empty building where he'd spent the night. He must find somewhere to buy a knife very quickly.

Afternoon

After the scare with the man called Saqui, Azim went into hiding. He now saw the empty house down by the river as home, a wretched home but better than other places he had slept in over the last year. Here he could guard the bag and the money. Venturing out would have to wait until it grew dark. Then he would risk sneaking up the road to a little shop that sold food. That was where he wanted to go. He could take the long way round, to and from the shop – up one of the back streets and down past the ruined castle, so that he always approached the empty house from the rear.

He had money. Lots of money. Enough to buy whatever he wanted. What he didn't have was any sort of friend. Not since he left home had there been anyone to laugh with, to fool around with, to trust. He'd been in this town only a couple of days, and all the people he had met in that time he now had to avoid. Added to them, were the people he hadn't yet met and didn't want to: police and soldiers and Immigration Officers; and the hunters that he was sure couldn't be far away. He wasn't locked up any more, but the empty house was a like a cold and uncomfortable jail. He wanted fresh air, the sun on his back, and the open road. He told himself to stay where he was, not to go out. But as soon as possible he would have to get away, to keep moving.

And moving this time would be different from the way he had escaped from the Farm. He would plan this getaway. There were hills to the west of the town. He had seen them. They were not as big as the mountains at home, but they were wild and open, and they offered freedom. That was where he would go. He would take to the hills, and leave the worries and dangers of the town behind him. It would be cold in the hills. Azim knew about cold. He knew it killed like hunger – every bit as silently and suddenly. He still had no sheepskin and no blanket. When he went into the hills, he would need to take matches. There would be little to burn in the hills, but there might be old wood, dry wood, and old parched grass. And it was unlikely that anyone would be searching for him there. It was possible that he would find sheep and goats up there, feeding on the hills. If he had a knife, he could kill a sheep. His brother had shown him how to do that long before the Taliban took him away to teach him how to kill two-legged creatures. With a knife and a fire, Azim told himself, he could have roast meat. Man, that *would* be good.

But he still had no knife, only the shard of glass, and he had no means of making fire. If he had matches, pine wood was good for fires. It was full of oil. Dead wood might be better. There might be nowhere to shelter for the night. There would surely be nowhere to buy the food he needed. He must lay in stores: bread, biscuits, perhaps some tins of beans with ring pull tops, dried fruit, nuts…

But how much room was there in the bag for all this food?

He thought of getting rid of some of the money, but rejected the idea. He had to keep all the money. He must take it all across the world and present it to Uncle to pay off the debt. Once that was done, he would be truly free. He would live once more in the high hills, and look after his goats. How wonderful that would be.

He was surprised to find how tired he still was. The overnight journey under the lorry had been terrifying and exhausting. He would rest now, then he would buy the things he needed for his journey. Azim curled up on the floor of the deserted house and slept. When he woke up, he sensed that much time had passed, but he didn't know how much. Perhaps a long time, for now he was hungry again. It was still light. He knew it would be risky, but he had to leave his hideout and go shopping.

It would be safer to keep to the back streets. He passed houses and what looked like some sort of drinking room. There were men in it, women too. This was a strange land. He moved on. He found a different food store and bought three sandwiches, a big bottle of water and some apples.

The young woman in the store placed everything in a plastic bag. This was good. He put his handful of money into the bag. He walked until he came to an open space where many cars were parked. No one would notice if he sat on the ground and ate his sandwiches behind one of the cars. He ate them quickly and threw the empty wrappers under one of the cars. Now for the trainers, a knife and a sheepskin. And perhaps a cigarette lighter that he could use to make fire. Back home, Uncle used a huge lighter to make fire. Uncle called it his Zippo.

Azim got to his feet. He walked on for a hundred more paces, and reached a shop that looked promising. In the windows were saucepans, plastic bowls, hammers, rucksacks, waterproof capes, saws, dog leads and broom handles – and, there, in the very corner of the window, knives of various sizes, all with wooden handles and sharp pointed blades.

He pushed the shop door and went in. Behind the counter was a white-haired woman. She smiled at him. He smiled back. Everyone smiled in this town. She spoke to him but in UK language that he could not understand. He would have to show her what he wanted. He pointed to the corner of the window where the knives were.

The woman looked concerned. She spoke again, and looked at him as though he was supposed to say something back. All he could do was point again at the knives and repeat his mantra: "Yes, please, for me."

As soon as it was clear that Azim was determined to buy a knife, the woman stopped smiling. She looked worried.

Azim rummaged in his plastic bag until he found a 50 note. He held it out and pointed again at the knife. The look of worry on the woman's face changed to one of alarm. She shook her head and said something else. It was obvious that she wasn't going to sell him the knife.

Azim's eyes flicked round the inside of the shop. On one shelf, next to the rucksacks, there were pairs of boots, strong boots, walking boots, the sort of boots that would be good for climbing the high hills, good for someone on the run.

It took a long time, and Azim had to try on several boots before he found a pair that was comfortable. Again he held out a 50 note. The woman smiled, took the note and gave him a small coin. Again he pointed to the knives. Again she shook her head, but she was smiling now. Azim accepted that he could not buy the knife on his own. He would need someone's help. It would have to be the man called Saqui because there was no one else who could speak his language.

He sat on the floor of the shop and fastened the laces on his new boots. He held out his old shoes. The woman pulled a face and said something. Then she smiled again and took them, holding them by the tips of her fingers.

She said something that might have been a polite 'thank you', or might have been a joke, though she wasn't smiling like she had been when he'd first entered the shop.

"Thank you, please, for me," he said.

Azim left the shop, stamping his feet in his new boots. They were fine boots. In these boots, he could walk up the high hills and down the other side, all the way to the sea. But first, he would go back to the empty house, where he and the bag would be safe. Later, much later, he would find the courage to go to the Shop of Chips and make peace with the man he wanted to be his friend, the man called Saqui.

Azim didn't know what made him think that he was being followed, but as he walked down the street he became aware of a silver coloured car keeping pace with him on the other side of the road. Why would it do that? There was little traffic on the road, no reason why a car should crawl along at walking pace. He began to panic. A primitive fear gripped him. He sensed that, inside the car, there were people… people who might be looking for him… hunters…

He took off down West Street as fast as his stiff new boots would let him. A couple of times he risked glancing back over his shoulder. The silver car was still keeping pace with him. There was no way he could outrun it if he stuck to the pavement, but the cinder track that led down past the old house wasn't far away, and it was all downhill. It was an almighty risk to take, but it was the only way out. Azim swerved across the road and on to the cinder track. He glanced back. The car wanted to follow him, but had to wait for traffic coming in the opposite direction to pass before it could make the turn on to the track.

There was the empty house, his hideout. No. He mustn't go in there. He had to lead the hunters away from where the bag was hidden, like a bird would lead predators away from the nest of eggs. The big bottle of water in the plastic bag bashed against his leg. He chucked it away, and sprinted across the waste ground between the house and the river. It was tough going, dodging through the rubble and between piles of stones. Ahead was the footbridge over the river. Should he take that, or make for the meadow straight ahead? No, not the meadow. That was all open ground, with nowhere to hide. On the other side of the footbridge there were trees, bushes, thick undergrowth.

As he rushed across the bridge, he looked back. He could see only one hunter. The man was on one knee, fifty paces or more away. He could have been tying a shoelace, but he could also have been preparing to shoot. Azim didn't wait to see if the man then took up the shooting position – both arms stretched in front of him and both hands grasped together to take aim. Azim knew about guns. As a child, he had seen men take up the shooting position back home. During the long journey across the world he and the other boys had regularly been threatened by men with guns.

He knew better than to wait for the crack of the gun or to feel the pain of a bullet entering his leg, his arm, his body. Or to feel nothing because the bullet had torn his brain away. He threw himself forward, diving into the undergrowth. There was no crack of a gun being fired, no sudden pain. The Hunter hadn't fired.

Azim reached the cover of the trees. Maybe he was safe here. But *why* hadn't the hunter fired?

*

The hunter's name was Kyle, and he hadn't fired because this was far too public a place. Any old pensioner walking a dog might have turned up and seen what was going on. Then Kyle would have had to kill the pensioner, and maybe the dog. The whole thing would have got out of hand, when what was wanted was a quick neat job. The Chief at the Farm had been insistent on that point.

"Find the Kid and the bag," the Chief had said. "I want that bag back with the money in it. And I want the Kid neatly killed. I don't care how, but I don't want a mess. And when you've killed the brat, I want pictures… photos we can show as a warning to others."

Then there was the handicap of his assistant. The Chief had insisted that young Coleson – a pain in the arse if ever there was one – should accompany Kyle on this mission. The Chief had said he wanted Coleson to learn the business. Kyle knew better. Coleson was there solely to keep an eye on him and make sure he didn't do a runner with the money once the Scumbag Kid was dead. The Chief had blabbed on and on, about how Kyle could coach Coleson until he was ready to take over as the Farm's resident hitman. Kyle disapproved. Any contract killing was better in the hands of a freelance killer. Freelance hitmen were cheaper and more experienced. Before Kyle had become a hired assassin, the Army had spent a lot of time and money teaching him how to kill, and he'd done his share of killing. Then came cuts in the Defence Budget. Kyle was chucked out on to Civvie Street. He'd found new killing fields in Central Africa, as a mercenary, but that had come to an end after the massacre that still haunted him.

But the other reason why Kyle hadn't fired from the bridge was because a dead Scumbag Kid wouldn't be able to lead him and Coleson to the bag of money.

The two hunters had been in Rhayader for two hours. The lorry driver had put the Chief on the trail of the runaway Scumbag Kid, but spotting the Kid so quickly had been an immense piece of luck. Even so, they'd found him almost too early. One lesson the Army had taught him was that you never commit yourself to action without an escape strategy, without knowing how to tidy up and get the hell out. In this case, that meant knowing how and where to dispose of the Kid's body. On the drive from Bristol, Coleson had jabbered about a reservoir just a few miles from Rhayader. He'd suggested that was where they should dump the Kid's corpse.

It wasn't a bad idea, and as soon as Kyle and Coleson had checked in at an old pub in the main street, they'd taken a ride out to examine the reservoir.

Kyle's military experience had given him some knowledge of what happened to dead bodies that were left to rot. He knew that if you disposed of them in water, you had to make sure that the body was weighted down, otherwise it would reappear on the surface of the water after a few days.

"We'd have to fill the Kid's pockets with stones, so that his body sinks to the bottom. It decomposes. The good thing is that fish feed off it, especially the face."

Coleson wanted to know why that was good.

"Because it makes it bloody near impossible for anyone to identify the body."

The return trip to Rhayader had been made in silence. Not until they were driving over the river, towards the pub, had Kyle opened his mouth. He'd stopped the car opposite a little supermarket and told Coleson to get out and buy some cans of beer. Coleson had wanted to know what was wrong with the beer in the pub. Kyle had sighed, as though he didn't want to lose his temper but was being forced to.

"You fancy a night in the bar with the locals, do you? Chatting with them about what's brought you to Rhayader, and what we do for a living?"

Coleson had got out of the car and gone to do as he was told.

And then Kyle spotted the Kid, and made a rapid three-point turn, to the fury of other drivers. He drove slowly down the street, keeping just a little behind the Kid – also to the fury of other drivers.

But the Kid was smart. He must have sensed that he was being followed. Near the bottom of the hill, just before the bridge over the river, the Kid shot across the road and legged it down some side path. In the Merc, Kyle sat and swore, held up from making a right by bloody traffic coming the other way. He watched the Kid sprint past a cluster of what looked like empty buildings.

"Come on, come on, you bastards! Let me through."

At last he made the turn. Kyle accelerated past the old houses, but the track came to an end. The Merc could go no further. He braked sharply, snatched his handgun from under the dashboard, and set off on foot.

The clouds were thick and low. Visibility was poor. Kyle had difficulty making out the Kid, running over some kind of footbridge. Kyle took careful aim at the Kid's legs. All he wanted to do was to bring the Kid down. He took first pressure on the trigger, but then his finger froze. This wasn't supposed to be his hit.

"Shit."

This was a lousy commission, nursing a total novice in the art of execution. And the pay was miserable. Five thousand quid. A few years ago, Kyle would have insisted on ten grand minimum. But the market was slow these days. Back in London you could get a killer who'd be happy to pick up a contract killing for less than a thousand. This was a bad time for the profession.

Kyle wiped the sweat from his forehead, and stood up. There was no point in kneeling or crouching any longer. As he looked around, checking that no one had witnessed this little scene, he realised that his body was shaking. That was a bad sign. That wasn't professional; that was stupid. He kept telling himself that he'd been right not to risk a shot; a dead Kid without the money was of no use. He had been right not to fire. He had no doubt about that. But he did have other doubts, and he knew that he was failing in his attempts to convince himself that he'd done the right thing. It had gone against his nature not to fire.

Kyle sat in the Mercedes for a long time. He wouldn't let it happen – he wouldn't go soft. The Scumbag Kid must die, but Coleson wouldn't be up to doing the business. The Chief would get what he wanted. But Jesus, what a mess this could turn out to be. Kyle wanted a drink, but knew he wasn't supposed to have one – not with these new pills the Doc had given him. He slowly turned the car round.

*

As he did so, Gwynedd Hughes came marching up the hill. She was in a good mood, because she was on her way to meet her best mate, dear lovely Sam Harper. Their friendship had come to a painful end when Sam had moved to Bristol with his Mum eighteen months ago. But Sam was going to spend the rest of half term in Rhayader, and Gwynedd was going to fan flames of love with all her might. She hadn't replied to his latest texts and e-mails because he hadn't replied to dozens of hers. She suspected that he thought she'd be on the platform at Llandrindod when his train got in. Well, let him think that. Let him know what it was like to be disappointed. He could wonder where she was all the way on the bus from Llandrindod to Rhayader. Do him good. Teach him a lesson. She pictured the scene of their meeting, in the car park up the road. There'd be…

She wasn't looking where she was going. She stepped off the pavement, causing a car to have to brake sharply. From the silver-grey car came a long and loud blast on the horn that made Gwynedd jump. She gave the driver her favourite two-fingered salute.

"Piss off!" she called out, and walked on, thinking no more about it.

The car was a posh sort of car, a Mercedes, with those dark side windows that allowed those inside to see out, but denied outsiders the chance of seeing in. She couldn't see who was driving or how many passengers there were, but she was so happy, she didn't care who was inside. The car could have been full of robots or Creatures from Mars for all she cared. The car started up again with another angry blast on the horn. In return, she gave the driver another salute, then shouted.

"*Piss off!*"

The car stopped abruptly, and she prepared herself for a row with the driver, but decided she was too happy to start a shouting match with some BOF who was simply passing through the town. Whoever or whatever were inside, she gave them another gesture and then a friendly wave, with the hope that they'd see that in the car's mirrors.

Kyle watched the black girl in the driving mirror. He hadn't noticed many coloureds in this town, and it shouldn't be difficult to spot this one again. As soon as they'd done with the Scumbag Kid, he'd deal with the black girl. Kyle looked forward to that.

*

They'd told Sam Harper at the Hospital in Bristol that physiotherapy could start as soon as the plaster was off his arm. That was great, but then they'd told him that he'd have to keep the plaster on for at least three weeks. Sam had already discovered having his arm in plaster was a physical inconvenience and a mental pain. It meant he needed help opening doors when he was carrying something, and when he was cutting up food, and especially when he was dressing and undressing. He could manage pants, socks, T shirts, trousers and even sweaters on his own. It was shoes and coats that needed two arms, or two hands. Becky was happy to help him; Sam wasn't happy to be helped. He *really* didn't want his mum managing him first thing in the morning and last thing at night.

More than ever before in his life he wanted to prove to himself that he could manage on his own, but today there seemed to be a conspiracy to prove him wrong. He been cooped up in three... three!... slow-moving trains ever since leaving Bristol. Becky had made a fuss at and between every station. The worst had been when they changed trains. Newport wasn't so bad. There'd been only a five minute wait between trains, and all he and Becky had had to do was wait on the same platform. But at Swansea, the wait between trains had been more than half an hour.

Becky had gone through what Martin called her 'Mother Hen Performance'- running up and down the platform, looking for what she called 'a responsible adult'. This was pointless. All the info they needed was available online. He could get it up on his phone right now: times and destinations, and how long they'd have to wait between trains. It made him very angry that Becky didn't listen to him. He wished there was someone he could talk to about his anger. It was at times like these that Sam most felt that hole in his life that had opened up when Dad died. That was seven years ago. It was only natural that Becky had fussed back then. But those days were over, because he was no longer a kid.

He leaned back in the uncomfortable train seat and thought about his friendship with Gwynedd. Then he thought about the wider circle of all his friends, not that it was really wide now, or ever had been. He and Gwynedd had started as playmates – two youngsters who lived near each other, went to the same school, and somehow rubbed along together. That had been Gwynedd's doing. She had taken him over when he first came to Wales. She had been the one to start everything: a race round the park, or through the streets, or up one of the steep hills that overlooked the town; a raid on one of the shops, where it had been his job to distract the shopkeeper while she slipped a Mars bar into her pocket; an attempt to catch fish from the river with a piece of curtain net and two bamboo sticks pinched from her Grandad's garden. And, once this pattern had been established, somehow there was little room for other friends, other playmates.

Over the next five years, the friendship had grown. Neither had a brother or sister, and they only had one parent between them – Becky – so they used to spend a lot of time together. Gwynedd talked a lot without thinking; Sam thought a lot without talking. But still the friendship grew. They became partners rather than playmates. There had been teasing at school – 'you love her, don't you… yes, you do. You love her'. Sam had never allowed himself to respond to these taunts. Gwynedd had often clenched her fists, threatened, and sometimes thumped the teaser.

All this had come to an end when Sam and his Mum left Wales and moved to Bristol. In this new environment and his new school, Sam had made new friendships, mainly with girls. But because none of them matched Gwynedd – laugh for laugh, smack for smack, dare for dare, he had wondered why this was. Maybe it was because he had no dad, maybe because of Gwynedd's early influence, maybe because girls could not be his rivals in the world of sport that played such a big part in Bristol school life.

He wondered if it worked the other way with Gwynedd. Since he'd left Wales, had she found new friends among teenage boys? In the old days she'd behaved as though girls were one step behind teachers as her natural enemies. Sam remembered the almost daily rows and fights between Gwynedd and Mollie Pryce. He wondered if that had changed. It was now over eighteen months since the move to Bristol. Gwynedd could have a regular boyfriend by now. There'd been no mention of such a thing in any of her emails, but that didn't mean there wasn't one. Once or twice in the old days, she'd sort of flirted with Saqui, but maybe that was only because the two of them were almost the only non-whites in Rhayader. Had that been something that mattered?

He suddenly realised that this line of thought was making him feel like a lost little boy. Ridiculous.

He'd emailed Gwynedd a week ago. He hadn't gone into details. He hadn't put in anything about leaving Bristol. He just wanted her to know that he and Becky were coming for a half-term break. He'd made no mention of the row with Martin and the accident and his busted arm. He wanted to deliver the big surprise about coming back to live in Rhayader face to face, to cop what he anticipated would be Gwynedd's delighted reaction. But she hadn't replied. He emailed her again last night, letting her know exactly when he would be arriving at Llandrindod Wells Station, and ending with the threat that she'd 'better be there' to greet him. And again, there'd been no reply.

It didn't make any sense. She was usually much better at responding to emails than he was.

Ten days ago she'd sent one to him saying that it was the first email she'd written on her new phone. It was a crazy email, full of news about school and local gossip and how she was earning good money working at the Chippie. Sam hadn't replied, because that was when he'd had the accident and Becky had taken his phone away because she thought he wouldn't be allowed to use it in hospital – another typical example of Becky's fussing.

The train stopped. Sam looked out of the window. They were at Builth Road. Not far to Llandrindod now. The train pulled out, and there, lit by a warm autumn sun, were the mountains at the heart of Wales – black and green, russet and gold. According to Mr Richards, the teacher that Sam and Gwynedd had shared back in their Junior School days, these were the oldest mountains in the world. As a boy, he had grown up in the shadow of these mountains, and for the last eighteen months, living in Martin's house in Bristol, he had missed them. He gazed up at them from the jolting train, and saw a pair of red kites high up against the soft blue sky, circling, drifting lazily on a warm breeze. In Bristol all you got were seagulls. This visit was going to be incredible, or *incroyable*, as Charlie always said, showing off her French.

The train slowed down, over the bridge at Park Lane, over the little brook that ran through Rock Park, under Spa Road, and there was the station. Sam slipped his good arm through the strap on his rucksack, waited while Becky checked that nothing had been left behind, and followed her off the train.

He remembered every single detail of it, the old signal box, the little station building, the footbridge. But where the hell was Gwynedd?

"Where do we go for the bus to Rhayader?"

Why was Becky asking a total stranger? Why didn't she ask him? He'd caught the bus from here to Rhayader hundreds of times. Did having a busted arm mean that people thought you must have the brain of a four-year-old?

The bus ride to Rhayader took longer than he remembered. For three years he'd made this journey every school day, always sitting next to Gwynedd on this same bus – except on days when she'd got the hump or been suspended from school. It didn't seem right to be doing the journey without her. Why hadn't she come to the station? She couldn't have forgotten he was coming. She'd never do that.

At last. The bus climbed the hill into Rhayader. Here was Dark Lane. Here was journey's end, where the bus stopped in the car park. Sam checked the time on his phone. Dead on time. The ride was easier for the driver at half term. Half past four. Just like the old days when Gwynedd used to shove her way to the head of the queue to get off the bus and he used to struggle to follow her. And once off, the two of them would saunter down to the meadow by the river. Sam felt he had come home. Except that Gwynedd wasn't there. Sam was surprised by how disappointed he felt.

"Are you all right?"

"I'm fine." Sam didn't want Becky to start fussing again.

"Can you manage your rucksack?"

"Of course I can."

"It shouldn't be far to the cottage."

It wasn't. Sam knew it wasn't. He'd looked it up on a Google map, which he had shown to Becky three times. It was less than a five minute walk. They set off.

It was when they rounded the corner into West Street that both Sam and Becky became aware of some kind of argument taking place a bit further on. Someone was shouting 'Piss off!' and Sam recognised the voice. In the old days, before he'd left Rhayader for Bristol, he'd heard that voice utter those words almost every day. Gwynedd Hughes was causing trouble.

"Is that Gwynedd?" Becky had also recognised the voice. "Oh dear…"

*

This was not the time to hang about. Azim wriggled backwards until his feet found the trunk of a tree. It was safe to stand here, screened by trees. He squinted round one of the trees. There was no sign of the man with a gun. Azim moved on.

He was not sure where to go. There was a chance that the man with the gun didn't know about the bag being in the empty house, a chance that he didn't connect the house in any way with Azim. But there was at least one hunter who knew that the Kid with the bag was in town, and it was such a small town. Azim couldn't go on living like this. He had to find help. And the only place where he'd find that was with the man called Saqui. But Azim knew he couldn't simply walk up to the door of Saqui's shop. If the Hunter saw him do that, then Saqui too would be in danger. There was a lot to think about. Maybe he would have to leave this town tonight. The man – or men – hunting him knew he was here, and Azim knew they were out to kill him. Why hadn't the man on the footbridge done that already? The man had a gun. He could have fired. Why hadn't he?

Of course! It was obvious. However many hunters there were they couldn't kill him until they knew exactly where the bag was. For the short time that Azim intended to remain in this town, he had to make sure that he didn't lead any of them to the bag. And that made it considerably easier to know in what direction he should go. He had to find another way back into town. The footbridge, the cinder track, the street from the river up to the clock tower were all far too dangerous. The men with guns would have their eyes on all those places.

Azim moved upstream. In this crowded country, where everything was so close together, another bridge couldn't be far away. When he found it, he would go back to the town on the other side of the river. He had plenty of energy left. He could go on walking all night if necessary, but he must get back to the empty house as soon as possible. He would be safer there. He and the bag would be together. And after that?

He almost missed the bridge when he came to it. It was a simple wooden structure, only wide enough for one person to cross at a time. He crossed it at a run, then crouched down on the sopping grass. He raised his head. There was no sign of life, no one to be seen, no sound other than the ceaseless gurgling of the river and the steady swish of traffic on a nearby road. It was time to head back into town.

Azim was slowly recovering from the terror of the chase. Walking was good here, with soft grass underfoot. He made good progress. Soon he was on the outskirts of the town. This was the dangerous bit. There were people about – too many people.

He was getting near the crossroads. If he turned right there, the man Saqui's Shop of Chips would be down on the right hand side. But he didn't want to go there. He would go there later, not now; maybe tonight, maybe tomorrow. There were things he needed to do at the empty house. What Azim was looking for was a turning before the crossroads, a side street that would lead down to the river. There was one just coming up. Narrow, more like an alley than a street. No shops. Hardly any people. Dark and quiet. He walked slowly along, always ready to make a run for it if that was necessary. The alley seemed to go in the direction he wanted, dropping gently down. He couldn't be far from the river now. He'd have to take much care, in case the hunters were still watching out for him.

Above all, he had to find out if the bag was still safe. If it had gone, if the hunters had found it, maybe they'd go too. He'd be safe then, but the loss of the bag and the money would mean bad trouble for Uncle back in Afghanistan. With the money, Uncle would be able to pay back the men who'd lent money for Azim's journey to UK. Without the money, there would be killings. Even if the hunters had not found the bag, there could still be killings. One of the hunters had wanted to kill him half an hour ago. Money or no money, the hunter might still want to kill him. But Azim had to know whether the money was safe or not.

The alley curved towards the big street. It looked as though it joined the street somewhere between the Shop of Chips and the cinder track by the river. He would use extra care now. He would make no noise and no sudden movements.

It took him some time to summon up the courage to enter the big street, but he was lucky. There was no one about. No one loitering. No one waiting with a gun in his hand. Azim reached the empty house. There were no signs that anyone had been there. The door was as he'd left it. There were no new footprints in the greasy dust on the staircase. Azim climbed the stairs and entered the room he'd been using as a bedroom. No signs of a thief or robber having been here. There was the hole he had made in the floorboards.

With trembling hands, Azim put his arm in and felt under the boards with the tips of his fingers. Ah! There was the bag. He pulled it out, shoved his hand through the slit he had cut in the bag and took hold of one of the wallets. It was full of 50 notes. All was well. He placed the wallet on the floor and pulled another wallet from the bag. This was stuffed with a mixture of 50 and 20 notes. It was the wallet he'd taken money from earlier in the day, when he went shopping. Azim had broken the seal on this wallet, and there were some loose notes in the bag. He tried to cram them back into the wallet. It wasn't easy.

No matter. Everything was safe. But for how long? He needed to get the bag somewhere safer than this empty old house. The only place he could think of was the Shop of Chips. Perhaps the kind man who ran the shop, and who had given him water, had what was called a safe, like the one the Chief had at the Farm.

Azim decided it was time to find a new home for the bag, the money, and his own tired, cold, hungry, frightened body. Life on the run was tiring.

*

The reunion with Sam had not gone as Gwynedd had hoped. It had taken place on the pavement within seconds of her final call to the driver of the silver-grey car to 'piss off'. She had been shocked to see Sam's arm in a sling. What happened? What sort of accident? How bad was it? But Sam had not wanted to talk about it in front of Becky. He'd mumbled something about telling Gwynedd later. All he wanted at that moment was to get to this place called Lavender Cottage, thereby bringing this long and tiresome journey to an end. But Gwynedd went on and on with her questions.

"I think Sam's tired," said Becky. "Perhaps you could leave us to settle in, and we'll all meet up later. I'm sure you've got better things to do."

She was doing her politest best to get rid of Gwynedd. The girl's friendship with Sam had been fine a year and a half ago, though there had been that business with the dog fight when both Sam and Gwynedd might well have been killed, but Becky wasn't sure the friendship was suitable now, not with Sam and Gwynedd both being… well, older. And there had been that scene in the street not five minutes ago.

To Becky, the worst part of leaving Bristol would be Sam giving up his friendships with the youngsters at the College there. Nice lads and lovely girls. Gwynedd was wonderful, of course, but she was… she had always been a bit lawless. And though youngsters changed as they grew older, they didn't always change for the better. Becky knew it was wrong of her, but she couldn't help thinking that Sam could do better than Gwynedd.

"It's fine, Mrs Harper," said Gwynedd. "And I can give you a hand moving in. Just down here, isn't it? There we are. Lavender Cottage."

Gwynedd was aware of Becky's doubts about her suitability as Sam's girlfriend, but she gave Becky one of her best smiles. And even as she did so, she thought what a pity it was that people changed. Having no mum of her own, there had been a time when Gwynedd had viewed Becky as a sort of substitute mum. Right now, it sounded like those days were over.

Lavender Cottage was what Gwynedd would have called posh-cosy. Becky found the key left under an upturned flower pot by the back door. Gwynedd was first through the door. Sam followed. He swung the rucksack off his good shoulder and dropped it on the floor in the tiny hall. Becky muttered something about 'a cup of tea'.

"Ta, Mrs Harper. Two sugars, please."

Gwynedd stuck close to Sam. She picked up his rucksack and carried it upstairs. She selectcd the bigger of the two bedrooms for him, dumped the rucksack on the bed, and tentatively stroked his bad arm.

"You don't have to be that gentle," he said. "I can't feel anything."

"Oh, my God! It's paralysed!"

"Duh," he said. "Don't be stupid. It's Velcro-ed to my chest. You can't feel anything through Velcro."

She wanted to hug him and couldn't. He glanced at his watch, and remembered Gwynedd's time-table from the old days.

"Aren't you supposed to be getting your Grandad's tea? We could meet later at the Chippie."

Gwynedd smiled. So he remembered about Grandad Dave and his strict timetable. And the idea of meeting at the Chippie was a good one. She'd have to be there, because she'd promised Saqui that she'd work there every night during half term. The Chippie was where she and Sam used to go in the old days, when Becky had enough money to splash out on an evening treat of three small cod and chips. Sam smiled too. He'd lost touch with cod and chips in Bristol. Martin didn't allow the smell of hot fat and vinegar in his fancy house. Martin preferred the smell of whisky. Sam remembered the smell of whisky in Martin's fancy car on the night of the accident.

"We could meet before then," she said, "and we'd be on our own."

He put up little resistance to the idea, and it was arranged that they'd meet just after six down by the river.

Evening

Just over an hour later, Gwynedd sprinted into the park. Was he there? He was there! She'd been afraid that Becky wouldn't let him come. But there he was!

She rushed up to him, grabbed his good arm and kissed him on the cheek.

"Right," she said. "What happened? What have you done?"

"Everything's fine," said Sam. But he couldn't stop adding: "Why weren't you at the station?"

"What's wrong with your arm?"

Was she going to fuss, like Becky?

"Nothing's wrong. My arm got busted."

"How? Is it going to be all right?"

He nodded. "Yeah, yeah, yeah."

This was their favourite old haunt, the playground where they used to meet every weekday morning on their way to school, and where they sat and talked together on the way home after school; where they shared Welsh cakes or packets of biscuits or ice creams, and cans of Coke; where they tried and rejected the first cigarettes they'd ever smoked; where they'd talked about everything that mattered and a lot that didn't; where they'd tried to work out why adults were like they were; and where they'd experimented with kissing.

And here they were again, on a fine evening, not yet too dark to make out the high wooden framework that supported the swings and the climbing ropes in the play park. Sam gazed up at the bar across the top of the swings.

"Do you still fool about up there? Doing… what did you call them? Your aero-acrobatics?"

She didn't want to tell him that for almost two years she hadn't been able to face coming back here without him. She tried to make a joke of it.

"I'm not going to let you dare me into doing back flips in my glamorous new boots. Far too dangerous. Which reminds me. Your poor arm. What happened?"

They sat beside each other on the swings, trailing their feet on the ground. Sam thought back to the day of the accident. There'd been the row with Martin, about the way Sam treated his house, about Sam's lack of application to his school work, about the school fees, and about Sam's not appreciating how lucky he was to be given a lift to school day after day in Martin's precious car.

"It was a bad day," he said. "I was late for school. I forgot to pack my rugger boots."

"Is that how you broke your arm? Playing rugger in the wrong shoes?"

"No. There are spare pairs you can borrow, but you have to pay a fine."

"The school makes you pay a fine?" Gwynedd was outraged. "That's criminal. You ought to tell the police."

He shook his head. "No. Becky signed a form when I first went there, saying she accepted the school's disciplinary rules."

"Well, she ought to change her mind and unsign it. But how did you break your arm?"

She leaned across from her swing seat and starting stroking his hand.

"Martin picked me up from school. He was in a bad mood because I was late coming out to his car. He shouted at me to get in. I was saying goodbye to some mates…"

"Male or female?" She stopped stroking his hand.

"What difference does it make?"

Gwynedd was about to tell him it made an enormous difference as far as she was concerned, but realised that she really didn't want to hear about any Bristol girls in Sam's life.

"Never mind," she said. "Go on." She stroked his hand again.

"Martin started driving off before I was properly in the car, so I told to him to wait. He snapped at me, telling me to shut the car door and to shut up. I slammed the door…"

"Doesn't he like that?" Gwynedd made a mental note, in case she ever had the chance to slam the doors of Martin's car and annoy him.

"He had a go at me. So I opened the passenger door and said I'd rather walk. That really annoyed him."

"That's my boy," she said, and she stopped stroking his hand just long enough to kiss it.

"I was pulling the belt harness over my shoulder, and then… then I remember the smell of liquor in the car… whisky perhaps… And then there was a crumpling noise and I was thrown forward and back, almost in one move. My knees cracked down on the floor of the car…"

"He could have crippled you." The frightening image of Sam on crutches came into her head.

"… my left arm smacked into the passenger door, and then I must have passed out. And that's why we're here. Becky's leaving Martin. She wants to find somewhere to live here, in Llandrindod or Rhayader. She's kept in touch with friends here."

"Which is more than you have."

He ignored her sarcasm. He didn't want a row.

"She's going to start looking at properties tomorrow."

She slapped his good arm. "You mean you're coming back? We'll be going on the school bus together! And you've waited all this time to tell me that? You bastard!"

"I guess so." He didn't sound as delighted as Gwynedd.

"You make it sound like a prison sentence."

She felt a mixture of disappointment and anger. Didn't he want to come back to her? – that was the disappointment. Was he sad to leave the girls of Bristol? – that was the anger. But both emotions quickly died away. Sam was coming back. She leaned further over, and rested her head on Sam's good shoulder. She felt a slight shiver pass through his body.

"Pretend we've never met before," she said. It wasn't an original idea. She'd seen a couple do this in a film on TV. "Then we'll both be delighted with each other. Each of us will be, like, the best we've ever met."

She could see that Sam was trying not to laugh.

"What?" she said.

"You're nuts," he said. "Wait…" He could see that she was about to lose her temper. "… you're nuts in an incredible way."

In Bristol he would have used the French word 'incroyable', part of the current lingo of his Bristolian set. But he stopped himself just in time.

She thought about what he said for a couple of seconds, a long time for Gwynedd.

"Well," she said. "If you put it like that, Sammy, that's OK. I can live with that."

"Come on," he said. "Let's walk some more."

They started walking slowly, hand in hand, over the soft turf, but after a few paces Gwynedd let go of Sam's hand and bent down to pick something up.

"Someone's chucked a perfectly good bottle of water away. What a waste."

"You don't know it's perfectly good," said Sam.

"Course it is. The seal's not broken. I'm having that."

"It's a bottle of water," said Sam. "Leave it."

"But why would someone chuck it away? And why here?"

He had no answers to her questions. This was the old Gwynedd, always looking for a puzzle or a mystery.

"Just put it back where you found it, and give me your hand."

She laughed and did as she was told, squeezing his hand until he squeaked in protest.

They walked on until they reached the ruins of the old castle at the edge of the park. Gwynedd had walked hand-in-hand with boys before. There was Vinnie, whose palms tended to get a bit sweaty; and Little Huwie who was more interested in ghosts and the supernatural than the super and natural; and even Saqui, a couple of times. And she and Sam had often walked hand in hand, in the old days. But this was different. It was as though there was a difference between holding hands playfully and holding hands seriously, and this was serious.

They found a slab of stone to sit on.

"I thought you wanted to walk," he said.

"Yes. But there's other things I want to do."

She tried to get her arm round him, but his bad arm and the plaster round it and the sling all got in her way.

"I'm gonna sit the other side," she said. "So's I can grab hold of you."

They changed places clumsily, but then Gwynedd carefully stretched her arm behind his back, tucking her hand between the sling and his ribs, as though it was all a game and she was only threatening to tickle him. Sam guessed she wanted them to kiss, but he wasn't ready for that – not yet. And he'd decide when. She had tilted her head towards him, but he would decide when they had their first proper kiss. Now was too soon to share what was supposed to be an all-out, earth-shattering moment. He let his bum slide down the stone until he was lying on the ground. It was unnecessary because, at that same moment, she jerked her head away.

"What was that?" She spoke in a whisper. She took her hand from his body and sat up straight, like an animal that had sensed danger. "There's something moving over there." She joined him on the ground.

"Over where?"

"By the old house. The one with corrugated iron on it. There's someone coming out. There!... climbing over the wall." She was whispering, a rare thing for Gwynedd. "What's he doing?"

"He's just woken up."

"How do you know?"

"I can see him rubbing his eyes. And he's yawning."

"That doesn't mean he's only just woken up. He might simply be tired."

Sam disagreed. "Perhaps he's been sleeping there. Keeping out of the daylight. Waiting until it's nearly dark."

"Why?" said Gwynedd. "What's he doing?"

"How should I know?"

"Well, you seem to know everything, Mr Smart Ass."

"He's Asian," said Sam.

"Must be a mate of Saqui's," said Gwynedd. "Like, he's a cousin or something."

"Why? There are millions of Asians in the UK. What makes you think this one's anything to do with Saqui?"

"He's in Rhayader. So's Saqui. And Saqui knows this old house. Back in the summer, he had some fish go off, and he come here and buried them round the back there. Didn't want any of the customers to know…"

"Shut up. He's getting nearer."

They lay rigidly still. The figure hurried past them, and up the cinder path that led out of the park and back to Rhayader's main street.

Sam waited until he was sure the Asian lad had gone, and then stood up. All thoughts of kissing had gone from his mind.

"Maybe it's no big deal," said Sam. "It might be just a bloke who's been squatting there, and now he's leaving. He's carrying a big bag." He was relieved to be able to shift the focus from passion to curiosity instead. What Gwynedd wanted to talk about now was what was going on in the old house.

"Don't be daft," she said. "Who'd be squatting here? There's far better places to squat even in Rhayader."

"Looked them over, have you?"

Gwynedd delivered a light punch on Sam's good arm. She didn't tell him that there had been times when she'd thought about squatting, about getting away from Dave and the bungalow and setting up on her own.

"Maybe this guy's a druggie, then," said Sam, "and he wants somewhere quiet to do his needlework."

She peered at him. "You've changed. Such cool talk. My Sam's turned into a city slicker."

He pretended to take no notice, but felt pleased with himself. He knew that, in some way, what she said was meant as a compliment. "Are we going to hang around here all night? I'm hungry. I haven't had anything proper to eat all day. I wanna go to the Chippie."

"Saqui won't have started frying yet. Let's stay here. Wait and see what happens. Perhaps there'll be other druggies."

She moved close to him and put her arm round him again.

"I like it when there's only the two of us," she said. "I'm sure there's something awesome and brilliant we could do to fill in the time while we're waiting." She pulled him closer.

He knew what she was suggesting. The same idea had been with him a lot of the time on the train journey from Bristol. Sam could handle a kiss, largely thanks to Charlie and Nessie, who gave lessons in the art. But kissing his best friend would be different. Kissing with Charlie and Nessie was like rugger practice – it didn't matter if it all went wrong. Practice was about making mistakes and learning from them. Kissing Gwynedd would be like a crucial game, where you had to perform at top level, and he didn't yet know what his top level was. He wouldn't feel he was properly in charge.

Gwynedd had no doubts. She was ready to go, and she leaned towards him until their lips were a finger apart.

"Let's check out what he's been doing in the house." Sam still wasn't ready for passion.

"Awesome." There was sarcasm in Gwynedd's voice.

"Awesome? Awesome's so yesterday," he said. "Nobody in Bristol says 'awesome' any more. We say '*étonnant*'." He gave the word its French pronunciation. "You wouldn't know that word."

"You shut your face," she said.

"You shut yours first."

"You shut yours for ever!"

"We're supposed to be looking at the house."

"Supposing there's someone else in there?"

"There won't be," he said.

"All right then – how are we going to get you over the wall with your arm in that sling?"

"You're going to help me. You kneel down and I put my foot on your shoulder. Then you straighten up and over I go."

"I'm not having your filthy shoes on my best jacket."

"Take your jacket off."

"You take your shoes off. I'll be brave and put up with your smelly socks on my shoulder."

Apparently, the new Gwynedd cared what she looked like. It occurred to Sam that she must have taken considerable time and trouble preparing for his arrival, arranging her hair, painting her nails. He liked that. In a way it made him feel good.

Getting Sam over the wall was difficult, but they managed. Sam swung himself up with his good arm while Gwynedd shoved from below. With a little cry of 'shi-i-i-it-t-t-t!' he disappeared over the wall. There'd better not be anyone in the house, Gwynedd thought, not with the row he was making.

"Now you climb over." It was another of Sam's very loud whispers.

Gwynedd wondered if Sam ordered Bristol girls about. She had no idea what Bristol girls were like. She didn't really care. But she doubted that any of them could match the power of a Welsh girl in all her glory. She would give Sam something to remember. She would show him what the best boots in Llandrindod could do. She climbed over the wall, took three quick strides across the small yard between the wall and the front of the house and, at the risk of damaging one of her lovely new boots, kicked the door as hard as she could. The door collapsed. Gwynedd staggered in, struggling to keep on her feet.

She heard him groan.

"You idiot! The door wasn't locked."

"How was I to know that?"

"You could have tried it first," he said.

It was time to change the subject.

"We should have brought a torch," she whispered.

"What's the point of whispering after you've made a noise like a cannon going off?"

"Oh my God but that's so awesome, Sam, so absolutely awesome!"

"What are you talking about?"

"I'm being a totally awesome Bristol girl, crazy about you, Sammy, darling, Sammy, Sammy, darling…"

"Shut your gob."

"Brilliant."

There were no signs of human occupation on the ground floor. They approached the stairs.

"Somebody's been here recently," said Sam.

"How do you work that out?"

"The treads on the stairs. They're clean. They're not covered in grit and dust. Someone's been using them. At least we can see where they're safe."

There were two rooms on the upper storey – one facing the road, one facing the river. The first room contained nothing but litter, a couple of cardboard cases that had collapsed with the damp that impregnated everything, soot that had fallen down the chimney and spilled on to the floor, and a bent and rusty filing cabinet – nothing of any interest. The room facing the river was much the same: plenty of rubbish, a few broken floorboards that had been wrenched up and scattered on the floor, a pile of plastic sacks, and some broken glass.

"Nobody's living here," he said. "We might as well go."

Gwynedd had picked up a shard of glass and was examining it closely. "There's blood on this."

"Don't be daft."

"There is. I'm not surprised. It's sharp as a carving knife." She thought of sucking her thumb noisily, to trick Sam into thinking she'd cut herself, but gave up the idea. Once upon a time, yes. But she was more mature now. It was the sort of stupid thing Vinnie would do.

"Come on," he said. "But watch your step. There's a big hole in the floor here. Plant your fabulous new boots there and your foot would go right through the ceiling of the room below." He used his phone to shine a light into the hole. "Hang on a minute."

He knelt on the floor, reached into the hole and picked up a piece of paper.

"What have you found?"

"Bloody hell! It's £50."

"Ketchup's on you tonight then." She thought he was joking.

"Honest. It's a £50 note."

He went on his good hand and both his knees.

"What are you going to do?"

"See if I can find another."

"I'll help you." Gwynedd settled beside him.

Their faces were very close. She could feel his breath on her cheek, feel the warmth of his body. The setting was as unromantic as it could possibly be, but that didn't seem to matter. Gwynedd wondered if she should be looking at his lips, as though sizing up where to land the kiss, like so many of the kissers she'd seen in so many of the films that Dave and she had watched on TV. She didn't really want to look at his lips. She wanted to look into his eyes. She moved her head a tiny bit closer. He moved his a tiny bit back.

"Not now," he said.

"Then when?" She didn't understand him. There was no one about. They were all alone. Hadn't he dreamed of her, and this, like she'd dreamed of him, and this? She shoved her face right up to his. Their lips were again a finger apart, until she leaned further forward and kissed him smack on his mouth.

"That's for good luck," she said. Her hands were shaking.

Fifty pounds and a kiss that he hadn't expected, or wanted, but had to admit that he'd enjoyed. That was enough excitement for one day. Sam struggled back on to his feet.

"Come on."

"Where are we going?"

"To the Chippie. If this lad *is* something to do with Saqui, isn't that where we'll find him?"

"Then what?"

"We show him the £50 note, say we saw him drop it, and that we've come to return it."

Gwynedd knew that morally it was the right thing to do. From the look of the kid, he needed £50 more than she did. On the other hand, that banknote would have paid for more than one of her new boots, and it represented nearly five nights work in the Chippie. Perhaps it was time she asked Saqui for more money.

"How about another kiss?" she said. "For more good luck. Maybe we'll find another £50 note. We could go on kissing all night and in the morning we'd be millionaires."

"I don't know what it is about you," said Sam.

"What do you mean? Aren't I attractive?"

"Awesomely attractive." He felt obliged to say that, not because of the kiss, but because he was now aware of the trouble she'd taken over her appearance. It was like feeling he had to say something complimentary to Becky whenever she'd come back from having her hair done, except that a part of him also meant it.

Gwynedd was thrilled. "Go on," she said.

"You attract all sorts of weird happenings. Often dangerous, always a bit mad."

She thumped his good arm.

"You mean I'm special," she said.

He gave a little sigh. "Yes. I suppose I do."

"Well, give us a Goodnight Kiss."

"Why? I thought we were going to the Chippie?"

"Kiss first, Chippie later. Kiss and Chips."

On the way to the Chippie, Sam received a text from Becky:

What time will you be back?

He sighed.

"What?" said Gwynedd.

He showed her the text. "What she really means is 'You should be here'. I have to reply. We go through this every time."

They laughed.

"What time are you going to tell her you'll be back?"

"Ten." He started entering the text.

"Eleven would be better."

He thought for a moment. There was no way he was going to let himself be trapped between the wants of two women.

"No, no, no, no, no," he said. "Ten."

He sent the message. "We've got three hours," he said.

She had been shaping up to kiss his cheek, but changed her mind.

"We need to talk," she said.

"Really? I thought we were going to make passionate love. Unless it rained."

They had switched sides. She was now the one who wanted to be serious.

"What are we going to do about the lad we saw if he's not at the chippie? If it was him dropped that fifty quid note, something odd's going on."

"Perhaps he's one of a gang. We didn't properly search the whole house."

"Should we tell Saqui about the fifty quid note?"

"Do you want to?"

"Duh!"

"Duh?"

"Isn't that the noise you smart city slickers make when you want to make out that someone's just said something really stupid?"

"Duh!" he said. "Of course it is. So you *do* want to tell Saqui about the 50 quid note?"

"Yuh. In a manner of speakin', like."

"I think we should keep the 50 quid hidden until we know more about this lad. We don't even know if he's anything to do with Saqui."

"Wanna have a bet on it?"

"Not £50, I don't."

"Come on," she said. "I'm late for work."

Despite the warmth in the Chippie, they received a cold welcome. Saqui was pleased to see Sam, but he was furious with Gwynedd.

"Look at all my customers!"

Gwynedd looked. Admittedly there were more customers than usual on a Wednesday night, but it was hardly like the first day of the January Sales.

"So?"

She gave the impression that she wasn't interested. Her eyes flicked to and fro, looking for some sign of the mysterious Asian lad.

"You are forty-two minutes late," said Saqui. "The customers are waiting to be served."

"All right, all right." Her eyes stopped moving and she looked straight at Saqui. "We're late because we've been watching your cousin." There was a look of sweet innocence on her face. "We saw him come out of that wreck of a place down by the river. What's he doing there? Growing mushrooms?"

Saqui had been rattled by Azim's sudden appearance at the Chippie that morning. He had feared that local people would assume that there was some connection between him and the poor lad. He didn't doubt that Gwynedd had seen Azim, and he wasn't surprised that she'd leap to such a conclusion. But it was stupid to think he was his cousin.

"Which cousin are you referring to?" he said. "The one in Cardiff or the one in Merthyr?"

"Neither. The one that's living in that house. Or maybe he's living here."

"There's no one living here," said Saqui. He looked genuinely puzzled. "Not even me. You know that. You see me lock the place and go home. I do that every night."

Gwynedd didn't know what to say. The old building where the Asian lad was squatting was barely two minutes' walk from the Chippie. He must be some sort of relation, or friend, or fellow countryman. And why else would the Asian lad have popped up in Rhayader? But Saqui looked as though he was telling the truth, and Sam was peering at her as though she'd gone nuts. She had to say something.

"I'm talking about the lad down the road. He's the same colour as you."

"So," said Saqui, "anyone who comes here from Bangladesh, or Pakistan, or India, or Sri Lanka or Afghanistan must be my cousin? Vinnie and Sam are the same colour. Does that mean I should assume they are cousins? Really, Gwynedd, I'm ashamed of you."

Saqui put on his managerial frown, the look on his face he used the night Gwynedd had dropped the huge jar of pickled onions on the floor. But it was the look on Sam's face that hurt Gwynedd far more. He looked as though he disapproved of her, and she couldn't bear it.

"Now, come on, Gwynedd!" said Saqui. "We need another bucket of chips here. And more cod…"

*

The visit to the derelict house had reassured Azim to a small extent. He knew that the money was safe because he was holding the bag in his hand as he walked slowly back up the hill from the river. But he couldn't go back to living in that house. It was too near where the hunter had chased him. He had to find somewhere else to spend the night, and he had to find it quickly. It was already getting dark. He could just see the stars in the night sky - nothing like as many as you saw back home, but a clear sign that it would be a cold night. His hope was that the Saqui man would let him sleep in the Shop of Chips. Azim could make a bed for himself on the floor, behind the counter. No one need know that he was there. No one except Saqui.

Azim made his way through the back alleys to one of the streets that met at the crossroads. What he was looking for was an alleyway off that street, one that would lead to the rear of the Shop of Chips. He slowed his speed, walking with great care, pretending he was looking in shop windows whenever other people came along, turning his back on the road whenever a vehicle passed. When he was still a hundred paces or so from the crossroads and from the corner that led to the Shop of Chips, he found what he wanted - a gap between the buildings, wide enough for a horse-drawn waggon to pass through. Azim made his way slowly through the gap into a small open yard where cars were parked.

Most of the buildings here were tall at the front, but with low extensions at the back. Memory told him that the Saqui man's shop was smaller than the rest. There it was – one storey lower than the others. That must be the back of the Saqui man's place. This was good. There was a small van parked very close to it. If he climbed on to the top of the van, he might be able to haul himself on to the roof of the extension. It was a sloping roof, but not steeply pitched.

Azim sat on the ground and took off his boots; clomping around in boots on its roof would make a lot of noise. He tied the laces of his boots together and slung them round his neck. He peeled off his socks and stuffed them in the pockets of his old jeans. This wasn't like climbing rocks back home. Bare feet would give a far better grip on both the smoothly painted van and the roofs of the buildings around him. Even with the bag of money, getting on to the van roof was easy. He put one foot on the top of the front wheel and hoisted himself on to the bonnet, then grabbed the aerial above the windscreen and hauled himself on to the top of the van.

The rear doors of the van were almost touching the wall of the building. He put the bag on the roof of the van, then reached up and grabbed the guttering, testing its strength. It seemed sound enough. He placed the bag on the guttering, then put his right foot next to it, and pushed off from the van with his left.

The guttering sagged but didn't break. He was now on the roof. He lay flat on the slates, his left hand tightly gripping the bag. He stretched out his right arm, feeling with his hand for the ridge of the roof. It was just too far away. He couldn't reach it. He was stuck... unless he could move sideways along the guttering, to the end of the building. If he could do that, he might be able to climb to the ridge by grabbing the edge of the slates that extended about a thumb's length beyond the edge of the bricks.

Slowly, shifting the weight of his feet as gently as he could and dragging the bag with him, Azim moved along the guttering... There, he was safe. The guttering was strongly supported here. And there was plenty of moss in it to cushion his bare feet. He allowed himself a moment's rest. But never relaxed his hold on the bag.

He couldn't stay here long. Someone might see him from one of the other buildings that overlooked the courtyard. It was time to go. He reached out with his right hand, grabbing the edge of the slate. With his left hand, he dragged the bag as close as possible to his body, then risked letting go of the bag for a tiny moment so that he could shove his left arm through the handles of the bag, and loop it over his left shoulder. The bag almost slipped from his grasp, and threatened to slither down back on to the roof of the van. It took a desperate jerk of his shoulder for Azim not to lose the bag. Once he was sure the bag was safe, he reached a little further with his left hand, flattening his body against the slates. Once his left hand had a firm grip, he reached beyond it with his right, and dragged himself a little higher. Left over right... right over left... bumping the bag along with him... a strong arm's length at a time.

He reached the top of the roof and swung his right leg over so that he straddled the ridge. The rest was easy. He worked his way over the roofs of three other buildings, until he came to a flat roof beyond which was what must be the back wall of the Shop of Chips. In the wall overlooking the flat roof, there was a window. When he reached it, Azim discovered that it was shut fast, perhaps bolted, perhaps nailed to the frame. It was impossible to find a gentle way of opening it. Azim didn't want to smash it open. Anyone hearing the noise of a window being smashed would want to investigate. He examined the window closely. It was already badly cracked. If he could scrape away the old putty on the edge of the window, it might be possible to jiggle one of the pieces of glass until it was loose and then pull it out from the frame.

The putty came away in chunks. Good... good... this was good. He pushed gently on one piece of glass. It yielded but did not break away from the frame. Paint alone was holding it in place. But if he could shift it a little more, he should be able to make a gap big enough to get his hand in and grab the piece of glass before it fell.

Gently... gently...

The paint gave way. The piece of glass fell back into the building before Azim could get his hand on it. There was a clatter as the glass hit the floor and smashed to bits. Azim silently cursed his clumsiness. There was nothing he could do but wait to see what harm the noise had done.

All was quiet. Nobody shouted. No lights flicked on. No torches were turned in his direction. And the bag was still safe. The hole in the window made the next stage much easier. Azim took one of his socks from his jeans and pulled it over his hand like a mitten. Now he could take firm hold of another piece of cracked glass and work it loose. Piece by piece, laying each one carefully on the flat roof, Azim made the hole big enough for him to push the bag through and then place it gently on the floor. That done, he squeezed his body through the same hole in the window.

He was in.

He listened intently, straining his ears for any sounds of other humans. There were noises coming from downstairs, the sort of noises to be heard in any café or shop: people asking for things they wanted to buy or to eat, other people accepting their orders. Someone laughed. He thought he heard both male and female voices. He thought he recognised one voice as that of the kind man who had given him water, the man called Saqui. What mattered was that there were no sounds of human activity coming from this upper floor.

He picked up the bag, took two steps into the dark room… and a third…

*

Someone with his arm in a sling isn't much use in a Chippie. Sam leaned against the wall. He could see how busy Gwynedd was, running the paddle through the bubbling oil to make sure the chips were evenly fried, picking up pieces of fish with the tongs to take them off the hot plate, adding the chips and swiftly wrapping up the parcel, handing it to the customer, taking the money and giving change. Saqui was in charge of the whole operation. He cooked all the food – fish, pies, saveloy, sausages in batter, and the chips. He and Gwynedd made a good team, but an extra pair of hands would have been helpful. Sam rubbed his sling. His arm seemed to be OK, but the test would be when the Hospital took the sling off, and that wouldn't happen for another couple of weeks.

He wondered what would happen during that time. Would Becky find somewhere to rent here in Rhayader? Would Martin kick up a fuss? What would it be like to go back to school in Llandrindod? It would be weird to be once again travelling on the same school bus as Gwynedd every morning and every afternoon. She'd changed in some way. The old Gwynedd, the one that looked for laughs and trouble, was still there, but there seemed to be a sadness in her that he'd not been aware of in the past. He wondered…

His thoughts and the bustle of the Chippie were interrupted by what sounded like a heavy gun going off. The sound had come from upstairs.

*

Azim had taken one step too many. His bare foot hit a heavy object. He lost his balance and fell and his head struck a large empty canister that had once held fifteen litres of cooking oil. The canister toppled over, making a sound like a heavy gun going off.

Azim panicked. He was terrified. The people downstairs had all stopped talking. He had to find somewhere to hide the bag and hopefully to hide himself, and he must do that quickly. A door had opened downstairs and voices were coming nearer. There was the sound of someone coming up a staircase. Where? Where could he hide the bag? Behind the empty oil drums? No, it would be too big. He tried the door on his left. It opened. The room was bare. There was a cupboard, under the eaves of the roof. He bundled the bag in there, shut the cupboard door, and managed to turn round and take a couple of steps away from the cupboard before the Saqui man, the kind man who had given him water, burst in and switched on the light.

There was time for them to exchange a couple of short sentences before a young woman joined the Saqui man. She had run up the stairs, clumping in her big boots, and she looked very excited. Azim felt it would be right to be frightened of her. Behind her was a third person, a young man who had one arm wrapped up and strapped to his body, as though he had been wounded by a flying piece of shrapnel or a bullet. This was a dangerous settlement.

The Saqui man said something to the young woman in a language Azim didn't understand, but assumed was English. The woman shook her head. There seemed to be an argument between them, because when the woman said something to Saqui, he shook *his* head. Then the other young man spoke quietly to the young woman and pointed down the staircase. The woman shook her head again, but the man insisted. Azim could see that the man wanted her to go back downstairs, but the woman was reluctant to do that. The young man took hold of her arm. Now, all three people – Saqui, the young man and the young woman – were talking at the same time, and there were shouts coming from the shop. The smell of burning fat flew up the stairs, and there was more shouting.

Azim heard Saqui telling him to stay where he was, and then Saqui pushed past the young woman and the young man and hurried downstairs. Azim had no idea what was happening or what any of them had said, but he could feel the hot air racing up the stairs. Fire. They were frightened of fire. This was terrible. If the Shop of Chips went ablaze, they could all be killed and the bag and the money would go up in flames. Perhaps that would be his punishment for taking the bag in the first place, and the deaths of these three innocent people would be his responsibility.

The young man said something to the young woman, and they followed Saqui downstairs.

Azim switched off the light.

In the Chippie, steam and smoke filled the air. Saqui was desperately turning off the deep fryers and trying to clear the Chippie of customers.

"Please, outside, everyone. All is under control, but it will be quicker if we can work alone. We have to drain away all this oil, and then start again. It will take time."

None of the customers moved. There was nothing worth watching on television. They all wanted to see the oil drained and the new start.

Saqui was a businessman.

"You will all have your money refunded and your orders replaced free of charge if you go out now."

The customers moved out on to the pavement.

"Gwynedd! Get the fire gloves. And something to put the burnt fish in. And the chips. Quick as you can."

Gwynedd did as she was told. Sam watched her. He could see that she knew what she was doing. Bit by bit, bucket by bucket, Saqui and Gwynedd brought the Chippie under control. The customers returned. Some of them refused Saqui's offer to refund their money: all of them wanted to see the drama through to its end. This would be a story to tell for days to come.

Sam listened as he watched. Mingled with the sounds of chatter and of Saqui and Gwynedd's clearing-up work, was the noise of something being dragged across the floor upstairs. A corpse? Hardly. But it was something quite heavy, and there was only one person who could be dragging it. He was about to go upstairs to investigate when there was a call on his phone. It was Becky. She was hungry.

"Don't worry if you're busy," she said. "But if you did have time to bring me a small bit of cod and a small portion of chips…"

She didn't need to finish the sentence. Sam knew exactly what she meant and what he should do. He went over to Gwynedd.

"Where else is there in town that does fish and chips?"

She looked at him as though he was a traitor.

"There's nowhere as good as this."

"I know, I know. But Mum, Becky, wants fish and chips and I can't tell her what's going on here."

The shocked look disappeared from Gwynedd's face. "Oh right. There's a place in North Street. Nothing like as good. And more expensive."

"That'll have to do. I'll be as quick as I can. Keep an ear open for what might be happening upstairs. You'll be OK?"

"How should I know?"

There was that anger threatening again, but she fought it down. There was nothing Sam could do here with his bad arm, and it might be better for him to be out of the way.

"You'll come back?"

"Course," he said. "See you later."

Sam left the Chippie.

*

From the pub bedroom across the street, Kyle watched the small crowd assemble outside the Chip Shop. Crowds interested him, especially crowds that gathered for no apparent reason. Crowds often meant trouble, sometimes violent trouble, and Kyle was always interested in violence. All his adult life, he'd earned his living from other people's trouble, mostly on a small scale – like this Scumbag Kid business – sometimes on a grand scale.

He remembered his final mission in Central Africa, three years ago: the crowds on the streets, the sudden burst of gunfire, people running in all directions, bodies falling, writhing in the red dust. And afterwards, the bodies swelling in the heat. Small bodies, many of them. The bodies of children caught up in crossfire. The flies crawling on their lifeless faces. The stench of death.

All that killing. So, what did it matter if one Kid was going to be killed? If one young lady was going to be painfully punished for her cheek? Kyle had suffered plenty of pain, much of it at the hands of his father.

There was a smile on Kyle's face. The light in the upstairs room had been switched on for only a couple of minutes. But that had been long enough for him to recognise the little Asian lad jabbering away to the Paki bloke that ran the Fish and Chip Shop. The Scumbag Kid was hiding out there. Fabulous. There was no need to go chasing off all over the place trying to find the Kid. He was right across the road. He made a mental note to send Coleson to check that there was no rear exit from the Chip Shop.

Kyle took a swig of beer from one of the cans Coleson had bought. He remembered what the Doc had said but, what the hell... This was a celebration. The job was as good as done. The beer was poor stuff, no bite to it, no comfort in it, but it tasted like vintage champers.

"Something going on across the street," he said.

Coleson got off his bed and joined Kyle at the window.

"Something to do with the Kid?"

"Here's something for you to think about," he said to Coleson. "Suppose the Kid is with his Asian mate in the Chip Shop. Exactly where would he be?"

Coleson shrugged his shoulders. "How the hell should I know?"

"Is he likely to be downstairs, in the shop with all the other customers?"

"You tell me."

"I'm asking you." Kyle was enjoying himself. "Take a look at the window over the shop. What do you see?"

"Sod all."

"Well, that's a bloody shame because there's a lot to see. In the first place, there's no lights on in that room, so probably there's no one there. In fact, you might think that there'd been no one there ever since I came back. Everything's pitch dark."

Kyle paused.

"So?" said Coleson.

"You're a sulky little bastard, aren't you," said Kyle. "So, the likelihood is that room's a storeroom." Kyle paused again.

Coleson went on sulking.

"An unused storeroom would be a good place to hide. Good place to doss down. The Kid probably doesn't have anywhere else to live. Your Chief said that this Kid hadn't been in the country for more than two weeks before he legged it from the Farm. The Kid's been on the loose in this dump of a place for nearly twenty-four hours. That's time enough to have found the Chip Shop and an Asian mate, and to blag his way into living there. But first things first. Get round the back of the Chip Shop and check there's no rear exit. Go on. Off you go. Now!"

Kyle noted Coleson's reluctance to leave. At some point, Coleson would have to be taught a lesson. That could wait. Business first, pleasure later.

He started planning the hit. It should be a simple matter to flush the Kid out, grab him, get what they wanted from him, and then kill him. All it needed was a bit of preparation: pack, and pop the cases in the Mercedes, ready to leave whenever the moment was right. Then, back to the room, where he'd show Coleson how get the shooter ready, how to fix the silencer and the telescopic sight – the night-sight could come later, if needed. All they had to do was wait. Sooner or later the Kid would show himself at the window. The later the better – there'd be no one else about. And then, ping! It wasn't a matter of shooting to kill, not with the first shot. All that was needed was to shoot to frighten. The Kid would know he'd been pinpointed. He'd panic, he'd make a dash for the cash, and hit the road with the bag in his hand. And this time, Kyle and Coleson would be ready. Once the Kid was out of the Chip Shop, the second shot would blow him away.

Kyle calculated it would take less than thirty seconds for them to get down the stairs and out of the pub – gun in hand. Forty seconds more would be enough to cross the road, grab the bag of money, hoist the Kid's body on to Coleson's back, nip back to the pub car park, start up the Mercedes and drive off. They'd registered under false names and Kyle very much doubted that the nice young lady behind the bar had made a note of the Merc's registration number. Driving on empty roads in the middle of the night, he and Coleson could be back at the Farm in less than two hours. He'd hand the Kid's body and the bag over to the Chief, and get his five k. He'd even settle for four k. The Chief could have the Merc back, and any problems that went with it.

Kyle relaxed, and smiled. A thought had just entered his head. He'd make sure he got more than five k. There was no knowing what the Kid might have done with some of the money. Kyle didn't see why he shouldn't help himself to a couple of handfuls from the bag, and blame any shortage on the dead Kid.

He would have been less happy, less relaxed if he had known that Coleson was not obeying orders. Instead of making sure there was no back door to the Chip Shop, Coleson was sitting in the saloon bar of the Lamb and Flag, drinking and cursing his luck to be working with Kyle.

THURSDAY

Morning

Sam lay in bed in his room under the eaves at the rented cottage. He could hear rain rapping on the skylight. He didn't want to get up. It had taken hours to clear up the mess at the Chippie last night, and at least an extra hour to reassure Becky that nothing terrible had happened. When he got back she was waiting up for him, despite the text and emails he'd sent from the Chippie, explaining why he was going to be late. Not until he'd managed to convince her that all was well did Becky reveal that she'd had a long and difficult phone call from Martin. She was always doing that; spending ages worrying about the little 'nesses' of life (lateness, forgetfulness, untidiness) before getting on to the real problems. How different she was from Gwynedd, who dropped everything if there was the slightest chance of taking part in a drama. Despite this, he had slept well.

He checked his phone. No messages, but it was time to get up. Gwynedd would be knocking for him in ten minutes, and lateness was not one of her 'nesses'; unlike rudeness, loudness and often thoughtlessness, all of which she excelled at. Because he was in a hurry, Sam didn't bother to fit the sling on his busted arm until he was already dressed. The arm seemed OK. A bit tender, and probably still not solidly mended, but getting stronger all the time. He couldn't wait for the day when he could chuck the sling away.

*

At the bungalow, Gwynedd's day threatened to start with a row. Dave complained that his early morning cup of tea wasn't outside his bedroom door when he went to get it at the usual time.

"I told you yesterday evening that I'd be back late. You don't listen, that's your trouble. Obviously if I was going to be back late, this morning's cuppa would be late too. What time did you look for it?"

"Half past seven. The usual time."

"You should have looked for it at half past eight," said Gwynedd. "That's when I put it there, and it was boiling hot."

"How was I to know that? Half past seven's the time for a morning cup of tea, as you well know."

"I ought to. That's the time I've been leaving it at your door almost every morning for the past five years. But it's half-term. Remember? Which means I have an extra hour in bed."

She didn't tell him that she'd been awake long before six, when the rain started, turning over in her mind last night's strange happenings. There was a whole lot of stuff about Azim, and about the narrowly averted fire at the Chippie, but there was also what had passed between her and Sam. Of the two, she had to admit to herself, at the moment, that her stuttering romance with Sam didn't quite match up to the excitement and mystery surrounding the lad called Azim. On the one hand, there had been the exchange of a little kiss, in which she had taken the lead. On the other hand, Sam had found a £50 note lying on the ground, and that doesn't happen every day. And, anyway, one good thing about the Mystery of Azim was that it had given her a perfect reason to go round to Sam's cottage the moment she'd seen to Dave, who could go without his bloomin' *Daily Mirror* for once. As for his breakfast, that would be served immediately.

As she juggled with the three different utensils needed to cook Dave's mushrooms on toast and poached egg, her mind repeatedly re-ran everything that had happened last night, from the first sight of Azim climbing over the wall, and finding the £50 note, to Azim's sudden and noisy entry into the floor above the Chippie. At the end of the evening, as soon as they'd cleared up the Chippie, she and Sam had sat and talked with Saqui for a long time. As a result, Gwynedd now knew considerably more about Azim. She knew his name, and that he had a whole stash of £50 notes. Saqui had seen Azim with a couple of them, and then there was the third, the one that she and Sam had found at the empty house. Where had they come from? It was only the second time in her life that she had seen a £50 note. Years ago, her parents had sent her one for her birthday, inside a card with the scribbled message 'Buy yourself some fun with this, Best Wishes, Bronwen and Frank'. No mention of love, no kisses, and not even 'Mum and Dad'. That was a sad thought. She dumped it, and went back to thinking about Azim. The lad was in some kind of trouble, so bad that he was frightened even to tell Saqui about it. She was glad that she hadn't said anything about the £50 note she and Sam had found. She'd save confronting Azim with that banknote until another time.

She took Dave's breakfast through to the living room. He'd already switched on the TV. He patted the seat next to him on the sofa.

"Sit down," he said. "Give us a bit of company. You got no school this morning."

"I got better things to do than watch the goggle box." She felt bad about saying that. She knew how lonely he got, and how frightened. But she couldn't hang around waiting for some kind of health crisis that might not come for years yet. She had other things to think of.

In all this, the most exciting thing she knew about Azim was that he was scared stiff of somebody or something. Ever since she'd seen his ragged figure climbing over the wall down by the empty house and running across the cinder track, Gwynedd had decided to become involved in Azim's affairs. And that couldn't wait. She'd fetch Sam out of the rented cottage and they'd go to the Chippie together. She put on her anorak and clamped Dave's old hat on her head.

She heard Dave drop his knife and fork on the plate and drop his tray on the floor of the living room. It was the signal that he had finished his breakfast.

"Coming!" she shouted.

She went to collect Dave's tray from the living-room.

He didn't like the sight of her wearing his hat.

"You got no cause to wear that. Makes you look like a bloke."

"Pity it doesn't do the same for you when you wear it."

She watched him feeling about for his stick.

"Lucky for you it ain't within reach," he said. But he laughed as well. "Where are you off to?"

"I'm meeting Sam Harper." She waited for Dave to react. He didn't. "You remember Sam? The one with the dog that you refused to have in the house?"

"I remember the Sam that nearly got you killed. He ought to have been locked up. You can tell him that from me. Got your mobile?" he said. "In case I need you."

"I've got *my* mobile. Have you got yours?"

"I dunno where it is."

"We go through this every time."

Gwynedd took out her mobile and selected Dave's number from her very short list of contacts. A muffled ring tone came from down the back of the sofa. Dave took no notice. He was busy picking his teeth. Gwynedd handed him the mobile.

"Don't lose it." She kissed his forehead. "Bye-bye, Grumpy," she said.

"You'll be back to make my dinner? Promise?"

"I promise."

She took the tray to the kitchen. The washing-up could wait. What couldn't wait was collecting Sam and going up to the Chippie to have words with Saqui and to collect the tenner he owed her for last night's work.

She grabbed Dave's ancient umbrella, and rushed out into the rain.

*

Gwynedd reached the cottage and banged on the door. It was immediately opened by Sam, as though he'd been waiting for her. Becky was hovering in the background. There were smells of bacon, coffee and toast.

"Have you had breakfast?" said Becky.

"That's very kind of you," said Gwynedd. "But me and Sam's in a bit of a hurry. Tell you what, you make us a take-away bacon butty while I help Sam into his waterproof, and then we'll be off and leave you in peace."

"Where are you going? It's pouring with rain."

"We're meeting up with some of Sam's old school mates. So that he'll be up to date with all their news when he starts back with us at school."

"What mates?"

"The old gang. Mollie..." Gwynedd would have bet a £50 note that Becky didn't know that Mollie was no longer a pupil at the High School and now lived miles away. "... Vinnie..." Becky didn't know that Vinnie had already left school. "... er, Little Huwie..." Becky didn't know anything about him. "… and, er, Kate… and, of course, Gustave."

One minute later, she and Sam were walking briskly up West Street.

"Little Huwie?" said Sam. "How long has Little Huwie played a leading role in your life?"

"I know, I know," she said. "But I had to say something."

"And Gustave?" said Sam. "Where the hell did Gustave come from?"

"I ran out of names. First stop the Chippie, right?"

When they reached the Chippie, they found Skinny Vinnie already there, sitting at a table with a weary-looking Saqui.

"I heard all about the fire last night," said Vinnie, "and come straight here, like. And Saqui tells me he's got this visitor. What's he called? Aslan, that's it. Sleeping upstairs. And the lad don't speak one word of English, which is ridiculous. This Aslan got to learn English right away if he's going to live here, isn't he?"

"Well, he won't come to you for lessons," said Gwynedd. She turned to Saqui. "How is he this morning?"

Saqui shook his head. "Not up yet. There's something preying on his mind. Something frightening him. In the end I locked him in the room upstairs last night. He seemed to be relieved. Said he'd feel safer. So I closed the Chippie and went home. When I opened up this morning, he was still here, but he wouldn't come down. I'd brought him some food, and bottles of water. He ate everything, drank a lot of the water but wouldn't say anything except to thank me over and over again."

"That's where you gotta look out, Saqui," said Vinnie. "You'll give him squatters' rights if you're not careful. He'll take over the place, and he'll have us all ordering goat and chips instead of small cod and chips."

Vinnie laughed. He always liked his jokes. Gwynedd said nothing. She was watching Sam, and she knew that he was listening for any noise from upstairs.

"The first thing to do today is get Azim a mobile phone," said Saqui. "I've been thinking. If he's going to stay here on his own at night, he's got to have some way of contacting me, in case anything goes wrong."

Vinnie finished laughing at his joke. He liked the idea that Aslan needed a phone. It opened up a chance of a little money-making.

"Right you are, Saqui," he said. "Can't be without a mobile these days. And I got a pal wants to sell one. Top of the range and he's only asking twenty quid. I don't know how well off for cash Aslan is, but you could lend him the money, eh, Saqui? Or we could all chip in a bit. I don't mind putting a quid towards it."

"I bet that's because your pal's only asking a tenner for the phone and you're going to pocket the rest," said Gwynedd.

"Hey, now, our Gwynedd. How did you know that?" Vinnie was shocked.

"Because you were trying to sell me that same mobile weeks ago. Only then, the price was a tenner."

"Oh, righto, Gwynedd. I'd forgot." Vinnie was unashamed. "Let's say fifteen quid then. Which is a bargain. And it's pay-as-you-go, like, which everyone reckons the best system there is. Mind you, someone will have to teach Aslan how these things work. Don't suppose they have them where he comes from."

"Vinnie's right," said Sam. "Azim must have a mobile. And that's only the beginning. We've got to look after him and equip him. He can't manage on his own."

"I think he's got a bit of money," said Saqui, "but I've no idea how much…"

Sam gave Gwynedd a look that said 'keep your mouth shut'. She understood, and said nothing.

"… and he won't know how or where to shop. Anyone could cheat him."

Gwynedd looked at Vinnie. "You listening?" she said.

Vinnie tried to look hurt.

"The first thing to do is make him comfortable here," said Sam. "He'll need a bed and a mattress, sheets, pillows, a duvet or blankets, something comfortable to sit on, towels, some more clothes…"

Gwynedd had to stop her mouth sagging open as Sam reeled off his list of Azim's needs. This was posh stuff. That was Sam the Toff – or, rather, Becky, his Toff mum. Gwynedd did not doubt that Azim needed all these things, but who was going to pay for them?

"Where's the money going to come from for all these things?" She was prepared to give up the £50 note she and Sam had found, but Sam's list would cost hundreds. After paying for her new boots, she still had a bit of money left in the box under her bed, and she'd give it up if Sam told her to, but she did so hope he wouldn't.

Sam looked at Saqui.

"I can help," said Saqui, "but..." He didn't finish the sentence.

With all this talk of money, Vinnie wished he'd asked more for his pal's mobile.

"I think we may find that Azim has more money than we think."

Gwynedd had never heard Sam sound so serious, but it was Saqui who took charge.

"I shall talk to him."

Sam nodded.

"The rest of us will leave you two alone so that you can have a private conversation with Azim. He was terrified last night when he broke in and three of us rushed upstairs. Maybe he thinks someone's after him. And maybe he's right. But only someone who speaks his own language has a hope of finding out what's going on. Come on, Gwynedd. Let's go. You too, Vinnie. You let us know, Saqui, as soon as you've had a talk with Azim."

*

With a thick curtain of rain it wasn't easy to see through the Chip Shop windows from the bedroom over the pub, but Kyle could make out the figures of the black girl and the lad with one arm in a sling. The young man who ran the place was in there, too, with at least one more person – a thin male who'd arrived on a motor scooter.

If only this bloody rain would stop. Still, once the Chip Shop was open for business, they'd have the lights on and hopefully all would become clear. Kyle had done his homework. He knew when the Chippie would open because he'd been across the street to check opening times very early that morning, before it started raining.

Afternoon

The rain was getting steadily heavier, and the wind was driving fiercely against Gwynedd as she charged up the hill to the bungalow. She was in a hurry to give Dave his dinner and then race back into town. There was so much to talk about with Sam. All the business about Azim: people being after him, and Sam suggesting that Azim might have more money than they had realised. On top of that, there hadn't been a chance to discuss the wonderful news about Sam's return.

They had arranged to meet at Lavender Cottage, and this was why she'd given Dave the fastest dinner he'd ever had, and was now racing through the wind and the rain, on her way to the cottage that Becky had rented.

She thumped on the door. Sam opened it.

"Welcome to Lavender Cottage," he said.

"Lavender? Pong nice, does it?"

"We do our best," he said. "I'll give you the guided tour. We'll start on the upper floor. If you'll walk this way, madam..."

He walked in a crazy way, stamping his feet and swaying from side to side as he moved. She copied him. It was a bit of silliness they'd often shared in the old days. She was pleased when he looked round to check that she was joining him in the old gag.

Gwynedd noted the thickness of the lavender-coloured carpet on the stairs, the warmth of the building, the neat little touches – a pretty plant in a pretty pot on a window sill, a pretty picture or two on the walls, a cosy chair on a little landing. It was like a Dream Cottage.

"This place has got two bathrooms!" Gwynedd sounded shocked. "One of them's got a basin where you turn the water on with your elbows, like in those TV hospital dramas. And they've both got showers. It must have been built for really dirty people."

"The filthy rich." said Sam.

"Like Martin."

"Martin's not really rich."

"He is filthy, though, isn't he?"

He showed her his room. It was cleaner and neater than any bedroom she had ever seen, not that she'd seen many. They stood by the window and glanced at the big bed. She put her arm round him. He put his good arm round her. She tightened her grip. His didn't change. She kissed his cheek, gently. Then they faced each other and she suddenly realised how much he had grown. A year ago, she'd been slightly taller than him. Now, if she were to take her boots off, it would be the other way round. He was taller, and looked stronger. All thoughts of Azim went out of her mind. She wondered what Sam was thinking. She kissed his cheek a second time. Now his arm tightened round her waist. Gwynedd knew they were about to kiss, when Becky called up to them.

"Lunch is ready."

They went downstairs.

"Hallo, Gwynedd."

Becky looked at Gwynedd's boots. Gwynedd thought she was admiring them.

"Sam," said Becky. "You did tell Gwynedd to wipe her boots carefully when she came in, didn't you... No. I see you didn't."

Gwynedd looked back up the stairs. Her smart boots had spread some good Welsh mud on the gorgeous, thick, lavender-coloured carpet. Hastily, but too late, she took them off.

"Don't worry, Mrs Harper," said Gwynedd. "Give us a damp cloth and I'll rub that mess off in no time."

"No, no, no. Not at all. It's nothing," said Becky. "I'd much rather attend to it later."

They sat at the table in the kitchen-diner, laid for three, with bowls of steaming soup and hunks of brown granary bread on side plates all ready for them.

"Spar, is it? You can't beat a tin of Spar soup. My Grandad loves 'em."

"It's home-made," said Sam, before Becky could say anything. "Mum made it." He knew it was some kind of penance on Becky's part for eating takeaway fish-and-chips the night before. "No further calls from Martin?"

Becky shook her head.

"Good," said Sam.

The meal took ages. Becky had made some sort of eggy-spinachy tart. Gwynedd had never liked spinach, but she forced it down. With it was a salad that tasted of 80% garlic.

"I'm afraid there's no pudding." Becky made the news sound as though someone close had died.

Immensely relieved, as though she'd just been let off a school detention, Gwynedd did the best thing possible to ensure that she and Sam would be sent away.

"Let me help you with the washing-up," she said. Even if Lavender Cottage hadn't possessed a dishwasher it was unlikely that Becky would trust Gwynedd with plates and glasses that belonged to the owner of the cottage. Becky had experienced some of the results of Gwynedd's helping with the washing-up in the old days. Her offer was turned down.

Gwynedd and Sam were back upstairs in Sam's room, sitting on the big bed and holding hands.

"You really are coming back?" She knew he'd said that yesterday, but it still sounded too good to be true.

"Yeah. Back to Rhayader."

"And back to our school?"

"Yeah."

She threw herself upon him. He struggled to free himself from her grasp, and they both sat up.

"Mind my arm!"

"No more posh school? No more Fionas? No more Tatianas? No more Camillas?" They were names that had been in her mind for a long time, names that she connected with Bristol and with a character she called 'Sexy Sam, the Ladies Man'.

"Mum couldn't afford it. Not now she and Martin are splitting up. Will you mind my bloomin' arm!"

"I could give you an awesome good time," she said.

"At the Chippie? I didn't think Life could ever get better than that."

"Don't be rotten or I will break your bloomin' arm. Seriously, though, you are glad that you're coming back, that we'll be together again, aren't you?"

"Depends on what turns up. I'll let you know in a couple of years' time." He sounded serious. "Rhayader is lovely and all that, but it is a bit of a backwater, isn't it. I mean, it's a bit boring, isn't it?"

"Boring? Isn't finding a £50 note exciting?"

"Maybe."

"And you don't call finding a mysterious Asian lad squatting in an empty house exciting?"

"Maybe."

"And finding me? That's not the most exciting thing of all?"

"No. Definitely not."

"And isn't this exciting?"

She moved her face very close to his.

"Sam." That was Becky, once again calling from downstairs.

"We'd better go down," he said.

"First things first," said Gwynedd, and she kissed him. It was not an all-out kiss. But to her, it was soft and powerful at the same time. In all their years together, this was the first kiss she had given him, or anyone else, that went beyond friendship. "There," she said. "There's something that happens here."

They went downstairs with Gwynedd noticing that almost all traces of the mud she had brought into the cottage had been wiped from the carpet, and that there was a smell of some lavender-scented cleaning product in the air. As she pulled on her boots, there was a loud knock at the cottage door.

Sam opened it. And there was Martin, standing in the rain and looking sour.

"Where's your mother?" he said. "Get out of the way, I want to talk to her."

Martin ignored Gwynedd and pushed past Sam. As he did so, he shoved the end of a piece of string into Sam's hand.

"You can look after this. I've had enough."

At the other end of the piece of string was Ben.

Sam passed the string to Gwynedd.

"Can you take him outside and hold on to him? I want to check that Mum's OK."

Gwynedd and Ben went into the garden. It was still raining hard. The dog remembered her, and was delighted to see her, jumping and leaping in its attempts to reach a face he had licked many times in the past. She crouched down and patted him, shielding him from the rain.

"We don't like Martin, do we?" she said. "He boozes and nearly kills your lovely master, right? And he ties wonderful dogs up with cheap bits of string. Bloody nerve of the man."

Ben's tongue thrashed about in his efforts to lick her.

Sam came out of the cottage, and Ben almost tore the string from Gwynedd's hand as he rushed to his master.

"We're going for a walk," said Sam. "I think Mum will be OK. Martin insists he sees her 'privately', as he calls it. I think he's going to beg her to change her mind and move back in with him."

"Would she do that?"

"No idea. But let's get out of here."

"We can't walk in the rain," she said. "Come up the bungalow."

"Will your Grandad let Ben in? I thought he once said he'd never have a dog in his house again."

"He's not like Martin," she said. "He can be reasonable when he wants to be, or when I make him."

*

Coleson was chucking empty beer cans in the waste basket of the pub bedroom. Kyle had told him to leave the mess, the girl from Reception could clear all that up. That was part of her job. But Coleson was getting desperate to find something to do. The strain of waiting to make his first kill was becoming more than he could bear.

Kyle was relaxed. He was standing at the window watching water gushing from the bottoms of the drainpipes on the shops across the street, and thinking what a miserable dump this was.

A call came through on Coleson's mobile. It was from his lousy big brother, the self-styled Chief, back at the Farm. It was not a friendly call. The Chief wanted to know how much longer he'd have to wait before he got his bag and his money back. When Coleson told him they'd found the Scumbag Kid, but hadn't so far been able to kill him, the Chief wanted to know why they hadn't. Coleson made signs to Kyle that he should take the call. Kyle shook his head. This was Coleson's Rite of Passage.

Kyle stayed by the window, looking out. There were no signs of movement at the Fish and Chip shop right now, but there had been visitors this morning. Kyle had watched the guy who ran the shop, arrive, unlock the door and go in. He was carrying a plastic bag. Kyle could see it wasn't empty. He would have liked to have known what was in the bag because, if it had been, say, food and drink, that might suggest that the guy had a guest staying at the Fish and Chip shop. A skinny Asian Scumbag Kid, perhaps.

Not long after the owner's arrival, another bloke had turned up on a scooter with a big box fastened to the back. It was the sort of box that was used by pizza delivery guys.

This was good. Whoever this new guy was, the box would make it easy for Kyle to recognise the scooter if he saw it again. Not long after that, the black girl had also come to the Fish and Chip shop, with her boyfriend, the one with the busted arm. It looked like there was some sort of meeting taking place, not a long meeting, because half an hour or so later, everyone had come out, and the guy owning the shop had locked it up again. This time, he wasn't carrying a plastic bag.

Four people had gone in. Four people now came out, but Kyle was pretty sure there was a fifth person inside, and that person was the one that his nervous partner was going to have to kill.

*

Ben sniffed the finger that was pointing at him and gave it a respectful lick.

"Smell my dinner, can you?" said Dave. "Bloody awful dinner it was, too. What was that you give me, our Gwynedd?"

"It's called Arctic Harvest," she said. "Boil in a bag."

"The names they give things these days. Why've you brought this lad and this bloody dog here?"

"The dog needs somewhere to live."

"What about you, lad?"

"I'm staying at Lavender Cottage," said Sam. "With my Mum."

"I remember her," said Dave. "Good looking woman. Widow."

"You fancy her," said Gwynedd.

"Don't be ridiculous. The only thing I fancy is a decent glass of beer."

Dave winked at Sam.

"We'll look after your dog. I know the couple that own Lavender Cottage. Stuck-up pair. Are they letting you breathe in their cottage? Yes? Well, I am surprised. That's not like them."

The afternoon turned out far better than either Sam or Gwynedd had expected. Worn out by the strain of travelling all the way from Bristol in Martin's car, Ben went to sleep at Sam's feet. Gwynedd fetched tea and biscuits from the kitchen. There was no mention of Asian lads or £50 notes. Instead, conversation turned to absent parents – Sam's dad and Gwynedd's mum and dad.

"You've neither of you got dads," said Dave, as though he'd only just thought of that.

"What was my Dad like?" said Gwynedd.

"I've told you all that before."

"Tell me again."

"I didn't like him. He was a handsome beggar – it's from him that you get your good looks. But with him, sadly, you couldn't say 'Handsome is as handsome does'."

It was the first time he'd ever said anything about her having good looks.

"Did he love… your Rachel?" She had never been able to refer to Rachel as 'my Mum'. Rachel was Dave's daughter, and that was as close as Gwynedd was prepared to keep her memory.

"I never knew. Rachel, your Mum, reckoned he did, else she wouldn't have gone off with him. Deserting you, like. I could never forgive him that."

Gwynedd hesitated before asking her next question. She didn't want to upset Dave.

"Did Rachel love him?"

"Oh God, Gwynedd. I don't want to go there." He was blinking now. "Yes, she loved him. She was crazy about him. Thought the sun shone from under both his armpits. From the moment she saw him, she didn't have eyes for no one else. Not me. Not your Nan. Not even for you, when you came along. Your Mum would have done anything for him. If he'd told her to throw herself off the cliffs above Aberystwyth, she'd have done it with a smile on her lovely face."

"Do you think she loved him so much, there wasn't any love left for anyone else?"

Both Dave and Gwynedd were surprised by Sam's question.

"You've got me there," said Dave. "I dunno what to say. What d'you think, Gwynedd?"

There wasn't much that Gwynedd thought she could say. She could tell Sam how much she envied him when he complained about Becky. Every time he grumbled about his mum, Gwynedd wanted to point out how lucky he was to have a mum to moan about. And most of his complaints were to do with Becky making a fuss of him. Gwynedd had no memory of anyone ever making a fuss of her. Dave loved her, in his funny old way, but the only things Dave fussed about were his meals, his early morning cups of tea, and his television. He used to fuss about his smokes, but not since he'd given up smoking. If Sam was right about people having a limited amount of love to give, then Dave should have had a little bit more love to give her when he had stopped his beloved smoking. If so, she hadn't noticed it.

"What about when people love more than one person?" she said.

For all his complaints about her, she knew Sam loved Becky. What she wanted to know was, did he have some left over for other people? Was there someone in Bristol he loved? A girl-friend at school? Would he ever love someone in Rhayader? Someone who was sitting right next to him? Someone willing and available? She didn't dare stare at him in case her feelings for him were written all over her face.

Ben woke up, shook himself, and barked. Dave raised his stick.

"Don't you dare hit my dog!" Sam grabbed Ben and held the dog in his arms.

Dave put his stick down. "Well, Gwynedd, there's love clear enough. Your Sam loves his mum and he's still got some left over for his bloody dog. Mind you, he's got it all wrong. It weren't his dog I was going to hit. It was him. You ask him a fair question about what happens when a bloke loves more than one person, and he don't answer.

He sits there, quiet as a tombstone. That's what got my back up. But wasn't there somebody else he used to fancy? Mollie Pryce, wasn't it? Yeah, I remember you telling me, Gwynedd, about how he fancied Mollie Pryce."

Gwynedd glanced at Sam. He was looking at her. There was anger on his face.

"What?" she said.

"You say such stupid things," he said. "You get these mad ideas in your head."

"You don't speak to my grand-daughter like that. I'm telling you." The old man was furious. "You stand there with that bloomin' mutt in your arms and your mouth shut tight as a rabbit trap. Why don't you open your gob and tell my Gwynedd what you like about her? That's all she wants to hear. Put that dog down, wash your hands, and take my Gwynedd into the kitchen. You don't have to say anything about love, just be nice to her and then the pair of you can get me a cup of tea and some biscuits."

Sam and Gwynedd did as they were told, save for one of Dave's instructions.

"Don't you dare say you love me. Not now. Not straight after he's told you not to." Save it for another day, she thought.

"How am I supposed to know about love?" said Sam.

"But you know about loving your mum."

"Yeah, but that's different, isn't it."

"How should I know," said Gwynedd. "I don't have a mum. Or a dad. How am I supposed to know anything about love?"

"So, neither of us knows about love."

They looked at each other and laughed.

*

The rain stopped. The wind dropped. Half an hour later, Sam and Gwynedd were climbing the hill behind the bungalow, with Ben bouncing along beside them. Sam thought it would be easier to say what he wanted to say in the open air.

"Maybe we could find out more about love together," said Sam. And immediately, he wished he hadn't.

Gwynedd stopped walking. Silently, in her mind, she repeated to herself what Sam had just said, then flung her arms round him, and kissed his cheek.

"You need a shave," she said.

"I had one five days ago."

"You need another one. And who taught you how to shave? Martin?"

"You're joking," he said. "I'd never take advice from him."

"Is Martin going to put up a fight to stop Becky leaving him?"

"What can he do?"

"He could try bribery," said Gwynedd. "You can do anything if you've got enough money."

"It's all over. She's left him."

Gwynedd wasn't convinced. "But suppose Becky wants to stay with Martin because she thinks you need a father figure?"

It was a question he'd asked himself many times.

"I dunno."

"A father figure who's a drunk?"

"He's not drunk all the time."

"He was on the night of the accident. When he nearly killed you."

"He didn't nearly kill me. I was in hospital for only two days."

She wasn't convinced, and she wasn't sure he was convinced.

"Maybe it all depends on what's happening between them right now," she said. "Do you want to be there, with her?"

"I want to be here with you."

"Why don't you phone her? You could pretend you were phoning just to say you're all right and Ben's all right, and then it would be only natural to ask her if she's all right."

It was a good idea. If things were going wrong, he could be back at Lavender Cottage in under ten minutes. If all was well there, he would be free to stay with Gwynedd.

He phoned. The news from Becky was that Martin had left, but he wasn't immediately going back to Bristol. He would find somewhere to stay in the district. Becky said that she was sure Martin would want another meeting, and another and another and another, until she gave in. But that wasn't going to happen.

Sam asked what Martin had said about Ben. Becky told him Martin was adamant; he wouldn't take 'that bloody dog' back.

"He'll take you back," she said. "He knows he'd have to if he wants me. But he's gone for now, so you and Gwynedd enjoy yourselves. Celebrate, even if it's only at the Chippie."

"Thanks, Mum." The call ended. Sam put his phone back in his anorak pocket and, with his one good arm, grabbed hold of Gwynedd.

"Mum says everything's fine. She said we could go and celebrate."

He kissed her. The kiss was long, and would have been longer if the Velcro fastening on his sling hadn't started to slip so that they had to bring the kiss to an end.

"Goodness," she said. "It's good to know that you didn't learn that from Martin."

"I made it all up myself," he said.

She wondered if that was true. "Do Bristol girls kiss like that?"

"What makes you think I've been kissing Bristol girls?" A part of him wanted to tell her about the texts and emails that he'd been getting from Charlie. He didn't want to brag about it, far from it. He wanted her to understand that, though there were girls in Bristol – a couple of whom he had kissed a bit like that – they meant nothing to him. But that would take some explaining with Gwynedd.

"You didn't kiss like that before you went to Bristol. And I don't believe you could have made that all that up by yourself." She thought of the sad, hurried little kiss she'd given him right here, in this very same place, more than a year ago.

"There's this amazing website that teaches you how to do it."

She punched his good arm. "Don't be silly," she said.

"That's not fair," he said. "How do you expect me to be the world's greatest lover with both arms wrecked?"

They walked on until it began to get dark.

"What time is it?"

Sam consulted his phone.

"17.23."

"We've got to go back. Dave's tea..."

They walked back in silence. Sam was thinking about the strange happenings at the Chippie, and the mystery figure creeping into the derelict house down by the river, about the £50 note and the fear that had gripped Azim.

Gwynedd was thinking about Becky. Back in the old days Becky had become a sort of mum to her. She'd helped her at times when Dave would have been useless and embarrassed. She'd taken Gwynedd shopping to choose her first bra, and had talked to her about menstruation; she had bought Gwynedd sanitary pads in readiness. The day her periods started, although she knew what to do, it was a shock and Gwynedd's first thought had been to run down the road to tell Becky. Becky had made her a cup of hot chocolate and a hot water bottle and they had sat chatting cosily on the sofa together, as friend to friend. Becky had always been kind to her like that. But things had changed.

Then, it was as though she and Sam were brother and sister. Gwynedd wasn't sure how Becky would feel now about Sam having a black girl-friend.

Sam, too, had been thinking. As they neared the bungalow, he said: "It's always Dave, isn't it."

"Dave's all I've got."

"You've got me."

"Yes," she said. "That's true." But as she hugged him, she suddenly shivered. She had a frightening fear that she might not have Sam for long.

Evening

The Shop of Chips was crowded with customers. Upstairs, as he lay on the pile of blankets and rugs that Saqui had brought him, Azim could hear the noise of many people talking in the room below, could feel the heat generated by their bodies, and could smell the hot oil that was cooking fish and chips. All was well.

Saqui had been up to see him, and to tell him that a friend called Binnie was coming to the Shop of Chips later that night. Binnie would bring with him a mobile phone. This was going to be Azim's mobile phone. Saqui had said the mobile phone would mean that Azim could call and speak to him any time Azim was worried. Saqui had made it sound as though this mobile phone would make everything and everyone safe. Azim doubted this was true.

He still hadn't told Saqui, or anyone else, about the bag, the money or the hunters. The bag was now hidden in the darkest corner of the room Azim was living in. It couldn't stay there for long. There was the danger that someone would find it. Saqui had made it sound as if Azim could live in the Shop of Chips for ever, but Azim knew that couldn't be. He would have to leave sometime. He had a task to perform and a journey that he had to make. He had to carry the bag of money to Uncle as soon as possible. It would be a long journey and it would take a long time. Azim couldn't take the bag on a plane – the soldiers and the police at any airport would search the bag, and then keep the money for themselves. To walk across all the land that lay between the Shop of Chips and Uncle's house in the Afghan mountains would take more than a year, and there would be so many dangers on the way. The hunters would pursue him in lorries and cars and jeeps, and would soon catch up with him. But if Azim could find a boat, then he would have the best chance of getting safely home.

Azim was looking forward to receiving the mobile phone. He had heard of and seen such things, but he had never owned one. Saqui had said that, with this mobile phone, Azim would be able to send messages to Saqui and even speak with him.

"You will be able to tell me that you are safe."

Saqui had made it sound as though he knew Azim was going to leave. And Saqui was right. Azim could not stay long in this room above the Shop of Chips. He could tell from the level of the sun on the few times that it appeared that winter would soon be coming to UK, and that here, as in anywhere in the world, winter would make travelling much harder.

But, for a little while, for another night or two at least, Azim would stay here, to rest and make preparations for the first part of his journey – the walk to the sea. There was a river in this big village. Uncle had taught Azim that all rivers lead to the sea. When he was ready, Azim would follow this river until he reached the sea, where there would be boats to take him to the other side of the world, to his homeland, his true home, and his goats.

It was quieter downstairs. It sounded as though people were gradually leaving. Azim could now distinguish other noises: the sound of the TV, high up on its shelf on the wall opposite the shop door; the voice of the black girl; the hissing and spluttering of food as pieces of fish and saveloys in batter were dropped into the scalding oil.

He heard the sound of a scooter engine, revving outside the shop. The revving stopped, and Azim heard the shop door open and close, then another voice, which sounded like one he'd heard this morning. Perhaps this was the man who was bringing the mobile phone. Azim listened hard. There was what sounded like an argument with the black girl, and then laughter. Then he heard the sound of feet climbing the wooden stairs. Two people's feet, he reckoned.

There was a gentle knock at the door.

"Yes, please, for me."

The door opened. Saqui entered with a man Azim had never seen before. Saqui said the man was Binnie, the man with the phone.

It didn't matter to Vinnie that Azim couldn't understand a word of what he was saying. The important thing was to get the message across.

"See, like, Aslan, I got this mobile especially for you. So's you can keep in touch with your cousin Saqui. Sam, downstairs, he don't know nothing. Right? He's, like, saying it's an old phone because the numbers on the buttons are, like, a bit worn. But you know how to count, Aslan, don't you? It was your lot invented proper numbers, wasn't it? One… two… three… and so on. And all you have to do for texts is remember, like, press one once for A, twice for B, three times for C, and so on, through the buttons… D… E… F… So, like, if you was wanting to text your name, it'd be, like, Button 1, press once, and there's your A. Then press Button 7 four times, and there's S. Button 5, three times, there's L. Back to A, Button 1 once, and finally Button 6, twice for N. Then you got Aslan."

"His name's Azim," said Saqui. "A… Z… I… M."

"Better still," said Vinnie. "Only four letters. Button 1, once. Button 9, four times. That's Z…

"He won't be sending texts. Azim doesn't know the English alphabet."

"Go on?" said Vinnie. "You're havin' a joke. But, any roads, you listen to this ringtone, Azlim. You hold your mobile and I'll call you on mine."

He shoved the mobile into Azim's hands, took out his own mobile and punched in a number. Azim's mobile shivered in his hand. He dropped it as though it had stung him. The mobile clattered on to the floor, setting off the ringtone, the first four bars of *Men of Harlech*.

"Good Welsh ringtone," said Vinnie. "You wouldn't get that in Africa."

Saqui explained to Vinnie in English and to Azim in his own language that he would teach Azim how to use the mobile before he locked up the Chippie that night. He handed Vinnie ten pounds and pushed him out of the room.

"I thought we'd, like, agreed fifteen," said Vinnie. "Oh, yes. An' anytime you want a Zippo lighter, Azlin, you let me know. I can get you one cheaper than eBay…"

Vinnie was still talking as Saqui guided him downstairs.

Left alone in the upstairs room, Azim fiddled with his new mobile for a while, then lay down on the pile of blankets and went to sleep.

*

Kyle had seen the black girl and the one-armed lad shuffling up the street and going into the Chip Shop hours ago. He'd watched from the window of the pub bedroom all evening, noting that the place was unusually busy. He'd also seen the arrival, late, of the man on the pizza delivery scooter. A lot of the coming and going of the one-armed lad and the black girl puzzled him. Did they know about the bag and the money? He assumed that the guy who owned the place did. Why else would he be sheltering the Scumbag Kid?

Kyle had everything planned. At some point tonight the owner guy would lock the place up with the Kid in it, like he'd done last night. That would be the time to put the plan into action. The only uncertainty was the location of the bag. There was only one way to find out.

He'd spent a lot of time planning the details of this killing, with the promise of little reward. The Chief had been back on the phone to Coleson, threatening to cut the money he'd pay for the killing if it wasn't done tonight. Well, be that as it may. If the Scumbag Kid really did have the bag, with what? – a hundred grand in it? More? Once the money was in Kyle's possession, maybe that was where it should stay. It shouldn't be hard to find a way of killing Coleson as well as the Kid, and dumping both bodies in the reservoir. But that was a decision for later. Right now, Kyle wanted to go through the plans for tonight one more time.

A rifle bullet can do other things besides killing people. It can travel a very long way in a very short time. The right sort of bullet, fired from a high velocity gun can pass through a pane of glass leaving only a nice neat little hole. And the bullets that Kyle had brought with him to this lousy dump were very much the right sort. And so was the high velocity rifle.

He reckoned he had the plan all sorted. When the time was right, with everyone else tucked up in bed, he would be in position at the window of their room, with his surly apprentice Coleson by his side. On Kyle's order, Coleson was to fire a single shot through the window of the room above the Chip Shop. Kyle told Coleson that he was to aim high, so there was no danger of hitting anyone in the room. The bullet would whack into the far wall, making enough noise to wake the Kid, but no one else. And it was a cinch that once the Kid saw the hole in the window and the bullet in the wall, he'd put two and two together, and know it was time to go. And that's when they'd get him.

Perfect. But Coleson didn't see it that way.

"I don't know if this is the right way to go about it. In the middle of town. Can't we wait to get the Kid somewhere empty, like out by the reservoir?"

Kyle didn't answer. Those bloody images were coming back into his mind... the babes lying in the dust of Africa, with the flies swarming, and the blood drying on the dead faces. And he felt the wet heat that clogged your nostrils, and the dust that coated the inside of your mouth and the back of your throat. And he heard the buzzing of flies as they swarmed over the bodies, and the clumsy flapping of wings as vultures half flew and half ran away from their feasting while the convoy of mercenaries passed. No, it would be mad to make a massacre out of this. He was being paid to superintend only one killing. Why make extra work that he wouldn't be paid for?

For the next hour and a half, the gunmen kept their eyes on the room above the Chip Shop. There was no sign of movement. The last customers departed. The man on the pizza delivery scooter left. The lights were still on in the Chip Shop itself, and Kyle and Coleson could see the Asian bloke who ran the Chip Shop, the black girl and her one-armed boyfriend clearing up for the night. A little after ten the lights went out, and they left. The Chip Shop was empty.

· And five minutes later, there was a weak beam of light in the upstairs room, as though someone in there had turned on a torch, maybe from a mobile phone.

"We've got him," whispered Kyle.

He began to assemble the high velocity gun, taking great care to fit the silencer.

*

In the room above the Chippie, Azim lay under the blankets, fully dressed. He hadn't moved for some time. Immediately after Binnie's departure, Saqui had given Azim a lesson in use of the mobile phone. Azim was a quick learner for he had seen people using them on Afghan TV, and Uncle possessed a mobile, though he had never allowed Azim to use it.

Azim had pretended to be asleep when Saqui had looked in several hours ago, because he didn't want to speak to anyone. He had made up his mind. He would leave tonight. This was a dangerous place, with dangerous people in it. There was the Hunter, maybe more than one hunter. There were people who suspected him of being a thief, people in shops and cafés. Even the people that Saqui said were his friends, people who smiled and looked as though they were trying to help, even they must be dangerous. Azim felt he had known nothing but fear here. He was ready to go.

He would take the money with him. He had already pulled the bag from the darkest corner of the room, and it was now under the blanket with him. If anyone found it, at least they'd have to fight to take it from him. He was also ready to take the food that Saqui had brought him, several packets of dried fruit and nuts. He would put the food in the bag, and also the shard of glass – his only weapon. And once he had all that in the bag, he would make for the hills. The Hunter, the man who had been out of breath on the footbridge, would not be a Man of the Hills. He would not have the skill or the stamina to cross the mountain land on foot, and Azim would make sure that the route he followed kept well away from roads. And not even Saqui and the friends of Saqui would be able to keep pace with him in the hills. He would be truly alone, and there were always hiding places to be found in hills and mountains. Azim decided he would make his own way over the hills and mountains to the sea and freedom. He would not follow the course of the river that flowed under the bridge. That went too near the crowded parts of this big village. He would find a river of his own in the hills.

It would be like a pilgrimage, a lonely journey on foot. Uncle had frequently lectured him on how it was every man's duty to make a pilgrimage – a journey that was not only an act of Faith, like the Hajj, but also a test of manhood. Uncle had described pilgrims as men who dressed in two sheets of white material and a pair of sandals. Would his journey still qualify as a pilgrimage if he wore sweatshirt, jeans, and heavy boots? He made a silent promise that he would take off the boots whenever possible.

All he had to do was wait until the big village was asleep. Then he would start.

Sometime later he switched on the mobile that the strange Binnie man had brought him. He wanted to know what time it was. The display showed 01:07. He would wait a little longer.

*

From their room on the other side of the street, Kyle and Coleson saw the pale light in the room over the Chip Shop. The Scumbag Kid must be awake. It was time to make their play.

Kyle picked up the rifle and adjusted the night-sight. It didn't matter that there was no sign of a human figure. The place to aim would be dead centre and a little over halfway up the far wall of the room above the Chip Shop. No fear of killing the Kid, but near enough to make him wet his pants and then bolt for wherever he'd stashed the bag.

He passed the gun to Coleson.

"For Chrissake aim high. We don't want to kill him until he's got the bag with him. Right?"

Kyle opened the window of the pub bedroom, so that there was a gap just big enough for Coleson to push the muzzle of the rifle through.

Coleson steadied his sweating hands. He took a deep breath. And he remembered that he must squeeze the trigger, not tug at it…

*

Azim heard the bullet whack through the glass and into the wall. It was a sound he'd heard before, when the Taliban had killed Uncle's goats, and many other times, so he recognised it immediately. The hunters had found him. They had come to kill him. He must go now. He switched off the mobile.

This had to be the start of his pilgrimage. Azim snatched up the carrier bag of food that Saqui had brought him. His hand reached out for the blanket. He would be sleeping rough for the next few days. It would make the nights more bearable, but it was heavy and cumbersome, and it would slow him down. It might even make it easier for the hunters to spot him. The blanket would have to lie where it was. He grabbed the bag of money and put his arms through the handles, so that its weight was on his back and his shoulders, like a rucksack.

He felt his way to the broken window at the back of the building and climbed out on to the roof. He moved as fast as he could, praying that there wouldn't be another Hunter positioned in the yard below, ready and waiting for him. He crawled along the ridge, dragging the carrier bag behind him. When he reached the end of the roof, he peered over. Praise be to Allah, the van was still there. He dropped his carrier bag over the edge of the roof. It seemed to take a long time to hit the ground. Then he turned round, and crawled backwards until his body hung over the edge of the roof. Holding on to the ridge with his left hand, he reached down with his right to grab the guttering. This was the tricky bit, with the weight of the bag pressing on his shoulders and threatening to pull him over the edge. If he fell between the wall of the building and the back of the van, he could well break a couple of ribs. But if he pushed off with one of his legs, he should be able to swing his body away from the wall, and then drop on to the roof of the van. He kicked out with his left foot.

There was an almighty clanging and booming as he landed, boots first, on the roof of the van, followed by banging and clattering as he staggered towards the front of the van. There was no point in waiting to see if anyone had heard the racket. Noise didn't matter now. What mattered was speed. He seized the van's aerial, and slid down the windscreen to land on the bonnet. The last bit was easy – leaping down in life is always easier than climbing up. He simply jumped from the bonnet on to the ground.

Azim picked up his carrier bag. There was no one about. He could take risks now. He ran across the yard and down the little passage that led to the road. Here he turned left, away from the street the Shop of Chips was in, until he came to the side road that led downhill. As he hoped, it led to the river. He was upstream of the derelict house, but not far from it. He approached the house carefully – there was a chance that the Hunters might be waiting somewhere near.

If the Hunters were waiting for him, this would be where they destroyed him, because he would be all that stood between them and the money. But if he could get away with the bag, well away from the town, then perhaps the Hunters would leave Saqui and all the others alone. Once he was clear of the town all he had to do was let the countryside swallow him up.

He had a sudden idea. There was one more thing he could do before he left, one last message he could leave behind for Saqui and that strange black woman and the young man with the injured arm.

He took a 50 note from the bag and placed it neatly on the ground, at the base of the low wall to the rear of the derelict house. To make sure the note didn't blow away, he covered one corner of it with a half brick. It was impossible for any passer-by to notice it. Only people with a special interest in this area, in the derelict house would ever come near enough to see it. Azim's hope was that Saqui might come here searching for him. Saqui would find the note, and would know that his friend Azim was alive. If the Hunters found it, too bad. They, too, would know he was alive, but they wouldn't know where he was going.

And there was one thing more to do. The carrier bag with his fruit and nuts was white plastic. It would show up clearly if it was caught in the headlights of any vehicle. He'd have to get rid of it. He crammed the small packets of fruit and nuts through the slit in the bag of money, on top of the notes, and threw the plastic carrier bag away. That was better.

He crossed the bridge. A hundred paces further on there was a turning to the right that looked as though it led up into the hills. The clouds had cleared away. There was now a bright moon. The sky was full of stars. The air was cold, but it was clean. It was time to start his pilgrimage.

Azim headed for the hills.

*

In the pub bedroom Coleson waited, rifle in hand, fighting down panic.

"What do we do?"

Kyle heard the fear in Coleson's voice. He didn't share it, but clearly something had gone wrong. The Scumbag Kid should have been out of the Chip Shop long ago. He should be lying on the pavement, with blood seeping from the hole in his head made by Bullet Number 2. But, as it was, Bullet Number 2 hadn't been fired yet. Its target hadn't appeared. Where the hell was the Scumbag Kid? Waiting upstairs for a second bullet? No way. He had to show himself, to come out on to the street, either bringing the bag with him or making a rush to wherever he'd got the bag hidden.

Unless Bullet Number 1 had hit him. Surely not! Impossible. Kyle had seen Coleson aim high enough to pass over the top of a fully grown man, let alone a kid. Unless the Kid had been bouncing on a mattress like it was a trampoline. No…

"Where the hell is he?" Kyle kept his voice low. He wasn't going to show Coleson that he was angry.

"Maybe he's got the bag hidden away somewhere else..."

Kyle nodded. There were so many places to hide a bag in that dump across the road – under the floorboards in the upstairs room, or in the attic, the loft, under the stairs, under the eaves... somewhere pretty bloody inaccessible. The bag had been stashed away so well it was taking the Kid a long term to get at it.

"Keep the gun at your shoulder. Keep your eyes on the street door of the Chip Shop. He has to come out there."

Coleson did as he was told.

Any second now...

But another minute passed, and the Kid still hadn't emerged from the Chip Shop, with or without the bag.

Jesus Christ, thought Kyle. Was there a back way out of the building?

His mind raced. What should they do? Even in the middle of the night he couldn't send Coleson charging through the town with a rifle in his hands. They'd have to do the business with hand guns. Should they leave the rifle here, or sling it in the boot of the Merc before heading to the back of the Chip Shop? Were they ever likely to come back to the pub once they'd killed the Kid and got the bag? Jesus, what a mess. The Chief would have a fit.

First things first. Get the bag, then kill the Kid. Everything else would have to wait.

Kyle snatched the rifle from Coleson, chucked it under the bed, strapped on his shoulder holster, grabbed his black leather jacket, and beckoned to Coleson to follow him.

They moved swiftly and silently down the pub staircase. The nice young woman behind the bar had given them a key to the back door of the pub, in case they fancied a late night out, so that they could get back in. Whether they would want to get back in now depended on how long it took to find the Scumbag Kid, get the bag, kill the Kid and dispose of the body out at the reservoir.

You earned your money in this game…

Night

It was still dark. Azim was happy about that. He felt safe in the dark. Out here in the open, there would be plenty of warning of the approach of a car or truck. He would see their headlights miles away on this road. He had decided not to stick to his pilgrim vows and avoid roads. Marching over the rough grass and outcrops of rock was tough going. The road surface was too good a surface to be ignored. Though the road climbed steeply, it was easy walking. The sense that he was headed for the hills spurred him on. Ever since he had come to this small but strange and dangerous country, he had missed the comfort and the strength to be found in the massive highlands at home. The Farm had been a place of misery, set in low-lying flat land, where the rainwater collected quickly but took its time to dribble away. Up here, down to his left, he could see a young river, tumbling and twinkling in the soft and hazy moonlight. It gave him a sense of superiority to look down on water.

For the last few hundred paces, the road had brushed the edge of a strip of woodland. The trees were poor stunted things that had spent their whole lives lashed by rushing winds. Nonetheless, Azim kept the trees in mind. Trees offered safety and a place to hide from the probing headlights of any car. As yet, he'd been overtaken by not a single car. This suggested that, as yet, the Hunters were not on his trail. But now, the land to his right was opening out. He was above the tree line. No matter, he would see headlights long before any vehicle got near him.

The air was the best he'd tasted since he left home. The sound of the clump of his boots mixed peacefully enough with those of the munching of grass coming from the fattest cattle he'd ever seen, and with the snuffling of the sheep who stepped neatly out of his way as he stomped past. He felt the wind's increasing power hitting his face.

He wondered how long he'd been walking... maybe an hour. Then he remembered his mobile. That would tell him the time. He fished it out of the bag and switched it on. There was no signal, but the clock in it was still operating: 03.27. He had been walking longer than he thought, more than two hours, but he still had plenty of energy. He would walk until his legs could go no further, or until his feet began to blister. He slipped the bag off his back and reached inside for the packets of fruit and nuts. He ate two handfuls, and hooked the bag back over his shoulders.

He came to a fork in the road. Straight ahead the road was level, heading in the same direction as it had from the moment he'd left the town. To the left, however, the road plunged down towards a bridge over a river that fed into a big lake. But the river looked as though it was flowing back towards the town, and Azim had no wish to go that way. It was an easy choice; he would go straight on. What he was hoping for was a river flowing in the opposite direction. Somewhere ahead there must be a watershed, like the watersheds in the mountains at home; a sign that you were heading into new country.

He was thirsty. There was plenty of water nearby, in ditches, in pools by the roadside, in the streams that tumbled below him. But was any of it safe to drink? Sheep and cattle pissed on the land every day, and the rain washed any parasites in the piss into the streams. Azim had seen the effect of animal diseases back home – cattle with almost skeletal bodies, with swollen heads, and sheep limping with black disease. He had been brought up to take the greatest care when drinking untested water.

He reached a point where a hill stream flowed out from under the road and tumbled swiftly away. He left the road and clambered down to reach the stream, cupped his hand in its water and brought it up to his face. He sniffed it. It smelt pure. He dabbed a little of the water on his lips and splashed some over his face. That would have to do for the moment. He wouldn't risk drinking any of it yet. Higher up in the hills there would be cleaner streams.

He climbed back on to the road. There was no stiffness in his leg muscles, no soreness in his feet. He looked at the mobile. There was still no signal, but another 50 minutes had passed. Was 50 a good number, or a bad number? It had been the number on the notes, and it was the notes that the Hunters were after. He must hurry. There would be perhaps another two hours of darkness. He could easily walk for much of that time, and every mile he covered took him further from the Hunters.

He hadn't yet reached the watershed. The landscape was deceptive in the way that upland landscapes always are. Time and again Azim was convinced that he had reached the high point of his trek, only to discover another ridge a few hundred paces ahead, and then another, and another. He was hungry and thirsty, but he had no idea how much further he had to go. It would be foolish to eat before he needed, and then run out of food before he got to his destination – wherever that was.

Water was still not a problem. There was a trickle of a stream beside him right now, flowing back the way he had come. He was on a sort of plateau, wide and flat, with a sluggish river snaking its way along, creating mossy bogs speckled with clumps of tough grass. This was not a promising landscape for clean water or a comfortable place in which to shelter and hide once daylight appeared.

He decided that he would rest as soon as he found a suitable place. He hoped for an abandoned shepherd's hut, like the ones in the mountains at home – rough piles of stone roofed with poles and brushwood, and with fires permanently burning outside them. But he had seen no such fires since he had left the big village. Shepherds did not light them here in UK. Perhaps they had invented other ways of keeping warm. Anyway, there would be no fire for him tonight, and possibly no roof over his head. He looked up at the sky. The moon and stars were beginning to fade, and the air was colder – that penetrating cold that comes in the hour before dawn.

The plateau widened and the road levelled. It would soon be time for Azim to be true to the Pilgrim Code, to leave the road and walk wherever he could find a reasonably dry passage for his feet. There were few trees here. The only ones he could see were poor specimens, small, bent and bare. He needed to rest. He would have to stop as soon as he found some sort of cover.

He was almost past it before he saw it; the remains of a shepherd's shelter, three and a half walls but no roof. No creatures used it now – two-legged or four-legged – but Azim was not in a position to be fussy. The turf inside was wet but springy. There was enough of one wall to hide him from anyone passing on the road. The bag would do for a pillow. He would rest his head on a fortune.

He settled down, telling his stomach to be quiet. There were a few handfuls of nuts and dried fruit left, but he would need these to fuel the next stage of his journey. For the limited hours of daylight that nature allowed at this time of year, he would stay in this ruin. When it was dark, he would start again. He had no idea how much further he had to go.

And the wind was still gaining in strength.

FRIDAY

Morning

Sam lay on his bed and tested the arm. He couldn't bend it or lift it, because of the Velcro, but he reckoned he could twitch the muscles. He pressed down with the arm on the bed so that he could sit up. He swung his legs over the side of the bed, pushing again with the arm so that he stood up. So far, so good. Nothing snapped. The arm hadn't fallen off.

As he pulled on his clothes, he looked out of the window. Not a scrap of blue sky. Clouds everywhere, thick clouds moving fast, bank after bank of them. There would be rain today. Lots of it. He'd need a sweater, and pulling on a thick sweater would be a real test. The problem was that the right arm – the good one – wanted to play the major part in this operation, but he forced it to share the task equally with the left arm. It made him think of his friendship with Gwynedd. There had been times in the last 48 hours when he had felt that she treated him as though he was a busted arm. Well, he wouldn't let that happen today.

He heard Becky setting the table for breakfast in the little kitchen downstairs. He knew that she would make a fuss about the sling, that she'd tell him he had to wear it. But he would be ready for her this time. He'd be strong, but he'd also be reasonable.

Half an hour later, having lost the argument with his mother, Sam stormed off in the direction of Gwynedd's bungalow.

His journey was cut short. When he reached the bridge over the river, he met Gwynedd on her way to visit him, and on this grey morning he could see the gleam of excitement in her eyes while they were still a shouting distance from each other.

"There's been another drama up at the Chippie," she said. "Vinnie's texted me. Can't be sure, because his text's all a mess, but I think there's been a shooting at the Chippie. Vinnie's up there now. And the police are there. Let's go."

She set a cracking pace.

A small crowd had gathered across the street from the Chippie. Vinnie was attempting to help a policewoman fix a DO NOT ENTER tape along the front of the shop. As soon as he saw Sam and Gwynedd, he hurried over, pointing to the Chippie's upstairs window.

"See that? That's a bloody bullet hole. How about that, then? Someone tried to kill Saqui last night. This is a Crime Scene, like, and that's why we're sealing it off." Vinnie made it sound as though he was running the show.

The policewoman told him to move away, undid the length of tape he'd fixed upside down, and started re-fixing it.

"Don't be mad, Vinnie," said Gwynedd. "Saqui wasn't in the Chippie last night. He left the same time as me and Sam. No one's been firing bullets at Saqui."

"It's Azim," said Sam. "Someone's fired a shot at Azim."

He was sure this was something to do with the money Azim had, but wasn't going to say anything about that in front of Vinnie. Sam turned his back on the Chippie and looked at the pub across the street.

"The bullet could have been fired from that pub," he said. "Less risk for whoever fired the gun if he was in the pub...say, in one of the rooms upstairs."

"Or if *she* was in the pub," said Gwynedd. "It's not only *men* who do exciting things. Stupid things, yes, but not dangerous ones."

"A woman done it?" Vinnie's amazement increased. "That's Mr Rees's pub. Does he know about this woman? Or, you mean, like, *Mrs* Rees was trying to kill Aslin. You could be right. That Mrs Rees got a terrible temper on her sometimes."

"If the bullet was meant for anyone in particular, it must have been Azim," said Sam. "Has anyone seen him this morning?"

"Not Aslin, no. According to that copper over there, Saqui's inside with a Police Sergeant. A bullet's been found embedded..." - there was relish in the way Vinnie rolled his tongue round the word - "... *embedded* in the wall. High up. They'll be taking that to ballistics. Tell you what... maybe your old enemy Len Mangle got something to do with this, eh, Sam?"

Sam shook his head. "He'd have used a shotgun, and a blast from a shotgun would have shattered the whole window."

"Here is Saqui." Gwynedd waved to him. He didn't wave back. "He looks in a bad way."

"Not surprising, is it," said Vinnie. "New window that size will cost quids."

Gwynedd had never seen Saqui so rattled. He didn't care about the window. He didn't care about the police. All he cared about was Azim. He told them that Azim had disappeared. There was no sign of him, no message to say where he'd gone. The lad's disappearance was shattering. Saqui had a vivid imagination, and he was frantic with worry about what might have happened to a young lad. He gabbled a list of some of the dangers... Azim beaten up... Azim so scared he'd thrown himself under a bus... Azim's body in the river... Azim high on drugs... Azim's body stretched out on the side of a mountain...

As Saqui jabbered away, Sam watched him closely. The words were coming out in a rush, but Sam thought Saqui was holding something back. Saqui would start a sentence with 'Maybe Azim's decided to...' or 'Maybe he's gone to...', but would then clam up as though he'd been about to say something he didn't want to say. It was reasonable to assume that, though Saqui knew more about Azim than anyone else in Rhayader, he wasn't prepared to share any of his knowledge.

They did what they could to comfort Saqui. They told him it was possible that the shot in the night had frightened

Azim, and he'd simply gone off to hide in some place until he felt safe again. They told Saqui that Azim would probably be back any time now.

Sam asked if the Chippie would be opening that night.

"It has to be," said Saqui. "I missed two hours last night and now I have to earn money to pay for a new window."

"That's the spirit," said Vinnie. "Business as usual. Like in those posters during the war: SHUT YOUR MOUTH AND CARRY ON."

Gwynedd wanted a private talk with Sam. She cut short the conversation with Saqui.

"We'll see you tonight then, Saqui. Let us know if there's any news, and don't worry. It's probably some kind of silly joke. Me and Sam's gotta go now… things to do. Give us a call the minute Azim turns up." She grabbed Sam by the sling. "Come on."

Sam knew where she wanted to go. It was where he wanted to go - to the derelict house down by the river, where they'd found the mysterious £50 note.

Once they were out of earshot, he said: "Best take the long way round. We don't want anyone to see where we're going. Not even the police. There's too much at stake."

"What do you mean?"

"Think about it," he said. "Azim's got plenty of secrets. None of us knows where he's come from, what he's doing here, how he got hold of that money, or how much he's got, or where the rest of it is if he has got more, or where he's gone. Those are just some of his secrets. At a guess, Saqui knows quite a bit about Azim, but he won't tell us what."

"Go on." Gwynedd put her arm round him.

"OK. Why won't Saqui tell us? And what's really bugging Saqui about the bullet hole in the window?"

"He's upset. Wouldn't you be upset?"

Sam nodded. "You bet I'd be upset. Especially if I thought whoever fired the shot wanted to kill someone I was looking after. Someone he's looking after. Someone who's a total stranger to this country. I reckon Azim's on the run, and he's possibly carrying around a lot of money. Money that he hasn't earned. Money that may well be the proceeds of crime. Or money that could well have been stolen. This could be, like, a major crime. Azim may not know who's after him. He certainly won't tell us even if he does know. He won't even tell Saqui. That's why Saqui's so worried about him and so upset. I'd be scared stiff if I was Saqui and thought that someone with a gun was after Azim."

She looked at him. She wanted to tell him how clever she thought he was, how brilliant, how good-looking. But he didn't give her time to say anything. He had more to say and she wanted to hear it. This was so much better than having a row. This was like the good old times they'd had together. "And there's something more, isn't there?" she said.

"You bet. Suppose the bullet was fired from the pub. No one but a weirdo would take a random pot-shot from a room in a pub at what looks like an empty room across the street. And Mrs Rees wouldn't have let a room in it to a weirdo with a loaded rifle. I know lots of people with guns do crazy things. They shoot at animals, and lights, and advertisement hoardings, and trains. But – shooting into an unlit room?"

"So what are you getting at?"

"I think that whoever fired that shot reckoned that Azim was in that room, and they did it, not to kill him, but to frighten him. I think whoever fired the shot was after Azim's money – that's assuming that Azim has a lot more money stashed away somewhere."

"What d'you think we should do?" she said. "Go to the police?"

Their journey through the back streets and across the park had come to an end. They had reached the derelict house.

"Not yet. If we did go to the police the only thing that would happen for sure is that Azim would get locked up as an illegal immigrant. I'm not sure that would be right."

"We need some sort of evidence," said Gwynedd. "It would help if we could find this big sum of money. And this is as good a place as possible to start looking. This is where we found the first £50 note."

"Looking here would be a waste of time. We've searched everywhere round here."

"That was Wednesday. Today's Friday. It could be like that old fairy tale... *The Magic Purse*, the one that kept on giving."

"On Wednesday you thought it was us kissing that produced £50 notes."

"Righto," she said. "Let's give that a whirl. There's no one looking."

"I wouldn't care if there was."

"You would if it was Becky."

"That's preposterous."

"Preposterous?" Gwynedd laughed. "That's the poshest word I ever heard."

Her laugh stung him even more.

"That's such a dumb thing to say. You know what - your trouble is you never stop to think before you open your mouth."

She didn't move.

"I'm going to search every bit of this place, and I'm going to find something." God Almighty, she thought, I'm being as childish as him.

There was a one minute silence, like the one on Armistice Day or at a funeral. At the end of it, Sam spoke first.

"You do the river side. I'll do the other side."

She wanted to rush up to him, fling her arms round him and give him the best kiss there had ever been in the entire history of love, but she feared that Sam might not be in the mood for passion and might not like it. She grudgingly admitted that he might be right. What mattered even more than love was Saqui's happiness and Azim's safety. For the moment.

They searched carefully. It was tiring work, bent over all the time, turning over bits of rubbish, running their hands through clumps of weed and grass, even looking in the patches of dying nettles. In the end, instead of splitting up, they searched as a pair, because Gwynedd thought that would be more fun and because Sam thought he could keep an eye on Gwynedd and make sure she searched thoroughly. But, deep down, they both thought there was little hope of success.

The rain came and went, slanting down as the south-westerly whipped it off the mountains and blew it towards England.

Gwynedd was about to suggest that they gave up when she saw what looked like a piece of paper flapping on the ground by the low wall at the back of the old house. She went over to take a closer look.

"Shit!" she said, and she called to Sam. "I was right. Look."

She pointed to a £50 banknote with a bit of brick covering one corner.

"What happens now?" she said. "Do we take it to the police?"

He shook his head. "This wasn't dropped by accident. Somebody deliberately planted the note here, hoping it would be found."

"What is it, then? A message of some sort?"

"The most likely person to have put it there is Azim. And you're right – it must be a kind of message."

"Suppose," she said, "suppose he put it here after someone had fired the gun at him. Suppose he wanted to show that he was still alive. Suppose it's a message for us and for Saqui. We're the only ones who know about Azim's supply of banknotes."

"Us and the guy with the gun."

"Oh my God," she said. "Poor Azim. I wonder where the hell he is."

*

After his all-night march, Azim had settled down to sleep, a little before dawn, on the springy turf among what was left of the dilapidated shepherd's hut. There was just enough of the hut left to shelter him from the worst of the rain. It had taken an hour for his body to get used to the contours of the ground, and another hour for his mind to find some sort of peace. The Hunters would be after him with their guns, but there were several roads out of Rhayader and he had chosen the least suitable for sleek, speedy, silver-grey cars. It wasn't until a dim lightening of the sky appeared over the eastern tips of the mountains, that Azim fell asleep.

He had no dreams. Mind and body were both exhausted. For almost five hours he was oblivious to all that happened around him: to the whining of the racing breeze as it passed through the gaps in the stone walls; to the munching of sheep and cattle grazing with their backs to the wind; to the small amount of early traffic passing on the road; and to the steady trickle of the infant black-water stream as it wriggled its way like a snake across the boggy plateau.

As soon as Azim woke, he switched on the mobile that the Binnie man had given him. The time on the display was 10:16. He now had to make a choice. He could travel by daylight, when there was a far greater risk of being seen by the Hunters or the police, or he could stay where he was for another seven hours or more until darkness came back to hide him, and then travel by night.

His decision was forced upon him by his stomach. He couldn't wait for dark. He had only a few nuts and raisins left, and the clouds moving up from the west threatened heavy rain. Besides, he wanted to be on his way, to get to the sea and to find a way out of this nightmare that he was living in. There were, of course, problems; he had known there would be from the moment he had snatched the bag in the Chief's office. He had not the slightest idea how far he still had to go. He might reach the sea in a day. He might have to stagger on for a week. But that was unlikely because UK was such a small and crowded place. One thing was certain: staying here wasn't an option.

He rolled over, got to his feet, and inspected the bag. The shard of glass was still there, and all the plastic wallets full of 50 and 20 notes. Right at the bottom were the coins he had been given as change when he had bought the cakes and his boots and food from Saqui – for Azim had insisted that he pay for his keep. There were quite a lot of coins, some silver, some dark metal – copper maybe – some a sort of dull gold. They all had a woman's head on them. He looked at the notes. They, too, had this woman's face on them. He hadn't noticed it before because the numbers on the notes seemed to be so important. He wondered who the woman was; she was obviously not a tribal leader because she was a woman. Perhaps she was the President of UK. He had no idea how much each coin was worth, but assumed they were not as valuable as the notes. Maybe the coins were for special use in some way. Perhaps there were things the coins could buy that notes couldn't. Even in his local Afghan town there were machines where you could exchange coins for cans of drink and chocolate bars, though only foreigners used them.

Azim sorted the coins into piles: one for the copper coins, one for the silver, and one for the dull gold ones. It was difficult to balance the piles on the turf. The pile of silver coins collapsed and several rolled away. When Azim grabbed at them, he sent the pile of copper coins flying. He could not bear the thought of losing any money, and tore at the grass searching for the coins. The problem was, he didn't know how many coins he had had in the first place, so he didn't know how many might still be missing after he'd found several of them. Money was precious. The money in the bag was the only money he had ever had. Every note and every coin mattered. His search became more desperate.

But his brain came to the rescue. Of course no coin was worth as much as any note, and he had many, many notes. Scrabbling for coins was a waste of time that should be spent getting nearer the sea. All would be well when he reached the sea. There would be boats that he could board, with or without the Captain's permission. Any boat would do, so long as it carried him away from this wild and dangerous land. Somewhere he would find a boat to take him to his part of the world – to Pakistan, perhaps, or to the United States. Azim believed that the United States must be somewhere near Afghanistan. How else could so many Americans have marched into his country? And, no matter how long it took, Azim would return to his own land, to his brother, to Uncle, and to his goats.

It was time to go. He pushed his arms through the handles of the bag so that it rested on his back, and set off, head down into the wind sweeping over the plateau. There would be rain soon. This was a land of rain. At home, it rained little. There was sometimes no rain for week after week. Here, they had a year's rain in a day.

He kept to the side of the road, except when there was a bend. There could be danger round any corner. During one of the wakeful periods in the night, Azim had worked out a strategy for dealing with corners. As soon as he saw a corner, he would leave the road and climb up the nearest hillside, then make his way below the skyline. He would stick to the high ground until he reached a point where he could see over the brow of the hill to check that all was safe around the corner. It meant a lot of extra walking – climbing and descending – but it would protect him from walking into a trap.

He was hungry. He needed meat. If he had brought his slingshot with him to UK, he might have been able to bring down a sheep out here in the mountains. He'd watched his brother do that many times, whirling the slingshot over his head and aiming at the sheep's legs. If the shot was on target, the stone broke the sheep's leg. The beast couldn't run, so it was a simple job to grab it and slit its throat with a knife, the sort of knife that every man carried at home.

Here, Azim had no slingshot and no knife. All he could try would be to grab hold a sheep and cut its throat with the shard of glass. That would be a long and messy business, and even if he could do that he had no way of making fire to cook the bits of sheep.

So, what little food he had must be rationed. He would reward himself with a nut or raisin every 200 paces. He started counting his steps. At first he made good progress, but after he'd covered a couple of thousand paces he realised he was being too generous with his rations. There was a risk that he would run out of supplies long before he found somewhere to buy more. There were no buildings anywhere to be seen: only hills and mountains, streams, sheep, and stunted trees, with buzzards flying overhead; and the road going on and on. The sight of it made his muscles sag. He cut his food ration to one nut or raisin every 400 paces.

The road was still climbing, towards what looked like a narrow pass between two of the highest mountains. Here, Azim reached what he had been looking for – the watershed. Tiny streams gushed down the steep mountain sides, bounced over rocks, tumbled into pools no bigger than Azim's boots, and then ran on, but in a new direction from that of last night. These streams were flowing westward. He was on course. He was heading for the sea. He had earned another raisin, and a drink. It would be safe to drink from these new streams. They had had no time to be polluted by man or beast.

The water was cold but it tasted good. Azim gulped down one handful after another, and then feasted on a nut. There was still no signal on his mobile, but it showed him that he had been walking for almost an hour. The little stream was getting wider. The steep descent that he had been hurrying along was levelling out. There were flat meadows on either side of the river and signs that he was approaching some kind of settlement, with a line of cottages and a farm. The noise of furious barking came from inside sheds and outbuildings. Afraid that people might come out to see what had disturbed their dogs, Azim clambered up the hillside until he was well above the farms and cottages.

A mile further on, he climbed through a barbed wire fence and entered a dark forest where the trees grew in rows, close together. This made for easier going. There was plenty of cover to hide him here. It was almost as dark as night in the forest, for the clouds were grey and low, and no light penetrated the thick mass of branches. When he heard the first car approaching, he dropped to the ground, with the bag under his body. The car passed at speed, and he realised all he had to do was keep still when traffic passed. Anyone in a vehicle would only notice movement. That was a relief, for getting to his feet was now painful. His knee was hurting. It had hit a stone when he had flung himself down. He climbed back through the barbed wire fence. It would be better if he slackened his pace, but that would mean his journey taking longer, and being without food for longer. He had half a dozen raisins and less than a handful of nuts left. He sat by the roadside, flexing his knee gently. It was not broken, only bruised. It would be all right if he kept going. It would be when he stopped that the knee would stiffen and make further walking difficult.

The road plunged down through the wood and was joined by another road. There were signs on the roadside, with unreadable names, and then another settlement. This was bigger than the first, a true village. A large building, with an imposing sign on it, stretched more than a hundred paces on one side of the road. A low wall ran along the other side. Beyond the wall the land fell steeply away into a deep tree-lined valley. There was the sound of rushing water. Azim crossed the road and looked over the wall. He saw a new river bursting through the trees and tumbling under three bridges, and plashing into pools in a series of waterfalls as it hurried to the sea.

Tired though he was, he limped on, round a sharp bend in the road, and there before him was a shop – the only one he had seen since leaving Rhayader. It was set back from the road, with the same big windows that the shops had in the town where he had bought the little cakes and the boots, and where he had lived above Saqui's Shop of Chips. And in the windows of this shop were what looked like packets of biscuits and bars of chocolate. He would need money for biscuits, lots of it, because he intended to buy lots of biscuits. Azim slipped the bag off his back, and took another 50 note from it. In the past few days he had learnt that there was always danger in shopping, but he would be on guard. Even with blisters on his feet, at the first sign of trouble he would make a run for it.

Azim pushed the shop door open and went in.

He was the only customer. A small, smiling woman said something to him. He guessed it was a greeting, so he nodded and smiled back. She said something else. It seemed most likely that she was asking him what he wanted. He pointed to the biscuits in the window. She smiled again and spoke more words. He didn't know what to do. He waited by the counter, hoping she would go to the window and pick up the biscuits, but the woman didn't move. She was waiting for him to do something – perhaps to pick up the biscuits. He took a packet from the window and handed it to her across the counter.

There was a dish of what looked like *jawari* cakes, only flatter. He picked one up. The woman shook her head and took the *jawari* from him. She said something that sounded like a question. He nodded, hoping this was the right thing to do. She put the *jawari* in a paper bag, opened her eyes wide, and gave him another big smile. Probably, she was asking if he wanted more. He held up four fingers. She popped three more *jawari* cakes in the bag, and placed it beside the biscuits.

In much the same way, Azim showed that he wanted two small bottles of water and two bars of chocolate. He was conscious that this process was taking a long time, and that the longer he was in the shop, the more risk there was that someone might want to know who he was, where he'd come from, and what he was doing. The woman asked him another question. He shook his head. This was enough. The woman wrote numbers on a piece of paper – perhaps a list of the prices of what he was buying. She held the piece of paper out for him to see. He offered her the 50 note.

The woman's eyes opened wider still, but this time there was no smile. She took the 50 note and held it up to the light. She said something to him. He shrugged his shoulders. She frowned. He picked up the biscuits and the chocolate, the water and the bag of *jawaris*, and put them in the bag.

The woman was watching him. From the way Azim lifted the bag she could see that it was heavy. She looked at the bag and seemed to ask him something, but not understanding a word she said, Azim didn't know what to say. He tried to smile and shrugged his shoulders. Still watching him, the woman pulled open a drawer at the back of the counter. From the drawer, she took a bundle of money notes. She added the 50 note to the bundle, then took five notes from it – one green and four brown. The green one said '5'. The brown ones said '10'. The President's face was on both of them. The woman added some coins from the drawer and gave the notes and coins to Azim. His shopping was over.

Munching one of the sweet cakes, Azim left the shop. He had spent a long time in the shop, and anything could have happened outside. The Hunters could have caught up with him. He glanced anxiously around him. It looked safe enough. People were gathering across the road – men, women and children - all staring at a notice board. He crossed the road and joined them – there was sometimes safety in numbers. There a map on the board, and depicted on the very edge of the map was the sea. A red line, with three large red dots on it, marked what must be a special route to the sea.

The crowd was now moving away from the board. Children were becoming excited. There was expectation in the air. Apart from a terrifying ride through something called Channel Tunnel, in the back of a truck loaded onto a waggon, Azim had never been on a train, never had anything to do with railways. But what he saw now were plumes of smoke rising into the blue sky. And what he heard was a noise that was half coughing and half spitting, that suddenly gave way to a frightening blast, a mixture of hoot and whistle. What he believed must be a train was arriving in what must be a station.

The train stopped. People – again mainly families - climbed out of the waggons. The engine's coughing and spitting noise was replaced by a hissing sound. This was the end of the line. In which case, presumably, the train would somehow turn round and head back the way it had come, back to the sea. He had to be on that train for the return journey.

The crowd that had been waiting for the train's arrival were now standing in line by a small hut. Through a hole in the side of the hut, a man inside was handing them strips of paper in exchange for money. Azim saw it all now. They were buying tickets. He must do the same. He joined the line. After a few minutes, it was his turn to tell the man in the shed what he wanted. The man appeared to know. He said something. Azim guessed it was something to do with buying a ticket, so he handed the man one of the brown notes. It had the number 10 on it. The man gave him a few coins.

No one was in a hurry to board the train. Azim guessed there was plenty of time. This was good. He was getting further and further away from the Hunters, the police, any immigration officers. The town on the map, at the end of the line, looked bigger than the town where Saqui lived, and it was on the sea. That was good. It would be easier to hide until he found a way of getting on board a boat sailing to United States.

Saqui! He had forgotten all about him. He must call him on the mobile at once, because Saqui was the only friend he had found since leaving Afghanistan. He hoped Saqui had been able to find the money he had left for him. He must let Saqui know that he was safe. But that was all. He wouldn't tell Saqui where he was, because if he did, Saqui would come chasing after him, to make sure he was safe. All he would say was that he was on his way to the sea. And he would thank Saqui for his help. There was an empty bench by the road. Azim decided to make the call from there.

He had not thought what he would tell Saqui. He didn't want to say anything about where he was or where he was going. Just to thank Saqui for his help and say goodbye. The thought of 'goodbye' was upsetting and frightening, but back home Uncle needed Azim's help and the bag's money.

Saqui had shown Azim how to make his mobile connect to Saqui's. Slowly and carefully, Azim now entered Saqui's number. A strange voice said something that Azim didn't understand. Then the strange voice stopped and there was a little 'beep'. There was no sound of Saqui's voice. The voice of the mobile gabbled words that he didn't understand. Maybe the voice was saying it was sorry.

Azim wondered if he should speak, and decided that it would do no harm if he said something and might do some good. Perhaps the mobile phone would speak for him later. He began his message. He told Saqui that he was safe and well but was not coming back. Then, and this was the difficult bit, he added that he did not want Saqui to come looking for him. He was going far away, where Saqui would never find him. He was on the point of thanking Saqui for all his help when several things happened at once: the train gave another loud blast on its whistle, the crowd of people began to board the train, and a large silver car drove into the station car park. Azim didn't know that silver coloured cars were common on UK roads, and assumed that the hunters had arrived. Panic seized him, and he felt as though his stomach had suddenly flipped over. Azim hurriedly ended the call, picked up his bag and joined the crowd.

The woman in the shop across the road had also been making a telephone call. She was worried about the young Asian lad and his £50 note, and she had mentioned him to every customer who'd come to her shop since. She had even pointed Azim out to them. She had thought of going across the road and telling Mr Hatton at the Vale of Rheidol railway station that perhaps they shouldn't let the Asian lad travel on the train to Aberystwyth without at least searching the lad's bag to make sure it didn't have a bomb in it.

That thought had so frightened her that she had decided not to bother Mr Hatton, but to phone the police instead.

*

After three frenzied hours spent on a useless search of the whole of Rhayader in the dark and the wet and the wind, Kyle and Coleson limped back to the pub a little before dawn, let themselves in by the back door, and reached the bedroom just as the police arrived at the Chip Shop in response to a couple of calls concerning a strange noise in the night, and an even stranger hole in the window over the Chip Shop.

"What do we do now?" There was anxiety in Coleson's voice.

"We take it in turns to get some rest," said Kyle. "You take the first watch. Wake me the moment you see anything of the Kid, the black girl, the one-armed boy, any of that crowd. Wake me if there's any sign of the bag. And for Chrissake wake me if the police come this way. Wake me if there's anything to report. Understand?"

Coleson did as he was told. Two hours later he woke Kyle.

"The Chief's phoned. He wants to know what's going on."

"You didn't tell him?"

"He was mad. He's giving us one more day."

"You idiot!"

"He's my bother."

Kyle shook his head. "Would you believe it. Well, that's his bad luck and your bad luck and you've both gotta live with it. You go to sleep. At least you can't mess anything up when you're asleep. I'll keep watch."

There had to be a new plan. Kyle sat at the window, racking his brains. They had 24 hours to find the Kid and get their hands on the bag. Kyle was convinced that, wherever the Kid was, he still had the bag. So he was the prime target. But there were other targets. That black girl looked the nosey sort who might work out some connection between the pub and the bullet hole. She needed putting away and so did her one-armed boyfriend. And the Chip Shop guy... he was in this up to the hilt.

An hour later, he woke Coleson.

"Get dressed. We're checking out, and then this is what we're going to do..."

Afternoon

A deeply worried Saqui had summoned a meeting. He, Gwynedd, Sam and Vinnie were listening to a voice message left by Azim on Saqui's mobile. It was brief, and they'd already heard it three times. Sam wanted to hear it again. The acoustic wasn't good in the Chippie, and it needed several hearings to identify a background noise towards the end of the message.

"Can't understand one word," said Vinnie. "I tell that Aslin he got to learn English."

"He says he's OK. But he's not coming back. He doesn't say why, but something bad is happening to him, I know." Saqui was working himself into a state.

"Did he say anything about the bullet hole in the window?"

Saqui looked miserably at Gwynedd. "Nothing," he said. "But I tell you, he is definitely not coming back."

"And you don't know where he's gone?"

"He was always asking me about the sea. 'Where is the sea? How far away is the sea? Were there big boats at the sea?' I told him I didn't know about the sea, but the nearest he would find it was Aberystwyth. I told him that was a town only for holidays. And he didn't know anything about holidays. He didn't even know what a holiday is."

"If you could all shut up for a minute, there's a bit I want to hear again," said Sam. "Right at the end."

Vinnie was bored. "Seems to me stupid, like, to be listening to something over and over again when it's a message only Saqui can understand, and it don't make sense even to him. No, don't look at me like that, our Gwynedd. You know I'm right."

"Shut up, Vinnie. This is important." Sam nodded to Saqui, who replayed the message.

"There," said Sam. "Right there. What's that noise in the background?"

"That's a train whistle," said Vinnie. "Thought you would have known that, Sam, you being a bit of a city slicker.

That's like the whistle up on the Vale of Rheidol railway. Out at Devil's Bridge. I bin up there on my scooter. Lot of bikers use that road. Best road around for two-wheelers, that is."

Sam was busy with his phone. "What time did you get this message, Saqui?"

"Just before I phoned you all. Twenty minutes ago."

"And it's now ten to two." Sam was running his finger across the screen of the phone, flicking through pages of an internet website. "Here we are… Vale of Rheidol… timetable… There's a train that left Devil's Bridge for Aberystwyth at 13.30…"

"How'd he get to Devil's Bridge?" said Vinnie.

"He must have walked it." Once or twice in her life, when she was on the point of running away from home, Gwynedd had thought of walking to Devil's Bridge because the name sounded exciting.

"Walked it?" Vinnie sounded disbelieving. "I reckon your Ashim's gone off his rocker."

Sam was still busy with his phone. "The train takes an hour to get to Aberystwyth… due to arrive 14.30."

Saqui shook his head. "That's no good. We couldn't get to Aberystwyth by that time."

"But at least we've got some idea as to where Azim might be heading," said Gwynedd. "Call him, Saqui. Call him now. Tell him to wait at Aber station until we get there. Vinnie can take me on the back of his scooter; Sam, you can go on Saqui's. I'll have to nip up to the bungalow for my helmet and to tell Dave he's getting no tea from me today. Meet you back here in twenty minutes… no, fifteen. Vinnie – you find a spare helmet for Sam. You are coming, aren't you, Sam?"

Please, she thought, please don't say anything about not wanting to leave Becky on her own. Please!

"You go to the bungalow," he said. "I'll send Becky a text so she doesn't worry. Meet you on the bridge as soon as possible."

Gwynedd could have kissed him, but there wasn't time. She hurried out into the cold wind.

As she ran up the hill to the bungalow, she glanced up at the sky. It was dark and threatening. The clouds that raced overhead were thick and heavy. There would be more rain soon, not a steady Welsh drizzle, but storm rain, stinging and soaking. There had been warnings on TV of gale-force winds, of likely damage and disruption. The emergency services were expecting trouble.

Gwynedd shivered, but then reminded herself that in an hour or less they should all be safe in Aberystwyth. Once there, they'd find Azim, and shelter in a café or in the little pavilion on the promenade. They would have to come up with some reassuring explanation to Azim – true or false – as to why someone had fired a bullet into his room in the middle of the night. If they could get Azim to talk, maybe the whole story would come out and the mystery would be solved. And then she and Sam would have time together to do whatever they liked. Perhaps there'd be £50 notes all round. She licked her lips. There was so much you could do with fifty quid… like, lash out on some stunningly smart clothes and some really wild nail varnish.

She reached the bungalow and found Dave in a good mood. He didn't make any fuss about getting his own tea.

"You go off and have fun with your mates. But don't go getting into any mischief. Promise?"

"I swear I won't." This wasn't mischief. This was a rescue mission. No one could find fault with that.

Gwynedd picked up the crash helmet that Vinnie had given her and left the bungalow. She was in two states of mind. Part of her was worried about poor Azim; the other part was looking forward to being with Sam. It was this part of her mind that failed to make sure she shut the front door of the bungalow properly. Always keen on an outing, Ben followed her out. She didn't notice him.

Swinging the helmet to and fro, Gwynedd raced back into town, with Ben trotting along behind her. This was more like it. She was almost sprinting by the time she came to the bridge. There was Sam, waiting for her, likc he said he would. She threw her arms round him.

"Mind my…"

"Never mind your arm."

"It's not my arm I'm worried about. It's my phone. I've put it in my sling because it's easier to get at…"

"Never mind your smarty-pants phone, neither. Come on. Up to the Chippie. We can…" Sam didn't finish the sentence. He had seen his beloved Ben, sitting on the ground, a few paces behind Gwynedd.

"What did you bring him for? He can't come on a scooter."

Gwynedd turned round.

"I didn't bring him. Dave must have let him out."

"Didn't you know he was following you?"

"No. And don't look at me like that. He's your bloomin' dog."

There might have been a row between them, but a voice called to them from the cinder track.

" 'Scuse me, guys…"

Gwynedd and Sam immediately turned towards the voice, both thinking this might be something to do with Azim and the fifty quid notes.

"Have you got a sec?"

The speaker was a bloke leaning on a silver-grey car parked down by the derelict house. The car looked very like the one that had nearly knocked her down the other day, but Gwynedd was curious rather than suspicious; many silver-grey cars drove through Rhayader. Despite the hurry to get to Saqui, she and Sam could spare a couple of minutes to see what this was about. Gwynedd moved towards the car. Sam grabbed her arm.

"Hang on a minute," he said. "You never know."

"Are you guys local?"

The bloke sounded friendly enough. It seemed a reasonable question. But Ben was clearly not happy. He was growling and backing away.

"It's fine," she said, partly to Sam and partly to Ben. Then, out loud to the bloke, she said: "I am. He's not."

"I'm only asking because we're trying to find someone who could identify this vehicle. We're very interested in its owner."

This was something to do with Azim, Gwynedd was sure of it. This bloke was probably some kind of plain clothes cop come into town because of the shooting. Yeah, the bloke had his hand inside his jacket, feeling for the pocket, going to show them his identity card. Ben continued to growl.

"It'll be OK," she said to Sam. "He's a cop and he's going to show us his ID." She called out to the bloke. "This'll have to be quick."

"Oh, it'll be quick," said the bloke.

Sam still wasn't sure. He trusted in Ben's judgement of people. And this guy sounded far too nervous to be a cop. Not only that, it was taking him a long time to find his ID. Sam was about to tell Gwynedd that he didn't think they should get involved with this guy, when he felt something hard pressing into the small of his back.

"Move to the car. Slowly."

The voice came from behind them. "Not a sound. This is a gun. It's a very quiet gun and if I have to fire it, no one will know it's gone off, except you. And you'll know for only a split second before you're dead. While you..." and now he pressed the gun into the small of Gwynedd's back... "...you will know for maybe two seconds before you, too, are dead. Got it? Good. Now, don't turn round, but we're all going to move very slowly behind this old house... That's it... Good. And now my colleague and I are going to frisk you."

Ben's growling grew louder.

In the same cold, quiet voice, the bloke with the gun spoke to Sam and Gwynedd. "Either you get rid of Lassie here, or I will."

He waved his gun in Ben's direction.

"Ben. Go home," said Sam.

The dog didn't move.

"Go home! Now!"

The bloke pointed his gun at Ben. Guns had been pointed at the dog before. He knew they meant danger.

"Go home, Ben. Please go home."

Sam was begging. The dog didn't move. The man held his gun at arm's length and pulled the trigger. There was a noise like 'phut', and a bullet pinged into the stones, missing Ben's head by a few centimetres. Ben turned and raced away.

"See what I mean?" said the bloke with the gun. "A nice quiet gun. Now we can carry on with the search. You do the boy. I'll do the girl."

"What are we looking for?" The bloke who had first called to Sam and Gwynedd sounded unsure of himself.

"Anything that might tempt them to create trouble."

"Oh," said the bloke. "Like a mobile?"

"You got it, Professor. Like a mobile."

"We'd better be quick," said the one called The Professor. "We can't hang around here too long."

"You be as quick as you like," said the voice behind them. "I'm gonna make a thorough job of searching this young lady. Arms out, and feet apart."

Sam and Gwynedd did as they were told.

Coleson, the Professor, was nervous. He made no attempt to search Sam thoroughly. He patted Sam's anorak, ran his hands up and down Sam's legs, and along Sam's good arm. He didn't touch the sling. Kyle, on the other hand, was extremely thorough in his body search of Gwynedd. It didn't take long for him to find her mobile, which he threw into the river. She thought the worst was over, but he stayed behind her, his hands wandered back and forth, up and down her limbs, and all over her body. It was an unpleasant experience for Gwynedd and, though she could not see his face, the worst of it was that she knew he was enjoying it.

Eventually, Kyle was satisfied. He patted her on the backside, as though she was some prize animal he'd bought at a cattle market.

"Into the car," he said, "and fasten your seat belts. We don't want any accidents… the back seat for you, One Arm. Black Beauty can sit in the front, next to me."

He gave Gwynedd a push in the back.

"And don't imagine you'll be able to leap out if the car stops for any reason." Kyle turned his head to face Sam. "The rear doors are fitted with child-proof locks. Wonderful motors, Mercedes."

Gwynedd made a mental note that perhaps the front doors weren't fitted with child-proof locks. If there was a chance of getting away…

Coleson sat in the back next to Sam. When Kyle turned to face Sam, Gwynedd got her first good look at him. He was tall, dressed in black leather and wearing shades. He was small but solid-looking, strong but with a little puffiness in his face. Gwynedd wondered how quick his reactions would be if she threw herself out of the car at a red traffic light.

"And don't think you can jump out and leg it." Kyle jabbed her arm with his gun. "Not while I've got this."

The jab hurt. She was powerless. There was nothing she could do. For one thing, there probably weren't any traffic lights between here and Aberystwyth, and for another, she couldn't leave Sam alone with these two bastards. They'd kill him immediately and then come after her. There was nothing she could do except wait and hope.

"If either of you makes any attempt to call for help, you will be shot in the knee, or both knees if necessary, and then in the elbows." The voice was matter-of-fact rather than sinister, but it suggested that threatening to kill or maim a couple of people was no big deal. "We've got plenty of ammo, and from what I've seen, the effect of a bullet in any one of those joints is extremely painful. And, by the way, my colleague also has a gun. Show them your gun, Professor."

"Let's get on with it, Kyle."

"You stupid bastard," said Kyle. "No names. We never use names in this business. Didn't your big brother teach you anything? Of all the stupid…"

Kyle pulled himself together. Bad things happened when he lost control.

"Where was I?" he said. "Oh yeah, the car's automatic, with power-steering, of course." Kyle turned to Gwynedd. "Which means I only need one hand to steer – a bit like your boyfriend here, with his arm in a sling. And that leaves my other hand free to hit, hurt, or shoot you. All set?"

"Why are you doing this to us?"

Kyle answered Sam's question.

"We're looking for a friend of yours. Little Asian lad. Don't know what his real name is. We call him the Scumbag Kid."

"Why? What's he done?"

"I think you know what he's done. You two have been very thick with him these last couple of days."

The man called Kyle was awakening all those instincts in Gwynedd which used to make her take on any teacher or social worker or anyone in authority. The difference here was that Kyle's free hand held a gun. No teacher had ever pulled a gun on her.

"I reckon you know the Scumbag Kid's real name. And what the Professor and I are hoping, for your sakes, is that you can tell us where he is."

Kyle leaned towards Gwynedd. She felt the gun pressing into her side, but said nothing. Kyle smiled, and pointed the gun at Sam.

A couple of minutes later, the silver-grey car was on the road, heading for Aberystwyth.

*

The little mountain train was crowded. Azim kept the bag trapped between his feet for safety's sake. To avoid eye contact with other passengers, he stared at the carriage floor. Many people in UK wanted to talk to you if you caught their eye. He did not dare to raise his head, even to look out of the train window, but was dimly aware that the train was passing through trees, clinging to the hillside, descending all the time, but not travelling with much speed.

He was afraid. He believed there was danger everywhere. He didn't know where he was going, or where he wanted to go, except in terms of reaching the sea. The sea would be a clean place. The Farm had been a dirty place. Other slaves at the Farm had told Azim that it was a hashish farm. The plants were grown in vast cellars lit by electric light. The hashish was marketed all over UK. The Chief had agents working for him in dozens of towns and cities. Azim couldn't remember the names of any of these places, but he thought it was highly likely that there would be members of the Chief's gang at the town the little train was heading for – the town on the sea. Azim already had at least one Hunter on his trail; perhaps there would be others waiting for him at the end of the line.

He risked looking up for a brief moment, like a man trying to gulp in air when he was drowning in the sea. The train, battling against a head wind, was travelling at little more than brisk walking pace, and yet no one had come out of the trees to steal a ride on it. The train here was unlike the only one that he had seen at home. There were no animals in the carriages. People were not sitting on the carriage roofs. No one was hanging on to the outside of the train. He noticed also that no one was leaving the train while it was moving, though there were no locks on the doors of any of the carriages. Whenever he liked, he could open one and leap out. He must remember that, especially when they got near to the end of the line. That was where there would be the most danger. Hunters could be waiting for him there, other men sent by the Chief – or the Police, or Immigration Officers. In the meantime, there was nothing he could do but sit tight until the train reached the end of the line.

Taking care not to reveal what else was in the bag, Azim took out the last of the cakes he had bought and ate it. It was a small cake, and after he'd finished it, he was still hungry. Except for the day when Saqui had brought him food, he had been hungry ever since he'd run away from the Farm. He looked down at the bag – all that money, and he was still hungry. The first thing he'd do when he got off the train would be to find something to eat.

*

The front door was as Gwynedd left it, still partly open when Ben returned to the bungalow. He squeezed through and went straight to Dave. The old man patted him. Dave found it easier to display his affection for the dog when no one else was looking.

"And how's my old mate?" he said. "Not gone out with our Gwynedd? Not wanted?"

The dog was shivering, though it was warm in the living room.

"I've had enough dogs in my life to know what that means. You frightened, boy, are you?"

He stroked the dog's head. Ben continued to shiver.

"Something wrong? What is it? Well, you don't talk Welsh or English and I don't talk doggish. Short of guessing, I can't come up with any answer to me own question. I'll feed you, and we'll see if that helps."

It didn't, and an hour later Dave put on his hat and coat and set off with Ben to walk to Lavender Cottage.

Becky answered the door. It took her a moment to recognise Gwynedd's grandfather.

"I've brought Ben," he said, unnecessarily. "I've no idea where our Gwynedd is, but she's likely with your Sam. The dog went off with her, but come back without her. I thought maybe you would know where Sam and Gwynedd was, and I wondered if we could discuss it over a cup of tea."

"I'm not supposed to let dogs in," said Becky.

Dave picked Ben up and tucked as much of the dog as he could inside his coat.

"No one'll know."

They talked for longer than Becky would have liked, not as long as Dave wanted. At the end of the conversation, it was still undecided as to where Sam and Gwynedd might be, but Dave had somehow put the responsibility of searching for them on to Becky's shoulders.

"You give your Sam a call on his phone box."

Becky promised she would, but didn't do so immediately. She had an appointment to view a property in ten minutes, and she was reluctant to phone Sam because he would probably accuse her of fussing.

It was a relief to get rid of Dave and Ben, but five minutes later there was another knock at the door.

It was Martin. Becky had been right, there was no way he was leaving Rhayader without putting up some sort of fight. He had spent the night in a local guest house, and said he had come to apologise, yet again, but what followed sounded to Becky more like a sermon than an apology. Martin still wanted her to come back to Bristol. They could make a fresh start. There had been misunderstandings on both sides. In a way, he was every bit as guilty as Sam… well, not every bit as guilty, but nearly as much… well, not really anything like as much, but there had been faults on both sides.

*

At the Chippie, Vinnie had brought his spare helmet for Sam to wear. Saqui was anxiously walking up and down, repeatedly asking 'Where the hell is Gwynedd?' 'Where the hell is Sam?' 'What the hell are they up to?' He had no number to call Sam but had already called Gwynedd's mobile three times, but it wasn't taking calls. Fifteen minutes, she'd said, and it was now twenty-five minutes since she and Sam had rushed off. Saqui was desperate.

"I'm going, Vinnie," he said. "I have to go. You coming with me? It will take us at least an hour to get to Aberystwyth on the scooter, and Azim must be nearly there by now.

"I'll, like, wait for our Gwynedd," said Vinnie. "And Sam, of course. Though I only got room for the one on my bike. I'll give you a call as soon as they get here, and then, well, either me and Gwynedd or me and Sam'll come straight to the railway station at Aber."

Saqui hurried away. It wasn't until he was well out of Rhayader that it occurred to him that he should have told Vinnie to lock up the Chippie.

*

Gwynedd stared in hopeless despair at the signs that counted down the miles to Aber... 25 miles from Llangurig... 20 miles from Pont Rhydgaled... 12 from Ponterwyd. All the time, a battle raged in her mind. She was desperate to think of some way out of this mess, but fear made that impossible. She and Sam had to come up with some plan of escape, some way of saving Azim and themselves. But she was too frightened for her brain to work properly. And, even if she could think of a plan, she couldn't speak of it. Occasionally, her mind thought about her mobile, lying on the bed of the river, back in Rhayader, but within seconds it had gone back to fear for her safety and Sam's safety.

She didn't know what she was most afraid of – silence or threats. She had been threatened with a gun once before in her life. But that time, the guy holding the gun had been nuts. The man called Kyle was more terrifying because he didn't rant, he didn't wave the gun around. He sat there quietly, occasionally flicking a sideways glance at her, or at Sam in the driving mirror. He seemed to think that she and Sam would lead him directly to Azim, like some Sat-Nav device. But she and Sam didn't know enough about Azim to be able to do that. They didn't know where Azim was heading, or what he was hoping to do. Aber was a big place, a city. There were streets full of shops, the harbour, warehouses and factories, hotels, the University. Azim could be anywhere. And Aber was now less than ten miles away.

Sam had different thoughts. From the moment they'd been taken prisoner, and once he had been sure that Ben was safe, Sam had not been scared. He remembered something his father had said to him when he was a little boy. He couldn't recall his father's exact words, but the gist of it was: 'People are divided into two groups – those who talk about the things they're going to do, and those who actually go ahead and do things'. This Kyle bloke had a big mouth, and a lot of his talk had been threats. Maybe he was more of a talker than a doer. This thought stayed with Sam throughout the silent journey from Rhayader. In his mind, Sam was estimating how big a risk there was that the men would carry out all they threatened to do. Even with a silencer on a gun – and Sam had seen no silencer on the guns he and Gwynedd had been shown – it would be difficult to keep the effects of a shooting spree hidden. If he and Gwynedd were screaming in agony, the two men responsible would find it hard to drive round Aberystwyth without drawing attention to their car and its prisoners. No. As far as Sam was concerned, the danger would come after they had found Azim, not before.

But, unlike Gwynedd, Sam saw Aberystwyth as too small a place for comfort. It might not prove all that difficult to find Azim. Sooner or later these men would demand to know why he and Gwynedd believed that Azim was coming to Aberystwyth. Sam didn't blame Gwynedd for telling them. He might have done the same, if they'd pointed the gun at her. He didn't know. But the journey was giving Sam time to think, and although no plan had formed in his mind, he could see what might be possible components of a plan. He still had his phone tucked inside his sling. He wished he'd turned it off, there was always the risk that Becky would call him anytime, to check if everything was all right. If there was a call, that would be the end of the only means of communicating with the rest of the world that he and Gwynedd had. But the younger man, the bloke who'd searched him, had been too anxious to make a thorough job of it, so perhaps there was still hope for him and Gwynedd, and for Azim.

The rain increased until it was belting down. Kyle switched the wipers to a faster speed. Sam could feel the wind hitting the car. This could slow them down, and that would give Azim longer to get away. Azim would have to find some shelter from this lashing rain, but where would that be in Aberystwyth? Saqui had said he'd talked of boats and a port. But there wasn't a port in Aber, only a small harbour and a marina. Once Azim realised there weren't any big ships there, where would he go next?

The car was slowing down. Visibility was not good from the back of the car, and Coleson had a lot to think about. Like the wipers, his mind was racing. In the first place, he wished he'd never taken this bloody job. Killing one kid was bad enough. Now, if he still wanted to make any money at all from this mess, it looked like he was going to have to take part in killing three kids. The Scumbag Kid had stolen a wad of money. You could say he'd asked for it. But the black girl and the lad with the bad arm had got involved with the Kid only because they'd felt sorry for the Kid, him being on the run and homeless. That was a different business altogether. And where was all this killing to take place? On the street? In the Mercedes? In this place called Aberwhatsit? There were too many risks involved. How big a risk was he supposed to take for a mere couple of grand?

Over the last few miles, he'd been looking at the problem in a different light. If he could get rid of Kyle, there were plenty of ways he could frighten the pants off the black girl and her boyfriend so that they'd take him to the Scumbag Kid. And then? Well, then nobody had to be killed. Without Kyle, he could tell the three kids to piss off and keep their mouths shut. And then? Then he could pick up the bag and the money. There'd be no need to hand it over to the Chief. He could pretend it had been lost or destroyed, or that Kyle had made off with it. And if he did that, he could keep the money for himself. The Chief hadn't said how much was in the bag, but it must be at least 50k, otherwise why all this bother? And 50k in the bag was a better deal than the promise of a mere two grand and the risk of a triple murder rap, which was what he was being offered now.

The problem was how to get rid of Kyle. It seemed like there'd have to be at least one killing, whatever way you looked at it. Coleson started to compose a flow chart in his mind, a way out of this mess. The first thing to do would be to kill Kyle, then stuff his body in the boot of the Merc, then drive out to the reservoir – the one where he'd planned to dump the body of the Scumbag Kid - then ditch the Merc in the water… It was the next step that was the tricky one. All of these things would have to be done in the dark, preferably in the middle of the night. It was the last bit that Coleson didn't fancy - having to walk in the dark all the way back from the reservoir to the car park behind the pub. Cities and towns were fine places. You could walk about them with no worries even in the middle of the night. Cities were never dark. There were always street lights and shop lights and the headlights of traffic. But out in the middle of nowhere, there wouldn't be any lights at all.

The rain beat down. The wipers flicked to and fro. New thoughts, new ideas flashed into Coleson's mind, each one more complicated and impractical than its predecessor. Get the money and the Scumbag Kid. Put the frighteners on the black girl and her boyfriend, so that they cleared out. Drive Kyle out to the reservoir in the Merc, so that they could get rid of the Scumbag Kid's body. Then, after they'd done that, he could kill Kyle, and dispose of *his* body in the reservoir. Then ditch the Merc, also in the reservoir, and make his getaway... How? Walking?... No, no, no. It was all crazy, bloody bloody crazy.

Kyle had no worries. There was plenty of time. As soon as he was sure that the girl and her boyfriend had been sufficiently frightened to put them out of action, he'd take out his mobile and send a long text to the Chief. The gist of the message would be that, despite Coleson's incompetence, all was well. The Kid was in Aberystwyth and they'd be picking him up any minute. It would all be over in the next half-hour, or hour at the most.

*

Azim had sensed that there was a feeling of relief in everyone on board when the little train left the hillside. But down in the river valley, the wind was ferocious and the rain was heavier and harder. Travelling at slower than walking pace and buffeted by the storm, the train reached a small station and came to a complete stop, as though exhausted. A man in uniform went from carriage to carriage. From the way the man spread his hands, Azim guessed that he was saying sorry to the passengers, or maybe this was how people prayed in this country. Most likely it was because the bad weather had made the train late. Some of the passengers muttered to each other. Others seemed to find all this some sort of adventure and spoke heartily to their children, as though they were taking part in a game.

He'd continued to stare at the floor. To do nothing. To say nothing. The only sound that came from him was the groaning of his empty stomach. After a long wait, with a brave hoot from its whistle, the train started to move, slowly lurching alongside the river. It crossed the river, and was joined by another railway, a bigger line, and then the two railways entered the outskirts of a big town. There were rows and rows of houses, enormous sheds, factories, and huge buildings that looked as though they must be parliament houses.

This must be near the end of the line. The sea could not be far away. Azim knew he must get ready to make his move. There would be guards and barriers, and men with rifles checking all travellers. He would have to avoid them. Which would be better? To be first or last off the train? Not first, and not last. But near last, when any guards searching for him might begin to worry that they'd missed him, that he'd already slipped through. At such times, searchers were torn between looking forward or looking back. So, it would be best to be nearly the last off the train.

The train stopped. Passengers collected their belongings, opened the carriage doors, and shepherded children out on to the platform and into the rain. Azim picked up the bag, selected a large man and a large woman as his cover, and stepped off the train with them. The platform was wide and long. The passengers fanned out, running for shelter under the roofs of the station buildings. This was good. The general stampede would make it far harder for any searcher to get a good look at everyone. On the other hand, Azim realised that with the bag he would stand out like a lamb among a pack of wild dogs. It would take less time than the blink of a hawk's eye for him to be spotted. There was only one thing for it…

There was no one behind him. He side-stepped to the edge of the platform, slid through the gap between the carriage and the platform, rolled under the carriage, and scrambled to his feet on the other side of the train. There was no one about. It seemed that no one had seen him. There were no shouts of alarm. No men with guns appeared. Azim moved swiftly along the side of the train, ready to roll back under it at the first sound of a gun being fired.

Out in the open, down by the rail tracks, he was getting soaked by the rain, but the way ahead was clear. There were no barriers, no guards, no checkpoints. He ran out of the station yard into a wide street. It was immediately apparent to him that this was a big town, but one that didn't seem to have many people living in it. There was no traffic. There were no cattle to be seen. No cars. No trucks with soldiers in the back, waving their rifles. No packs of scavenging dogs. No signs of life at all, save for his fellow passengers from the train, who were now scurrying to and fro, desperate to get out of the drenching rain and ferocious wind. There were plenty of shops but they were all shut. The rain and the emptiness reminded Azim of those times when the Taliban invaded his village during the monsoon season.

Azim crossed the wide road, the open space where there was always danger. What he needed – like when he jumped from the truck the night he escaped from the farm – was a dark alley. There was a narrow street to the left. He turned into it.

The side street ran down to what Azim thought might well be the sea, but it was hard to be certain, for he was now buffeted by a ferocious wind that almost threatened to wrench the bag from his shoulders. Progress was slow. He staggered along, stumbling several steps back as each gust struck him, and tottering forward in the moments when the wind freakishly dropped. Wind and what he thought was rain plastered his clothes to his body in an ice-cold embrace. He kept going. He had to find the port. He would get to the end of the street, to the sea. The port had to be somewhere near. But before that, hunger told him that he had to find food. Most of the shops were closed. Many of them had shutters over the windows.

He was almost at the bottom end of the street, when he saw a takeaway food store that had lights on inside. There was a sign on the frontage in letters that Azim couldn't read, but it looked like some kind of eating house. He fought his way through wind and wetness to the shop door. There were pictures of food in the window, dishes that were vaguely familiar to Azim – rice dishes, and kebabs, and what looked like dishes of olives.

One of the two men inside saw Azim's face peering through the window and took pity on the scraggy, half-drowned boy. The man hurried out and, before Azim had time to make a run for it, took him by the arm and led him into the shop. A second man came from a back room.

The two men sat Azim down at a little table. They smiled and nodded at him, as though they wanted to be friends. But they also asked a lot of questions, none of which Azim understood. They felt his clothes and shook their heads. One of the men fetched a towel, handed it to Azim, and mimed rubbing himself down. They were friendly. They smiled a lot. They pointed to the puddle of water on the floor formed by the drips that fell from Azim's soaking clothes. They laughed. One of them took off his shirt and mimed wringing it out. Azim shook his head. There wasn't time to dry his clothes. More than anything, he needed food. The men brought him a menu. Azim couldn't understand the writing on it, but the coloured photos of various dishes made ordering easy. He pointed to a picture of a *shish kebab* and said "Yes, please, for me".

There was more miming. One of the men held out his hand, rubbing his thumb and index finger together, universal sign language for 'We need money'. Azim was scared. Did they know what was in the bag? No, if they'd known about the money, they would have already dragged him into some back room, slit his throat, and taken all the money. Azim reached down, put his hand through the slit in the bag and pulled out a note. He hoped it wouldn't be a fifty; they always caused trouble. He was lucky. It was a brown one, a ten, part of the change from the shop where he had bought the cakes.

The men smiled again. One of them took a carving knife as big as a sword and began cutting slices from the large slab of *doner* meat; the other put pitta bread in a microwave and fetched plastic boxes of chopped onion and salad from the fridge.

Azim slumped over the table, with his head on his arms. For a while, he was safe. He would eat and then look for the port to find a ship to take him away from this cold and dismal land. The men brought him his food. They said something that Azim didn't understand. They mimed eating and then mimed shutting the shop. Azim got the message. He mimed filling his belly and then went to the door to mime leaving. But as he looked out, he saw to his horror what looked like foam-flecked water filling the street. Waves were flooding into town.

Two minutes later, with the bag on his back and with a takeaway parcel of kebab in one hand and a pile of coins in the other, Azim was once more out in the wind, the rain and the spray thrown up by the pounding sea. He looked about him. The Kebab men were placing sandbags across the bottom of the doorway into their café. As far as he could see through the rain and the spray, every shop was now shut.

He didn't want to go back up the street, to the railway. It was too dangerous. It was a place where police, soldiers, and his enemies might well gather. But did he have any choice? He had reached the sea, and that, too, was dangerous. It was a savage thing, that hurled water high into the air, where it paused for only as long as it took to blink an eye, before swooping down like a thousand great eagles, all diving to strike and kill. A curtain of spray, driven by the wind, whisked up the street, stinging his face and freezing his hands. Azim took one large bite out of his kebab, hugged the rest of it to his chest, and turned his back to the wind. He had to get out of this terrible town but, whatever the dangers surrounding him, he had to stay close to the sea. He had found the sea. Now he had to find a port. He had to get on a boat.

*

Saqui had been gone less than ten minutes before Vinnie decided he could wait no longer. Here was poor old Ashim gone goodness only knew where, and only Saqui out looking for him. Vinnie suspected Sam and Gwynedd were smooching somewhere. Either that, or Gwynedd had got pinned down at her Grandad's. He was a difficult old stick, Gwynedd's Grandad, but that was because Gwynedd never knew how to handle him.

Well, rain or no rain, Vinnie would do his level best to get this sorted.

He rode his scooter through the downpour up to Gwynedd's bungalow, and knocked smartly on the door.

A voice from inside called out over the noise of the television.

"It's not locked. Let yourself in. Unless there's something wrong with you. Like, you got the plague or criminal intent."

"It's me, Mr Hughes. Vinnie Roberts. Nothing wrong with me."

"I'll be the judge of that," said the voice. "Show yourself."

He's a good old stick, thought Vinnie.

Five minutes later, having been told in some detail what the Good Old Stick thought of him, Vinnie fled on his scooter. The old bastard's mad, he thought. You tell him his Gwynedd's disappeared, like, and he throws a fit. But it's only right and proper that people should know what's going on. It would be a kindness, therefore, to let Mrs Harper know that Sam had gone missing. She wouldn't throw a fit.

But she nearly did. That Mrs Harper went on something terrible, as though it was his idea to go to Aberystwyth. Adults, thought Vinnie, like, there's no way to understand any of them, 'cos they don't understand themselves half the time.

*

The wind grew still stronger. The rain belted down. The silver-grey Mercedes reached the outskirts of Aberystwyth. It was getting near crunch time. Sam reckoned that Azim must have arrived here an hour ago, maybe more, long enough for him to have moved on, taken a bus out of town – if buses were still running in this weather, which seemed highly unlikely.

Kyle flicked his eyes from the road ahead to the driving mirror, and then to Gwynedd sitting beside him. .

"Where do we find your friend?"

Gwynedd didn't know how to answer him. She believed that the moment the gunmen found Azim they would kill him, and that, therefore, she and Sam must do everything they could to lead the gunmen in the wrong direction. But she didn't know where Azim was, so she didn't know what was the wrong direction, and what would be the disastrous right direction.

Looking from the back seat at that same driving mirror, Sam could see that the man called Kyle was looking at him.

"Not here," Sam said. "He's more likely to have caught a bus somewhere… anywhere. Or maybe he'd have stayed at the station, hoping for a train to London."

"Is that what you both think?" Kyle's eyes darted again to Gwynedd.

"He did say something about going to Bristol," said Gwynedd. It was the only place that came into her mind.

"I don't think you're co-operating," said Kyle. "I don't think you're playing for the team. I think you've been telling untruths. I don't think your little friend is getting a train to London or Bristol or anywhere else. He wouldn't last three minutes in London and five minutes in Bristol. He's not smart. He's a dumb foreign kid from the mountains. I bet he's lost and wandering around in this bloody town. So sit back and enjoy the ride, kids." Again there was the sneer in Kyle's voice. "It may be your last." He took his left hand off the steering wheel and let it rest on Gwynedd's knee. She flinched away from him, as though she had been stung by a wasp.

192

Sam kept reminding himself of his father's words, about those that do, and those that only talk about what they're going to do. Gwynedd had no such comforting thoughts. She was already horribly aware that the man called Kyle posed a special threat to her. She wished she could think of some way to respond, protect herself, to fight back. But she couldn't.

In the same quiet, level, scary voice, Kyle continued to give a detailed description of what was about to happen.

"We take it slow round corners. If we see the Kid, no sudden braking. If he's going in the same direction as us, we pass him… drive on for a hundred metres or so. Then stop, and wait for him to catch up. If he's going in the opposite direction, same thing…we drive past, go on a hundred metres, then make a U-turn, drive slowly past…"

"For God's sake! Just drive the bloody car." There was panic in Coleson's voice.

Kyle took no notice. "… The moment he's level with us, you grab him and shove him in the back. Nobody'll see what's happening in this weather. And while you're doing that, I'll keep these two covered. If they make any sudden movement, any noise, we kill them both. OK? Once we've found the Scumbag Kid, he's the only one we need alive. Right. Take it steady."

No one in the car was prepared for what lay round the corner.

A wall of spray, as high as a house, was flung across the road in front of them. Pebbles and sand rattled and thumped against the roof and side of the car. Before the impact of the first wave had come to an end, another wave crashed down on them. Kyle instinctively jammed his foot on the brake. The car came to a halt.

For several seconds it was impossible to see ahead until a giant blast of wind whisked the spray away. Hitmen and prisoners peered through the windscreen. The promenade was deserted, save for one or two parked cars lying at strange angles to the pavement. The surface of the road was littered with debris, bricks, and slabs of broken paving stone as though an urban riot had passed through a moment earlier. Then another wall of spray crashed down and they could see only foam and water, and shingle torn from the beach.

"God Almighty!" said Coleson. "There's no way anyone could survive in that."

The next wave brought with it a length of twisted railing wrenched from the edge of the promenade.

Kyle's voice was still controlled. "We keep this side of the road. The impact's less here."

"What's the point? Anyone mad enough to be out in this gets smashed to pieces or swept out to sea. The bloody car'll be wrecked."

"We simply keep going."

But they didn't get much further.

There was a road block at the junction ahead. A number of police officers were struggling to erect heavy metal barriers across the promenade. Sam wished he could grab Gwynedd's hand and give it a gentle squeeze, to show that he hadn't given up hope. There was a small chance that the police might stop the car and want to see inside.

But the police weren't going to waste more time than was necessary to send the Mercedes on its way. The policeman waved his arms, pointing up the side road, indicating that the car should turn off the promenade and head away from the sea. Other police officers were waiting to place barriers across the entrance to the side street. The Mercedes was going to be the last vehicle allowed through. There would be no more access to the seafront.

The moment the car turned the corner, it was easier to see, so much so that everyone in the Mercedes recognised the thin and soaked figure scurrying along, a grey and black canvas bag strapped to his back. His head was twisting and turning, as though he was trying to look in all directions at once. He had seen the police roadblock, and his reaction had been to turn round and start walking away from the sea.

"Not here."

Kyle kept his voice low.

"We pass him, and we stop up by that lamp-post ahead. Then we wait. He can't get away. The police won't let him through their road block. All we have to do is wait. Remember, when I give the word, I'll unlock the car doors. You get out and grab the Kid. I'll keep my gun on our passengers. OK? We all wait quietly. Everything's going to be fine."

Coleson fumbled with his gun.

Sam could see that Gwynedd was twisting in her seat, trying to catch his eye in the driving mirror. He gave the slightest shake of his head. He wanted her to understand that she mustn't say or do anything to make the gunmen suspicious. He couldn't give her a clue as to what he was going to do. It was a long shot. He had no idea whether it would work or not. But he wanted her to be ready. She gave a nod of her head, a sign that she was on the alert. Good. The gunmen both had their eyes fixed on the car's wing mirrors. They were watching every staggering step that Azim made. Sam did the same. He prayed that the storm would keep raging, the sea would keep thundering over the promenade, and the rain would keep slashing down. The wilder the elements, the better the chance of getting away when they made a dash for it… if such a moment came.

Keeping his eyes on the image of Azim in the mirror, Sam began to unfasten his sling. The straps that went over his shoulder and round his back were tightly fastened with Velcro. It wasn't difficult to undo them if you ripped the Velcro apart, but it was impossible to undo them without making what seemed a loud scratching noise. Sam's hope was that the roar of the storm would drown out any sound made by unpicking the Velcro. Slowly, gently, bit by bit, he parted the fastenings.

Gwynedd realised what he was doing, but had no idea why he was doing it. She didn't know what Sam's plan was. She didn't even know if there was a plan. But she did know that it would help if she created a diversion.

"Why are we waiting here?" she said. "That's not the kid you want."

Kyle dropped his hand on her knee again. "You must think I'm one helluva dope." He dug his fingers hard into her thigh. "Get real." Back came the sneer. Then he spoke out of the corner of his mouth to Gwynedd, as though he was passing on a secret. "When we've got the Kid and the bag, and we're clearing up," he said. "I'll take care of you. I'm looking forward to that."

Sam worked steadily at the Velcro. The strap at the back was now loose. He started on the shoulder strap.

Azim was getting near. Coleson had his hand on the handle of the passenger door, ready to fling it open. Neither he nor Kyle was watching Sam or Gwynedd. Sam knew he had to time his move to perfection. When the moment came, he would have to swing into action at speed, shouting his orders to Azim and Gwynedd. But it was imperative that he waited until the gunman in the back seat was out of the car. That was the time when Sam had to make his play.

Azim was almost level with the back of the Mercedes.

"Unlocking the doors..." There was excitement in Kyle's voice.

Coleson flexed his leg muscles, ready to leap out. Sam unfastened the last section of Velcro. It was all about to happen, when suddenly everything changed.

Azim recognised the car beside him as the one that had chased him back in Rhayader. He tried to leap away from it, but he was too late. Coleson was out of the car. He made a grab at Azim but could only get hold of one of the handles of the grey and black canvas bag. He yanked at it and Azim was whirled round. The plastic bag containing the kebab went flying.

"Now, Gwen! Now! Open your door! Out!"

As he shouted these orders, Sam reached forward from the back seat and grabbed Kyle by the hair, jerking his head back as hard as he could. Before Kyle had time to recover, Sam wrapped the sling round the man's face, wound the straps round his head and fastened the Velcro at the back. There was a clattering noise as Sam's phone hit the steering wheel and dropped to the floor. One instinct was to let go of Kyle's hair and reach out for his beloved phone, but the will to escape overrode all concern for a mere machine. Kyle tore the sling from his face. Gwynedd fought her way out of the front passenger seat of the car. She collapsed on the pavement, but seized Coleson's arm and sank her teeth into his hand, the one that was clamped on Azim's bag. There was a snarl of rage and pain from the gunman. He lifted his other hand, the hand that still held his gun, aiming to bring the gun down on the back of Gwynedd's neck. Azim was too quick for him. He barged into Coleson, putting the gunman off balance so that he fell against the side of the car.

Sam was now out and round the back of the car. He grabbed hold of Gwynedd with one hand and Azim with the other.

"This way! They daren't shoot with the police coming up!" He was shouting the words as loud as he could.

Sam had no idea if the police were approaching. The words were meant for the gunmen's ears. He hoped they would take a look back to see what the police were doing. That would give him and Gwynedd and Azim time to reach the lamp-post and race round the corner. If they could do that, escape was possible. The gunmen wouldn't follow them on foot. Even in the empty streets of a deserted town, you can't expect to force-march three prisoners at gun point and not attract some sort of attention – from someone monitoring CCTV, from someone looking out of the window of a house or flat, or from someone dashing out to the shops. The gunmen would give chase in the car, which meant they would have to deal with one-way streets and traffic lights and, hopefully, other cars on the road – all in a town that was strange to them and in freak bad weather. The more corners he and Gwynedd could propel Azim around, the better their chance of escape.

For five lung-busting minutes they ran as best they could through the storm, along a jumbled succession of streets, in no fixed direction.

"We can't go much further," panted Gwynedd. "Azim's almost dead on his feet. We'll have to slow down."

"We can't stop," said Sam. "We've got to find somewhere to hide. Or some place where there's loads of people."

Gwynedd stopped. She looked back over her shoulder. There was no sign of pursuit.

"We've got to rest. And we've got to find somewhere that sells food. Catch him!"

Azim's legs had buckled beneath him. Gwynedd knelt beside him and massaged his hands. They were almost frozen.

"He can't go on. Food first and then some dry clothes, and then rest."

"How do you get dry clothes in a storm like this?"

"We buy them, silly."

"What with? Have you got any money?"

"Three pounds fifty. I thought my rich boyfriend would have money."

Sam fished in his pocket. "Not much," he said. "Perhaps Azim's got some."

"Another one of his fifty quid notes would come in handy."

"Ask him."

"How?"

"Show him some of your money."

They helped Azim to his feet and each took an arm to support him. Azim's face was pale with exhaustion. His teeth were chattering. But he understood what the black girl and the guy with the busted arm wanted. With difficulty he lifted the bag from his shoulders. He placed it on the pavement, sat beside it, put his hand through the slit in the bag, and plucked out one of the plastic wallets. He offered it to Gwynedd.

She turned it slowly round in her hand. "Bloody hell. He's got a fortune." She showed the wallet to Sam.

"You know what I like about you?" he said. "Something like this happens. We're running for our lives. We find thousands of pounds, and you *don't* say 'Oh my God!'" That would have been how his Bristol pals would have reacted.

"Oh my God!" she said. "You're right. But what do we do now? My mobile's gone. Your phone's somewhere in their car. We can't contact anyone."

Sam saw some advantages in having no means of communication. Becky couldn't contact him. If she knew what was going on, she'd be terrified. She'd get on to the police, and they'd find Saqui, and Saqui would tell them where to look for a boy and girl answering the descriptions of Sam and Gwynedd.

"What would happen if we went to the police?"

"They'd arrest Azim," said Sam. "They'd take all his money and cart him off to some kid's jail where he'd get bullied and beaten up. We have to keep the police out of this."

"Right," she said. "The first thing we have to do is get Azim into some dry clothes."

"No," said Sam. "The first thing we have to do is get the hell out of here."

"He *has* to have dry clothes. Look, he's shaking with cold."

"I'm shaking. Putting a mile or so between us and those thugs would warm us all up."

"He's got to have food. We all need food."

She sounded like a small child.

"You've only just eaten," he said.

She didn't understand.

"Raw meat," he said. "You must have bitten quite a chunk out of that gunman's hand."

He wanted to make a joke out of it, but she didn't want to respond in a jokey way. Both of them saw that they were on the verge of having a row. Sam didn't want a row, but Gwynedd's refusal to respond to his attempt at humour made him angry.

"There are men after us who want to kill us…"

Sam had a lot more to say, but Gwynedd cut in.

"I know, I know," she said. "But Azim's…"

"If we don't make a run for it now, we'll be killed."

"I know!" Gwynedd shouted.

Azim, a bundle of wet rags, flat out on the pavement, peered up at them. Sam and Gwynedd stared at each other. Though neither of them knew it, their thoughts were almost perfectly matched. Sam had just made up his mind that there was no use arguing with Gwynedd because she may well be right, and anyway, they had to work together on this. He also decided that only when he was with Gwynedd did life reach such a peak of intensity. Here they were, running for their lives, just like they'd done that night when Sam's dog Ben had saved their lives.

Gwynedd, too, remembered that time before, and decided that she must have sort of fallen in love with Sam that night… well, all right, if not then, she was falling in love with him now. Life – ordinary, dull, everyday life – became a whirlwind of excitement when she and Sam went into battle together. Only when she was with Sam, did she live life to the full. It wasn't easy. It was often dangerous. But it was always worthwhile. Especially afterwards – if there was an afterwards.

"All right," said Sam. "You win. But food first, and then dry clothes."

*

On the outskirts of Aberystwyth, Saqui gunned his scooter as hard as he dared. He could hardly see where he was going. The rain running in rivulets down the visor of his helmet was superimposed on the tears that filled his eyes. Every couple of miles, he had to stop and wipe his face. Miles back, he had given up all hope of making mobile contact with Azim, Sam or Gwynedd. There was no signal, which was hardly surprising in this storm. He believed that he was alone in his search. He was also convinced that he was the one who had let Azim down. This was a hopeless mission. Even if any of them got to Aberystwyth, there was only the faintest of chances that they would find Azim. And, if by some miracle they did find him, there was nothing any of them could do or say to make the poor boy come back to Rhayader.

On another scooter, Vinnie's attitude was different. He also wanted to get to Aberystwyth as soon as possible, but not because he was in any way worried for Ashim's safety or felt personally guilty about Ashim's plight. As far as Vinnie was concerned, this was simply a race to see who got to Ashim first. Vinnie wanted to win this race. It wasn't a fair race, because Saqui had started long before him. It had taken Vinnie so much time trying to find Sam and Gwynedd.

Vinnie had known that his one hope of winning the Race-to-Ashim had been to take a different route from Saqui. And Vinnie guessed that it was most likely that Saqui would have taken the main road that led north from Rhayader to Llangurig, and then headed west to Aberystwyth. That was the safe route. So Vinnie had decided to take the dangerous one. The thing was, like, that he could conquer all that danger and then he'd emerge the winner. Which was, like, brilliant.

*

Sam and Gwynedd found a convenience store that had the courage to stay open in the teeth of what was now a flat-out ferocious storm. Sam kept guard at the entrance while Gwynedd hustled Azim inside. She pointed to the sandwiches, pasties and pies. He pointed to the frozen pizzas. She shook her head, and tried to work out how to mime 'we haven't got anything to heat them in'. She pointed to the sausage rolls, but then had doubts.

"Hey, Sam. Does his religion allow Azim to eat sausage rolls?"

"How should I know? And hurry up, for God's sake."

"What is his religion?"

"How should I know?"

In the end, Azim settled for a fruit cake, several bars of chocolate and a litre bottle of water. Gwynedd approved of the chocolate. It would give Azim energy, and could be easily shared.

She took a £50 note from the wallet that Azim had given her, and passed it to the girl behind the counter.

"Haven't you got anything smaller, love?"

Gwynedd shook her head. All she had were dozens and dozens of £50 notes. Never before had she held so much money in her hands. It took her breath away. If they hadn't been in such danger she would have loved to daydream what she could do, how she could live if she had that sort of money. She and Sam could set up home in a little flat. On the day she left school, they could move in together. It didn't matter if Sam had to still be at school or college, doing his A levels. She wouldn't blow the fortune away like you heard people had done who'd won the lottery. She'd make it last for the rest of their lives. And to make sure it lasted, she'd get a proper daytime job, and then cook and clean the flat in the evenings, and look after Sam all the time. And they'd still have fun.

Sam called from the door.

"Get a move on."

Gwynedd tore the wrapper off the fruit cake and gave the whole cake to Azim.

"Eat," she said.

There was no need for words or mimes. Azim was ravenously hungry. With two bites he devoured half the cake.

The three of them raced out into the rain.

"Which way?" he said.

"No idea."

"Great. So helpful. No, look! There! There!"

Sam pointed across the street to a branch of Primewear.

"Perfect," she said. Gwynedd was amazed that Sam knew that Primewear sold clothes. There was no way Becky would have taken him shopping for clothes in any of their stores.

They went into the store.

The young woman at the till called out to them. "We're closing, my dears. Sorry. But with this weather, we can't stay open."

"Yes, you can," said Gwynedd. "We know what we want and we'll be very quick."

Sam took note of Gwynedd's idea of shopping for clothes when under pressure. With one hand, she dragged Azim round the store, like a toddler. With the other, she snatched T-shirts, sweaters and an anorak. At the checkout, she shoved all the purchases at the assistant, dropped two £50 notes on the counter, told the assistant to keep the change, and dragged Azim back to Sam.

"Round the back," she said. "He can change there."

They took Azim to a doorway in a small yard behind the store, where they were sheltered from the rain.

"You do this," she said to Sam. "Strip his old clothes off, and help him pull on the new ones – and mind your arm. Trousers first, and then pass the old ones to me."

"You've got three sweaters. All Extra Large. What's the point of that?"

"Azim needs a sweater. You need a sweater. I need a sweater. But none of us wants one that's too small. And you can bet it'll be cold tonight, and we've no idea where we'll be."

Gwynedd knelt on the wet ground and began a quick search of the contents of the pockets of Azim's old trousers. She found nothing. This was strange.

"Everyone carries something in their pockets," she said. "Keys, cash, Kleenex, mobile… something."

"The mobile!" said Sam. "The one that Vinnie sold him. It must be in Azim's bag."

Gwynedd tried to mime a request that Azim turn out the entire contents of the grey and black bag. He didn't want to do that. Gwynedd simplified the mime to 'lend us your mobile'. He understood. With hands that were still shaking with cold, Azim rummaged through the slit he'd made in the bag with the shard of glass. It took time, but eventually he found the phone. The signal was weak. The battery was low. But the phone was still working.

"Try Saqui first."

Gwynedd entered Saqui's number. There was no answer.

She tried Vinnie's number and got through, but the line was bad. Vinnie said it was good to hear Gwynedd's voice, but that he couldn't speak right now as he was 'screaming' down the mountain road from Devil's Bridge.

"Need both hands to steer," he shouted. "I'll call you when I get to Aberystwyth."

Vinnie ended the call. Gwynedd told Sam what he'd said.

"So there's no word from Saqui," said Sam. "And Vinnie won't be here for at least half an hour. And even when they're both here, they'll only be able to take two of us. One of us will have to stay and fend for himself."

"Or herself."

If it came to some kind of competition between her and Sam as to who could survive longest in a freak storm while being chased by homicidal maniacs, Gwynedd was confident that she'd emerge the winner. She didn't have a busted arm.

They both looked at Azim. He was recovering. He had stopped shaking. Food and dry clothes had brought about a miraculous cure. He could walk, but not for long and not at any pace. Had he been fit, he would have fought ferociously to survive. He had great skills to survive in the wild. In a town? Gwynedd was not so sure.

"Come on," said Sam. "We have to keep moving."

*

Kyle had nothing to report when yet another ill-tempered and threatening call came through from the Chief. Kyle explained that he and Coleson were still in Aberystwyth, and that any minute now they would have their hands on the Scumbag Kid and the money. It didn't satisfy the Chief in the slightest. What the hell was going on? Did it take an army to deal with one kid? Kyle exercised all his self-control. He repeated that he and Coleson were on the point of blowing the Kid away. Foul weather had hindered their operation. He told the Chief that, right now, the streets were more like rivers in Aberystwyth. The Chief wasn't interested. All Kyle got in return was an earful of threats. Kyle swore that he and Coleson would have the Kid and the bag within the hour. The call then ended abruptly, with another blast of angry threats from the Chief.

"He's like all the stuck-up fat-brained Army officers I've ever known," Kyle told Coleson. "Full of big-mouth orders but not prepared to listen to the guy on the front line."

Kyle was on foreign territory here, and he didn't like it. He felt the pressure on him. He knew his professional fee was in danger, but it wasn't a matter of the money involved; he could always help himself out of the 100k or more in that grey and black bag. This was about pride and reputation. It was all very well the Chief saying that he wanted the Scumbag Kid to be 'neatly' killed and disposed of. With this storm raging, the Scumbag Kid would get it any way that presented itself. It was the black girl's execution that Kyle would take trouble over.

Kyle reckoned that the most likely area where the kids would turn up was somewhere around the station. Sooner or later, they had to make a break to get out of town, by train, bus or taxi. There was enough money in that bloody bag for the kids to take a taxi to London. Whatever way they travelled, the rail station would be their point of departure. It would be best if he personally kept a special eye on the station.

*

A mile or so away, Saqui and his scooter were still battling with the gale, and he could barely see where he was going. He knew Aberystwyth well enough to find his way to the station but, with this storm racing through it, the place was like a ghost town. There were notices plastered along the front of the station. There would be no more trains or buses operating until further notice. If Azim had found his way to Aberystwyth, which Saqui still doubted, he wouldn't be able to find any way out. Saqui knew he had to keep searching. And the best way to do that was to start circling round the station on his scooter, gradually enlarging the radius of that circle, in the hope that sooner or later his path and Azim's would meet. There was a very real risk that they wouldn't, because either Azim was holed up somewhere off the streets - or he was dead.

*

Azim had finished his fruit cake and was quietly sitting in the doorway next to Gwynedd.

"I'll tell you where we'd be safe," said Sam, in what he hoped was a voice packed with genius and authority, "Constitution Hill."

"Never heard of it."

"Top of the cliffs at this end of the town. Where there's the Camera Obscura." Sam sounded very sure of himself

"Never heard of it."

"Yes you have. Mr Richards told us about it when we were top Juniors. Right on the top of the cliffs. We'd be safe there. They'll never think of looking for us there. Nobody'll be up there in this weather."

"How do we get there?"

"The Cliff Railway."

"Never heard of that either."

"Yes, you have…"

"You keep saying that. I'm sure *you've* been there. I'm sure Becky took you to all these posh places. Well, most of the time I don't get to go nowhere, right?"

"It's that way," he said, and he pointed towards the north end of the town. "And it isn't posh."

Gwynedd helped Azim to his feet.

"Come on, Azim, love," she said. "Sam reckons he's being brilliant, so you and me have to admire him and follow him and thank him. Even though Cliff's Railway won't be running."

"Yes, it will," said Sam. "It runs until the beginning of November."

"Not in this weather." It would be good if he could be wrong and she could be right for once.

"But today's special. They have a huge firework display on the top of the cliff, and crowds go up there to see it."

"In this weather?"

"Yes, it will be open. Because it's Halloween."

That was true. It was Halloween. Gwynedd's mind went back to Halloween Night two years ago. She and Sam had been in a mess then, running for their lives from Mollie Pryce's mad step-father. They'd had shotguns fired at them, a killer dog set on them, but they'd survived. Maybe this was some kind of omen, a Date-with-Destiny. It had rained that night, too, up in the mountains. But then, thought Gwynedd, you couldn't call that part of an omen. It nearly always rained in Wales.

"Come on then," she said. "Let's make a start."

"Hang on." Sam wanted to make sure they were doing the right thing. If only he still had his phone with him, he could have checked whether any trains or buses were still running out of Aberystwyth. It seemed unlikely. The wind was still a blistering gale, howling through the town. If there was no way they could get out of town, then they had to find the best possible hiding place. And one of the best hiding places would be in a crowd. Hundreds, maybe thousands of people would climb to the cliff-top to watch the Firework Display. He wondered what time it was. It was already dark enough for fireworks, but maybe it wasn't late enough. If only they had a smartphone.

"I'm gonna try phoning Saqui again."

This time he got through to Saqui. The two of them made hasty arrangements. Saqui was to contact Vinnie and wait for him at the one place in Aberystwyth that not even Vinnie could miss – the railway station. Then they were both to ride their scooters straight to Constitution Hill. Saqui said he knew the back roads that led to the top of the cliffs. It was complicated, and the last bit would have to be over wet grass, but it could be done. At Saqui's request, Sam then handed the mobile to Azim. He couldn't understand a word of their conversation, but it sounded like there were many exchanges in the Arabic equivalent of 'Yes, please' and

'Thank you' - all of which severely tested Sam's patience. But the phone conversation was mercifully brief.

Azim switched off the mobile. He was sufficiently aware of mobiles to know that little power was left in the battery, and that once the battery ran out, they couldn't keep in touch with any of these strange friends and allies.

The storm was at its height, with squalls of rain so heavy that it was impossible to see much in front of them. The wind was striking them with bruising force, and it felt as though the rain was cutting into their faces. Sam wondered how long they could keep going. Even here, at least a couple of hundred metres from the seafront, and with several rows of shops and houses between them and the beach, he could hear the pounding of the waves and the slapping noise when one of them hit the road. He, Gwynedd and Azim took it in turns to carry the bag, but it felt as though it was getting heavier all the time.

"So," said Gwynedd. "How do we get to this famous Cliff Railway?"

"This way," he said. "Up the back streets. At least we'll get some shelter from the wind there."

They reached the bottom of the Cliff Railway. It wasn't running. The two railcars stood at opposite ends of the slope – one at the top, the other at the bottom. The ticket office was closed. There was a notice pasted on the entrance. The Cliff Railway would not re-open till next Easter. There were also notices advertising the Massive Halloween Firework Display, but all these had CANCELLED straps pasted over them.

They sat on the boarding platform, where there was a little shelter from the gale. Gwynedd gave Sam a look of triumph, but she knew they were in a mess.

*

It was while Saqui was making the call to Vinnie telling him to come to the railway station that Kyle spotted him from the parked Mercedes. Saqui didn't notice the car, but Kyle recognised the scooter with the pizza delivery box on the back, and that the guy riding it was the Asian lad that ran the Fish and Chip Shop.

This was more like it. A stroke of luck at bloody last. The Chip Shop guy could only be here in this lousy dump because he too was looking for the Kid. Fine. Kyle would let the Chip Shop guy lead him to the Scumbag Kid. The two gunmen watched as the Chip Shop bloke's mate joined him.

"We follow as soon as they move," said Kyle. "They'll take us straight to the bag. I know they will." There was excitement in his voice.

"Then what?" Kyle might be excited, but Coleson was a bundle of nerves. "Do we kill the lot of them?"

"If necessary."

"All of them? That's a bloody massacre."

"No massacre. Just a repeat operation. Like a fairground shooting booth. Bang… bang… bang… bang… until they're all dead. It'll be easy. Dead easy."

But as Kyle uttered the words, his mind yet again threw up the monstrous image. Kyle stared through the windscreen. Was there something wrong with his eyes? In place of a grey Welsh town, he was looking at an African village, under a burning sun. He saw the swollen bodies of men, women and children, killed maybe days ago. His ears were full of the faraway echo of explosions all round him. He saw other bodies, small bodies, spin round as the bullets bit into them. He heard screams, and then there was a sudden silence. The sun was gone. The village was gone. The screaming had stopped. He was back in a grey city, on a day dark with rain, but he was sitting in a comfortable car.

"What's wrong?"

Coleson sounded concerned. Kyle reacted furiously.

"Nothing's wrong." Just my bloody luck, thought Kyle. Teamed up with a soft bastard when there's killing to be done. Think of the bag, think of the money, he told himself. How much of it has stuck to the fingers of these kids? They could have spent hundreds, and dished out thousands more to their mates. No one knew if 10k, maybe 20k hadn't already gone from the bag. If the job now involved disposing of five kids, then Kyle was going to demand 5k a pop from the bag for each kid he killed. What the hell, call it 30k for the lot.

Coleson sat in silence. He was on the verge of breaking down completely. It was all such a bloody mess. Kill one kid and you'd get a life sentence. With luck and good conduct you might be out in 12 years. Kill five kids? They'd bang you up and throw away the key.

"They're moving."

Kyle switched on the ignition. There was no fear of the kids hearing the sound of a Merc engine starting up with the rows their scooters made. He put the car's headlights on 'full'; there was no way he was going to lose them.

"What do we do about the Chief? He said we had to keep him informed."

"We don't call in until the job's done. When we do, use this." Kyle handed Coleson Sam's phone.

Coleson took it reluctantly. Kill all these kids? Jesus. He couldn't be party to that. All they needed was the bag and the money. Get that and make out they'd killed the Scumbag Kid. The Chief wouldn't know. The Kid would disappear. Maybe Kyle could be bought off with a few thousand out of the bag. Coleson himself would be happy with two grand. Take that and never have anything more to do with his lousy family, his lousy Chief. But what was going on in Kyle's crazy brain? Kyle wouldn't stop at killing all the kids, and nicking every penny of the money in the bag, and then putting the blame on someone else, anyone else… even his so-called partner. Kyle would make out that Coleson had taken the money, and the Chief would believe him. The Chief admired Kyle because he was a villain. He'd never admired his own brother. Coleson wiped the palms of his hands on the passenger seat of the Merc. It didn't do much good. What you wanted to dry your hands on was soft fabric, not swanky leather.

*

The black woman and the one-armed man had dragged him through the streets, fed him, given him dry clothes, and saved him from the Hunters in the silver car. Azim was grateful, but he was also exhausted. He had reached the sea, yes. There it was, dark and menacing, looking as though it was possessed of demons whipping it into a frenzy. But there was no sight of a boat.

There was magic all around him, good magic as well as bad. In the struggle with the Hunters, the one-armed man had suddenly grown another arm, which he was using to point to himself right now. 'Zam', he kept saying, while he jabbed himself with one finger from the new hand. 'Zam'. Azim repeated the word, wondering what it meant. 'Zam', said the man, and then he pointed the finger at Azim and said 'Azim'. Now Azim understood. 'Zam' was the man's name. The man did the same with the black girl, pointing at her and saying a word that sounded like 'Jennit'. Azim nodded. His two saviours were named Zam and Jennit.

Zam led the way up a steep and muddy path. Rainwater was draining fast from the cliff-top above, so that it was more like climbing a waterfall than a path. The climb was short, but dangerous, with the wind blasting in from the sea and threatening to pluck the three climbers from the ground and whisk them away. All three were gasping for breath when they reached the top.

They had come to the summit of Constitution Hill, to a plateau at the top of the cliffs. Directly in front of them were two large buildings, uninhabited by the look of them, for they displayed no lights inside. To their left was the cliff edge, and beyond that the sea, pounding and exploding in waves whipped by the wind. Along this cliff edge was a metal fence, running along the entire length of the cliffs from the top of the path they had just climbed to what looked like woods on the far side of the plateau. It was not easy to be sure. The night was heavy and dark with low clouds and no moon.

The fence intrigued Azim. It was made of metal, over head-high and capped with a row of wicked spikes. He guessed it was there to prevent anyone wandering over the cliff edge and falling to their deaths on the rocks below. It seemed to Azim that people would have to be very stupid to walk so near a cliff edge as to endanger their lives. Up in the mountains at home, when he was a little child, he had learned where it was safe to walk and where it wasn't.

Zam and Jennit tried the doors to the two large buildings. They were locked. It was impossible to get inside. Then Zam shouted something, and pointed to a brightly painted red and white timber cabin, little bigger than the ruined shepherd's hut that Azim had slept in the night before. The cabin was old and weather-beaten. It would have nothing to offer in the way of comfort or safety, but if they could find a way of getting inside it, they would at least be out of the wind. Zam shouted again, and led the way to the cabin.

Azim didn't see how this strange cabin with its peeling paint and drooping roof could possibly make them safe, not from madmen with guns. The only hope was that, at some point – please Allah, soon - Saqui would appear on his scooter and whisk Azim and the bag away. All well and good for Azim. But what would happen to Jennit and Zam? Azim had no idea where the gunmen were, but he had this horrible, crazy, creepy feeling that they weren't far away. There were no lights to be seen anywhere near, no signs of life, and nothing that offered help or hope. Azim's body had warmed a little during the climb up the muddy path, but in this biting wind it was rapidly chilling. They couldn't stay here for long. This was strange. It made no sense. They had a bag stuffed with money but nothing to eat. They could buy a palace with the money, but they had nowhere to spend the night other than this cabin. They were in danger of dying from exposure – like crippled animals on the hillside in winter.

Azim followed Zam and Jennit to the cabin. There was a padlock on the door, but the storm had torn the door from its hinges. Zam pushed it open, and they entered some kind of storeroom. It was full of wooden crates, nailed shut, with markings on them. The markings were in some script that was neither English nor Arabic. Windows ran along the length of one wall. He peered out through the dirty glass. There was not a light to be seen. They were alone on this cliff-top. But for how long? It wouldn't take any time at all for any hunter to see that the only places that needed searching were the three buildings...

Azim felt trapped. He had run as far as he could, but he could go no further. His fate was now in the hands of Zam and Jennit and Allah.

*

Gwynedd had guessed that if Saqui and Vinnie did turn up, they would come from the woods to the left. There was some kind of footpath leading from the woods across the grass. The wind dropped for a moment, and she heard the whine of a motor scooter. The noise came and went as the wind dropped and rose again. It sounded as though the rider of the scooter was having to rev the engine hard. Gwynedd put her hand to her ear. Could she hear two engines? No, there was only one.

A figure emerged from the woods, half riding and half walking his scooter over the mud.

"It's Saqui," said Sam. "I told you he'd make it." Sam felt as though he was gaining some rough sort of control over the situation, things were falling into place. He smiled at Azim, hoping to reassure the lad.

Sam and Gwynedd left the shack. Azim held back until he was sure that the rider of the scooter was Saqui, then ran to join them.

Saqui was gabbling. The wind whipped his words away. It was difficult to make sense of what he was saying. More than once he said something about a car following him, but it sounded as though it had become stuck in mud. Saqui pointed to the trees. He repeatedly said that he had come for Azim, and then pointed to his scooter and shouted into the wind that there was no room for anyone but Azim.

"I cannot rescue all of you."

He grabbed hold of Azim. They spoke rapidly together. Saqui was asking all the questions; Azim pointed first at Gwynedd, then at Sam. To Gwynedd, it seemed that Azim wanted Saqui to help them too. But what Saqui had said was true: there was only one pillion seat of his scooter.

Gwynedd looked at the large, plastic, pizza delivery box fixed on the back of the pillion seat. She unfastened the catch and opened the box. Inside was the spare helmet that Saqui had put there for Azim, and several pizza boxes. There was an unpleasant savoury smell coming from the boxes, as though they had been there for some time.

From the woods came the sound of another vehicle.

"Azim! Over here. Quick! Bring the bag." Gwynedd jabbed her finger towards the bag.

Azim didn't understand a word, but recognised the urgency and authority in Jennit's voice and saw where the finger was pointing He did as he was told.

"Sam, help Azim put on this helmet. Saqui, do you want these pizza boxes?"

Saqui shook his head. "They were supposed to be delivered last night, but I was so worried about Azim…"

"Good." She took the boxes out of the delivery box and dropped them on the grass. "Now explain to Azim that we're going to transfer as much of his money as possible from the bag into this box, and that you're then going to take him away."

"Hurry," said Sam. "They could get to us any second now." He listened. There was that noise of a vehicle engine. It sounded too high-pitched to be a car; more like another scooter. "Is Vinnie coming?"

"He's on his way."

"Good. The more people we have here, the more chance there is of you and Azim getting away."

Gwynedd was already packing wallets of money into the scooter delivery box. She doubted there was room for all the money, so she was picking out the bundles of £50 notes and packing them first. It was a good job that the notes were in wallets. If they'd been loose, her work would have been much harder, and the wind would have whisked most of them away.

"Come on, Gwen. Faster than that." Sam dumped a fistful of wallets into the box.

Gwynedd took them out. "We'll get far more in if they're neatly packed. You keep a watch out for any cars. And don't look at me like that. This isn't a time for arguing."

She packed the last of the £50 notes. There was room left for some of the £20 wallets. She had just made a start on them when another scooter burst out of the wood and began snaking its way across the soaking grass. It was Vinnie. Long before he reached them, Vinnie was shouting something and pointing back over his shoulder.

Sam took a quick look round. Saqui was fastening on his helmet and Azim already had his on. Gwynedd had almost filled the box on Saqui's scooter. Azim went to pick up the bag. Sam shook his head.

"Sorry, Azim," he said. "That has to stay here. Tell him, Saqui. We need the bag." He turned to Vinnie. "Here's a job for you. Put those pizza boxes in the bag."

Gwyneth snapped at him.

"The pizza boxes don't matter!"

"But the bag does - those guys want the money. They won't be interested in Azim if they think he hasn't got the bag any more. What matters is that the bag should look and feel heavy."

Vinnie began stuffing the boxes through the slit into the bag.

"Ok, Sam, but listen, I think a car was following me and Saqui up here. It got stuck in the mud half way up the hill and two guys got out to push it. Seems funny anyone would be wanting to drive up here tonight – unless they was looking for us."

The bag was now full of last night's pizzas. Gwynedd closed the lid of the delivery box and fastened the catch.

"Saqui, you and Azim go now," said Sam. "But not the way you came."

"There's another way," said Vinnie. "Over the golf course. There won't be no golfers playing in this weather, not in the dark. It's that way, over there." He pointed towards a wood where the wind was tearing leaves and small branches from the trees. "See the gap? You can go through that, then turn left until you come to the edge of the golf course. Straight across it, and then take the path to the left. Eventually that'll bring you out on a road. Simple as that."

Saqui nodded. He sat himself astride the scooter and told Azim to get on the pillion seat.

"What about you and Gwynedd?" he said to Sam.

"We stay here," said Sam. "With the bag. That's what the men want. When they see we've got the bag they won't bother with you and Azim. OK? Then go… go now!"

Saqui started the scooter and made for the gap between the trees. They were quickly out of sight.

Evening

The last of the light was fading. The wind was still fierce but the rain had eased. Sam looked about him. He turned to Vinnie. "Get on your scooter and take the same route that Saqui and Azim took. And once you hit the road, you go straight to the police. Any police. Doesn't matter where. Guys on the road, or if you can't find them, go to the police station"

"Why not phone them?" said Vinnie. "They'd get here quicker."

"Because they wouldn't believe a phone call," said Sam. "They'd think it was a hoax. And they'll be busy tonight with this gale blowing."

Vinnie looked at Gwynedd. She nodded. Sam was right.

"What are you and Gwynedd going to do, like?"

Gwynedd thought that, for once, Vinnie was asking a sensible question. What was happening now was all very dramatic, but her plan had always been to live with Sam some day, not to die with him any minute now.

"You go, Vinnie. Gwynedd and I will manage somehow."

"We got to get the police," said Vinnie. "I'm phonin' them now." He took his mobile out of his pocket and moved a little distance away.

Sam and Gwynedd took no notice. Sam was aware that Azim's departure with Saqui didn't remove the murderous threat of the gunmen. Azim was safe: that job was done. Vinnie had his scooter. How the hell were *they* going to get away?

"They'll be here any minute," said Gwynedd.

He didn't need to ask her who she meant by 'they'.

"What can we do?"

"Well, they don't know there isn't any money in the bag. Someone on the other side of the fence, with the bag, could hold the gunmen to ransom. If one of us was on the other side of the fence, he could hold the bag over the edge of the cliff and he could threaten to chuck it in the sea if the gunmen started waving their guns about."

"Or *she* could." said Gwynedd.

Her thoughts had shot ahead of Sam's.

"You said 'he could hold the bag over the edge of the cliff'. It doesn't have to be a 'he', it doesn't have to be you, it shouldn't be you, your arm's still not right, I could hurl the bag further than you, and I'm a better gymnast, I'd have a better chance of getting over the fence."

She had spoken without drawing breath. As she gasped for air, Vinnie butted in. The phone call to the police had evidently been useless.

"I spoke to a copper and he, like, didn't believe me. He says I'm havin' a laugh, like, an' if they weren't so busy

225

with the gale smashin' everything up and down the coast, he'd come up here and arrest me. Mad. It's all mad. We'd best all be goin'."

Gwynedd had got her breath back. "Never mind the police. We don't have to wait for them to get here. Vinnie, stay here!" She was screaming to be heard above the wind. "It's going to take three of us to get someone over that fence. Two people to chuck the third one over. I'm lightest. Sam, you and Vinnie have to throw me over. You link hands. I take a run, put my foot in your hands, and you chuck me over."

Sam and Vinnie stared at her.

"For God's sake," she said. "We do it like we did in the Juniors. Like in gymnastics, to get over the horse. But we have to do it now, or…"

She let out a frightened squeak. The headlights of an approaching vehicle flickered through the trees at the edge of the wood.

"It's too late." Vinnie reached for his scooter.

"No, it's not. Vinnie, grab your right wrist with your left hand. Now, grab my left wrist with your right hand… Vinnie! Like this!" Gwynedd grabbed Vinnie's wrists and showed him what to do. She glanced back at the woods. The headlights of the car had come to a halt. The figure of a man appeared, silhouetted against the lights. He was coming from the wood. It had to be one of the gunmen. He was holding something in his hand. It could only be a gun.

Gwynedd knew they had to do this now. The longer she thought about being thrown over the spikes on the top of the fence, the harder it would be. She picked up the grey and black bag and threw it over the fence. Her throw was almost too good. The bag came to rest at the very edge of the cliff.

"I'm going over now. Hold tight. If either of you loses his grip, I'm dead. We've only got one try at this."

The second gunman came out of the wood.

Gwynedd remembered Sam's bad arm. She wished she hadn't. Inwardly, she groaned, but she said nothing.

"If we mess this up," she said, "you two have nothing to bargain with."

"What about you?" said Vinnie.

Her mind was too fixed on what she had to do for her to reply, but Sam knew what she was hinting at.

"Ready?" said Gwynedd.

The leading gunman was running across the grass. They were going to be too late. But the ground was sodden with rain and the gunman skidded, slipped, fell and rolled over. There was still a chance.

Gwynedd told herself not to think about the spikes on the top of the fence. It didn't work. She immediately thought of the piercing agony she would suffer if she was impaled on them. She told herself not to think about that. Fear wouldn't help. She tried to scrape up some courage by remembering how she had successfully helped Sam over the wall at the back of the derelict house, but that had been a low wall.

Sam and Vinnie stood together, arms locked, knees slightly bent. Sam was staring at her with a look on his face that she'd never seen before. Whatever it was he was thinking, the sight of it made her feel that she mattered to him more than anything in the world. She took another look over her shoulder. Both gunmen were near enough to be recognisable. Black Leather Man was in the lead.

"Ready?" Gwynedd took a couple of steps back. Think high, she told herself. Imagine you're a bird taking wing.

"Ready." Sam's voice sounded as though there was something wrong with his throat.

"Here I come!"

She took a couple of long strides, like a high jumper approaching the bar. She let her left foot lead. It had never failed her in the past. There… she stepped firmly into Vinnie and Sam's good hands. Instantly, she felt the power of their lift. She swung her arms into the air and launched herself forwards and upwards. As she did so, a powerful updraft of air, caused by the wind hitting the cliff face and flying over the edge hit her and lifted her clear of the fence.

She landed heavily but managed to stop her body from rolling over the edge of the cliff, and gave a yell of triumph. She jumped up from the grass and grabbed the bag. In the fury of the storm that still raged about them, neither Sam nor Gwynedd heard the crack of a pistol as Kyle fired, though Gwynedd heard the bullet zing as it passed a few centimetres from her head.

She fought back the instinct to throw herself back on the ground. Both gunmen had seen the bag in her hand, had seen her holding it over the cliff edge. They were now only a few metres away.

"You put the bag down, or I'll blow your boyfriend's head away." Kyle grabbed Sam's hair and forced his head back, holding his gun against the side of Sam's head

"Any nearer and I'll drop this bag into the sea," she shouted, and the wind whipped her words to the gunmen.

Coleson came panting up. "That's not the Scumbag Kid," he said. "That's not the one we were sent to kill. None of them are."

Gwynedd stretched her arm a little further over the edge of the cliff. "I mean it," she said. "Back off or the bag goes into the sea. And all that money with it."

"She does," said Sam. "She does mean it." The gun was pressing hard against his head.

"If she drops it, all three of you die." He snapped at Coleson: "Cover the other brat."

Coleson protested. "We can't kill all three of them. Do that and they'll lock us away for good. They're only kids."

"What the hell does that matter? Kids die every day. Loads of them. Killed in wars… rounded up and shot and left to the flies… arms and legs blown away by land mines… bodies in the dust… And so what? There's millions more of them." Kyle was screaming.

"All we're after is the Kid, and the bag. Kyle, in God's name…"

"You stupid bastard. There you go again - using my name. You stupid, stupid bastard, Coleson." Kyle put his mouth close to Sam's ear. "You heard that? You heard what I said? What *his* name is? It's Coleson. That's his name. Coleson. Remember that, kid, if you get out of here." Kyle turned

229

back to Coleson, roaring at him. "You miserable little piece of shit. If you don't like what's going on here, go and sit in the car. Because, if you start to interfere, Coleson, I swear to God I'll kill you, too, Coleson. I can do this better on my own. There's only two of them this side of the fence, and I can manage two on my own, *Coleson*!! Watch me."

He pushed his gun as hard as he could against Sam's head, forcing Sam's neck to bend to one side.

Gwynedd knew that the stand-off couldn't last much longer. For one thing, her arm was getting tired. She was frightened she might get cramp and drop the bag by accident. Without the bag, they had nothing to bargain with. She was also scared of trying to change arms, for the same reason. For another, it sounded to her like the man called Kyle was going mad. This couldn't go on. Something had to happen.

Something did. In his rage against Coleson, Kyle had failed to keep an eye on Vinnie. From the moment Vinnie had seen that the gunman wasn't looking at him, Vinnie had begun to move slowly backwards, until he was in a position to slip behind the red and white shack.

And from behind the shack, there now came a sudden crack, as though someone had snapped a dry and brittle piece of wood, or someone had fired a gun.

Coleson whirled round. Kyle kept his eyes on Gwynedd and his gun steady against Sam's head.

"Go and see what it is!" Kyle was still screaming.

There was another crack, then a squeaking sound like an old door being opened for the first time in years, then the sound of splintering wood... then silence.

"It came from the cabin," said Kyle. "Take a look, Coleson."

Coleson shook his head. Kyle fired a single shot into the ground by Coleson's feet.

"I told you to take a look. It's the other kid."

Kyle's eyes were still on Gwynedd. The gun he'd just fired was back in place, against the side of Sam's head. Sam could feel the heat of its muzzle against his skin.

Reluctantly, Coleson began to move.

The sound of shattering glass came from the other side of the cabin, followed by an explosion and a blast of light.

"It's the other kid," screamed Kyle. "Go and bloody kill him."

Coleson edged his way nervously out of sight, round the corner.

The light from the explosion died. The sky was black, muffled in heavy cloud. There was not a glimpse of moon or stars. The only light remaining came from the headlights of the car parked in the woods.

"Coleson! You left the bloody lights on!"

Kyle was shouting, roaring. There was no answer.

Sam felt Kyle's grip on his bad arm weaken slightly.

Kyle shouted again. "Coleson! Where are you? What the hell's going on?"

There was first a glimmer of light from inside the cabin. It grew and became a glow.

"Coleson!"

Sam heard a sputtering noise, as though someone had thrown wet logs on a blazing fire. And then came a flare of light and a series of wild explosions from the cabin.

The moment he'd heard the first loud crack, and realised it wasn't his arm breaking, the ghost of a plan had begun to form in Sam's mind. With the fence between Gwynedd and the gunmen, all she needed was a few seconds start. And once she was up and running, maybe the gunmen would be distracted just long enough for him to sprint for it too. What was needed was something that would spread confusion among the gunmen. If Gwynedd left the bag on the edge of the cliff, and if he drew the gunmen's attention to it, the gunmen would have to choose between taking the bag or taking prisoners.

There was confusion, right here, coming from the cabin. Sam seized the moment. It was a risk they had to take.

"Gwen! Leave the bag! Never mind the money! Make for the end of the fence! But leave the bag!" Sam's hope was that, if he could make the gunmen believe the money was still in the bag, there was a slight chance they'd keep their eyes on the bag, and that somehow he and Gwynedd could slither away.

Kyle's eyes swivelled from the corner of the cabin to the girl behind the fence. He needed to look both ways at once. He was writhing with anger. Sam felt the grip on his arm weaken a little more. It was time to make a desperate move. Kyle half-turned to face the corner of the cabin, again calling for his partner. As he did so, Sam wrenched himself free from Kyle's grasp. Kyle spun round, dropped on one knee and brought the gun up in both hands, facing Sam. But his mind was in turmoil. It was raging like the wind around him. Kids. Coleson. Africa. The bag on the other side of the fence. Thousands and thousands and thousands of pounds.

Kyle was uncertain what to do. Shoot the girl. Shoot the kid. Shoot the girl. Shoot the kid who was now trying to sneak away. Kids. Kids everywhere. Kids dying. Kids with their bodies lying in the sun. Kids with a gale-force wind blowing them over. A kid sneaking away. A kid behind the hut. Coleson in the hut. The bag on the other side of the fence. A fortune at risk.

"You stay right there or I'll kill you." The words were directed at Sam, but the threat was meant for all those around Kyle.

Out of the corner of his eye, Sam saw Gwynedd moving fast along the other side of the fence. There was little space between the fence and the edge of the cliff, so she had to take great care. A false step could take her over the edge. But with every step she took, her chances of getting away were improving. In the darkness and the wind, it would take a lucky shot to pass between the bars of the metal fence and hit a moving target.

"Coleson!"

There was still no sound from the missing gunman. Instead, another volley of explosions shook the cabin. With each explosion came a burst of light – orange, yellow, red, silver, purple. Sam realised that this was some kind of crazy firework display taking place, not outdoors on an open space, but inside what was left of the cabin. There was smoke billowing away in the wind, the brilliant artificial stars were quickly fading to nothing, and the explosions died away.

Kyle's gun was still covering Sam. For five seconds or so, nothing happened, nobody moved. Then Kyle's self-control shattered. He turned his head from Sam and made yet another call to his partner.

"Coleson! Get out here!"

Coughing and choking, Coleson staggered out from behind what was left of the cabin. He'd been blinded and deafened by the explosions around him. There were dreadful burns on his face and he was clutching his head. There seemed to be something wrong with his legs.

"Cover the one-armed kid," said Kyle. "If he moves, kill him. I'll take care of the girl."

Coleson made no reply. With a terrible scream of pain, he slumped to the grass.

"Coleson! Get up! On your bloody feet..." Kyle was bellowing his orders. "Get up, you bloody fool! Coleson!"

Kyle's gun was now aimed at Coleson's body, writhing on the grass.

That was all it took. By the time Kyle spun round to check on him, Sam was twenty metres away, zig-zagging, as he'd been taught to do in rugger practice, towards the far end of the fence. Kyle dropped on to one knee, both hands on his gun. He was aiming to hit the kid in the leg, but his shot was too low. The bullet hit the grass a step behind Sam's flying feet. Instantly, Kyle was ready for a second shot. He'd aim higher this time. If he killed the kid, so what? His finger tightened on the trigger.

But the kid was moving fast, swaying from side to side. And it was hard to see clearly... The second bullet missed. And the third.

Away to the right, from somewhere near the biggest of the buildings, came the sound of a scooter starting up.

Kyle roared again. "Coleson! Get the kid on the bike. Aim at the lights on the scooter! Get up, you bastard!"

There was no reply from Coleson, and no sign of lights on the scooter. Vinnie had not switched them on. The high pitched whine of the scooter engine faded into the distance.

What the hell was Coleson playing at? Kyle took a step forward. From the inside of the wooden cabin came a flash of brilliant light, followed by the thunderous crack of an explosion. Giant balls of multi-coloured stars shot into the night sky, bursting high in the air. There were crackling volleys that sounded like a thousand gun battles, and rockets and comets that took off at odd angles and threatened to strike down anyone who got in their way. The smell of gunpowder, treason and plot swept across the field. Some explosions were muffled, as though they came from deep in the earth. Others were short and sharp as the fireworks leapt and lifted into the air. The cabin trembled and swayed. A succession of spluttering bangs was followed by more rockets fizzing and spiralling across the grass, flying erratically at just above ground level, like a flock of birds with damaged wings. The cabin began to break apart. Sections of it fell to the ground, landing on cases of more fireworks. It wasn't long before fire broke out, flames flickering within the ruins of the cabin, as still more explosions of light burst in the night sky.

Vinnie had managed to supply the people of Aberystwyth with a display despite its earlier cancellation. The crates in the cabin had been full of the finest fireworks that China could supply.

*

Gwynedd was on the wrong side of the fence, the sea side, the dangerous side. The gap between the fence and the cliff edge was less than the length of a school ruler in some places. But she had to move along this narrow, slippery ledge if she was to get away from the gunmen. Gwynedd was moving as fast as she dared over the wet and treacherously uneven turf, crawling on her hands and knees. The light from the exploding fireworks came in short flashes – one moment everything was almost blindingly lit up, the next it was in complete darkness. In the flashes of light, she could see Sam on the other side of the fence, twisting and turning as he sprinted towards the railway shed at the top end of the railway. She didn't dare look back to see what the gunmen were doing. She had heard one of them shouting the other's name. She had not heard any answering voice. But, with the howling of the wind and the crack and thunder of the fireworks, it was hard to tell what was going on. She had no idea what had happened to Vinnie.

A blaze of light, from what would have been one of the showpiece cones of the Halloween Firework Display, lit up her surroundings. There was the shed for the Cliff Railway, to her left, less than a hundred metres away. And it also lit up her crawling body. Surely, the gunmen could see her now. She had to move faster. She stood up; even shuffling upright was quicker than crawling, and every frightening step brought her nearer to the end of the fence. She knew that she faced another problem there - the problem of getting back over the fence. A few more careful and tiny steps, and she was able to see where the fence ended, right on the edge of the cliff. Sam was already there, on the other side of the fence, the safe side, waiting for her. She glanced back over her shoulder.

"It's OK," said Sam. "They've disappeared... for the moment."

Gwynedd stopped, and grabbed hold of the fence. Her arms were shaking. She looked down at her feet and saw how near they were to the edge of the cliff. Her eyes moved a little to the right. There was nothing there but black space, and she knew that at the bottom of that black space there were dark rocks, pounded by a sea as cold as death.

"It's not OK," she said. "It's terrifying. I can't stay here, I can't move on, and I can't go back."

Her head was aching with fear. Her mind seemed to be going mad. Had she really jumped over the fence? She could have killed herself. She heard Dave's voice saying something about how her mum would have thrown herself off this very cliff top if her dad had told her mum to do that. Had her mum done that? Gwynedd didn't dare look to see how far down the rocks were, rocks that would snap your back like a kid snapping a twig. She told herself she mustn't move. The only way to be safe was to stay exactly where she was, on the cold and wet grass, until someone came with wire cutters, and blankets, and all the strength in the world, to save her.

"You have to move," said Sam. "They'll kill us if we stay here."

He was asking the impossible. How could she move? Her frozen head hurt so, she couldn't tell her body to move.

"Gwen," he said. "You have to try."

She heard what he said, and there was something in his voice that cut through the pain in her head. He was begging her. Why? Was it for his sake? For both their sakes?

She took a deep breath. "What the hell can I do?"

"Can you reach the last bit of fence? With your left hand?"

"No."

"You have to try. And we can't hang about."

"No." She took another deep breath. She wanted to scream.

"OK."

Sam sounded so calm. Gwynedd wished he was within reach, so that she could grab him and smack him.

"Stop saying 'OK'. It isn't OK. Nothing's OK."

"OK… Sorry. Lie down. Now, with your left hand, grab hold of the fence where you are. Grab it right at the bottom, at ground level. Now stretch out your right arm and grab as near as you can to the end of the fence. Get your right hand on that last metal pole, halfway up the pole."

She could see where this was going. He wanted her to ignore the black space beyond the edge of the cliff, and the sharp rocks that lay in wait far below, and the murderous sea that was still pounding away.

"Then what?"

He spoke quickly, frequently looking back to make sure that the gunmen weren't in sight. "You bring your left hand up to your right. When that's firmly grasping the fence, you can take your right hand off the fence."

"What happens to the rest of me?"

"Don't stand up. Keep kneeling. Now, press your body hard against the fence and try to keep both knees on the ground."

"What if I can't?"

"You hang on with your hands and swing your body round the end of the fence. You're going to have to do that anyway. And I'll be here to grab you and pull you round. Think of the end of the fence as one of the poles at the playground in the park, back in Rhayader. Where we used to muck about."

"Which hand are you going to grab me with?"

"My left one."

"That's the one at the end of your bad arm."

"My arm's fine."

"We won't know that until either you've pulled me round or I'm falling into that black space…"

"Don't think about falling. It's all going to be OK... Sorry... It's all going to work." He doubled the speed of his speech. "It's a matter of the force generated on a circumference by a moving object fastened to the centre of a circle by a piece of string, or a metal rod, or in this case, a human arm. It's sort of like the way we keep revolving round the sun."

"There isn't any sun. There's only blackness."

"Do this, Gwen, and we can get out of here. I'm not budging until we've had a kiss on this side of the fence."

Fireworks and giant fireballs were still catching fire and taking off at irregular intervals from the ruins of the burning cabin. The wind was still battering the cliff and skimming across the turf at the top. A set-piece waterfall of shimmering silver stars made it possible for Gwynedd to see the expression on Sam's face. It was a nice face, and it was imploring her to trust its owner.

"All right, all right," she said. "Here I come. Oh my Goddddd...!"

She shut her eyes and kicked off with her right foot as hard as she could. The earth crumbled away beneath the pressure of her foot, and for a moment her body was hanging over the black space. She was convinced that she was going to fall. Then she felt Sam's fingers grasping the sleeve of her anorak, tugging on it as though he didn't care what happened to his arm so long as she was safe. There was a split second when she sensed rather than felt that his hold was weakening. He gave a little gasp, and she thought he was about to let go, but somehow he held on.

She clutched at Sam's sleeve and swung herself round the end of the fence. They collapsed together and rolled away from the cliff edge. She lay on top of him, breathless but triumphant, pinning him to the ground.

He was at her mercy. She could claim the kiss that he had promised her. She could tell him that she loved him. But the time wasn't right. If ever they did have a proper kiss, she wanted to feel that she could lose all awareness of what was happening around her. She imagined that a real kiss should take you into some other world. Here, now, she was too conscious of the wind, the wet and the whereabouts of Kyle and the other gunman. She didn't want a kiss, and hoped that Sam didn't want one either.

She stood up. "Not now, Sam," she said. "Please not now."

He struggled to his feet. "Yeah," he said. "Not now."

There was a sharp metallic ping! And a whining noise. A bullet had ricocheted off one of the spikes at the top of the fence.

Gwynedd rolled on to her side. Sam moved his weight on to one hand – his good one – and both knees. Another bullet whined past. Gwynedd pulled Sam down.

"Crawl," she said. "Head for the railway shed."

They wormed their way over the wet mud. No more shots were fired. As soon as they were inside the shed, they risked standing up.

"How's your arm?" she said.

"It's about as surprised as I am. I don't think it's broken, but I don't know. It's gone numb."

"Are they still coming after us?"

"Let's not wait to find out."

They started down the track of the Cliff Railway, stepping sideways so that their weight was more evenly balanced on each foot and there was less risk of tripping or slipping. The wind funnelled up the deep trench that had been blasted in the hillside to make a cutting for the railway, threatening to bowl them over. They both kept turning their heads to look upwards to the top of the track, terrified that the gunmen would appear any moment, guns blazing. Both Sam and Gwynedd knew they would be easy targets – slow moving and bunched together in a narrow space.

*

Kyle's rage was bursting inside every part of him – guts, head, stomach. He had given up shouting for his useless partner. That gutless fool was still lying on the ground, pretending to be dead. He'd either been deafened by the fireworks or had lost his nerve completely. He was a worthless coward.

Kyle's head was in chaos, incapable of remembering what had happened or what he had done. In what was left of Kyle's mind, Coleson was still alive and would have to be dealt with when Kyle had finished off the kids. Coleson would have a coward's death. Not quick. In the hands of an expert executioner, death can take a long time. After that? Well, Kyle would make sure that the Chief got to hear of his brother's treachery. Kyle would send a little memento of his brother – an ear, a finger or a toe. And the good news was that, once Coleson's last scream had died away, Kyle would be left with a fortune that he didn't have to share. There, on the grass, a few paces away, was the bag of money.

In Kyle's increasingly crazy mind, the value of the money in the bag was going up all the time. 100k? Think again. The Chief wouldn't have made all this fuss unless there was at least 200k in that bag. Or maybe a quarter of a million. Kyle's thoughts took off like a rocket. A quarter of a million? Where had that idea come from? Kyle tried to think back. Had there ever been a quarter of a million that was in the bag? Why shouldn't there have been? No one, except the Chief, knew for sure exactly how much was in it. And no one, including the Chief, knew what might have happened to some of that quarter of a million in the last few days. The more he thought of the phrase 'a quarter of a million', the more convinced Kyle was that there really was a quarter of a million in that bag. The bag that was so near, but too far away for him to reach from this side of the fence. Kyle racked his brains to think of a way of getting it. Every penny inside it could be his. The only people anywhere near were the black girl and the one-armed boyfriend. He couldn't see them, but they couldn't be far away. Kyle loosed off a couple of shots. If they were anywhere near, that would flush them out. No. There was no sign of them. Now there were no witnesses. He would finish them off later. Right now he was alone with the bag.

Kyle tried to reach it by squeezing his arm between the bars of the metal fence, but the bag was too large anyway to be pulled between the bars. His mind teetered on meltdown. A quarter of a million and he couldn't get his hands on it. There it was, in that filthy grey and black bag. He kicked at the fence. He cursed himself for allowing that black bitch to get away. She had been on the same side of the fence as the bag. He could have promised that he would let her go if she threw the bag back. There was no way he would have kept the promise. He'd have shot her and the boyfriend. Kyle gave the fence a few more angry kicks. A quarter of a million, maybe more than a quarter of a million in the bloody bag, lying there. On the wrong side of the fence.

Fireworks were still exploding. Eventually, people would make their way to the cliff-tops to see what was happening. Only the wind and cold was keeping them away so far. Kyle knew he must find some way of getting his hands on the bag, quickly. If only he had a length of rope with a hook on the end. It was possible that there was a tow rope in the boot of the Mercedes. In this game, you never knew when a bit of rope would come in handy… to truss up a corpse before dumping it somewhere, to drag a live victim through a fire, or for a simple hanging. But the Mercedes was back in the woods… Think, think…

A massive Roman Candle exploded nearby. In the flash of its light, Kyle saw something moving on the grass. It was black, and at first Kyle thought it was a dead rat. But its covering wasn't fur or hair, but cloth. The Roman Candle fired off another explosion and by its light Kyle realised he was looking at a human hand.

The hand had a bite mark in it. It was Coleson's hand. He'd forgotten about Coleson. Was Coleson supposed to be dead? Was that why Coleson hadn't responded when Kyle had shouted his name. Why wasn't the gutless fool wearing gloves? You always wore gloves when you were making a hit. But maybe the gutless fool wasn't dead. Maybe he was only pretending to be dead, waiting for Kyle to give up and piss off, leaving behind the bag and all the money. If Coleson was alive, Kyle might have to share the half million after all. In which case, it would be better if Coleson was dead. There was one way to find out.

Kyle put his foot on the hand and pressed down. There was no sound of protest from the owner of the hand, and the hand didn't move. It was Coleson's hand, no doubt about that. He replaced his foot on the hand and pressed harder. There was still no reaction. Kyle leant down, to feel if there was any pulse in the wrist – as he had been taught to do by the Army, 'in the event of front line emergency'. Then he had a second thought and stood up, smiling. That would be a completely pointless, stupid and wasted effort. He didn't want Coleson alive. He didn't want to share the money with him. He didn't want Coleson telling the Chief or the cops or anyone else what had happened. All Kyle wanted from Coleson were the keys to the Mercedes. Other than that, Kyle had no use for Coleson. The sooner he made sure that Coleson was dead, the better.

Kyle kicked away some bits of wood and rubbish. There was Coleson's body, one leg buckled beneath it, the other stretched out, and arms spread as though he might have been trying to protect himself. There was something wrong with his face. It looked scorched. Kyle went through Coleson's pockets. There were the keys to the Mercedes. Kyle straightened up, pocketed the keys, and took out his gun.

He would wait for the next firework explosion. That would drown the sound of the gun. He didn't have to wait long. A Vulcan Supremo took fire. But though there was a lot of sizzling and fizzing, there was not quite enough noise to drown the sound of Kyle's single shot to Coleson's head.

Now for the bag.

*

Sam and Gwynedd clambered down the railway track, checking what lay behind and above them. The gunmen were somewhere up there. Danger would come from above.

They heard the sound of a single shot fired from somewhere up on the stretch of grass.

Gwynedd grabbed Sam's bad arm.

"They lied to us," she said.

"What are you talking about?"

"The bloke who stuck the gun in our backs in Rhayader, when they kidnapped us. He said their guns were very quiet. He lied. They make more noise than the fireworks." She was shouting the words.

"Does it matter? And please let go of my arm."

She saw him wince with pain and grabbed his good arm instead. She wondered who was firing at who up there. Were the gunmen firing at Vinnie? Had Saqui and Azim not been able to get away? Were there more members of the gang?

"What's going on up there?" she said.

"We can't hang around to find out. We have to go on."

"I'll help you down. Lean on me. Good… that's the way…"

She wondered if there were other members of the gang down in the town. She wondered if there was any way they could possibly get out of this mess.

"Do you think the town's safe?"

"How should I know?" he said. "You know more about all this than I do. I'm only a poor wounded visitor from Bristol. All this started long before I got here."

He knew he had to sound as though everything was OK. He hoped desperately that they were through the worst of the danger, but there was no way of knowing. The pain in his arm made thinking difficult. It was all guesswork. He guessed they would be better in the town, but he could easily be wrong. Most of all he wanted to get off this cliff, out of this battering wind, down to somewhere that had lights and shelter and warmth. He also wanted to reassure Gwynedd. She'd taken the worst risks ever in the last few minutes – risking her life once when she leapt over the metal fence, and then again when she swung out over the cliff edge desperately reaching out for him.

He drew on his last resources of strength. He would see this through if it was the last thing he did.

"We should be all right," he said. "But we're not going to take any risks. We're going to climb right down to the bottom of the railway track. I'm going first, and we're going to keep as close as we can to the right hand side, where the rock face is highest. Take my hand with your hand... No, the other one. And if I squeeze it, you drop down on to the track immediately. It doesn't matter how badly you bruise your knees. Better that than a..." He thought it better not to finish the sentence.

"Than a bullet in the head? Is that what you were going to say?"

He squeezed her hand. "No! I wasn't going to say that... I was going to say..." He was too frightened to think of the right words to finish the sentence.

She could have finished it for him. Even with gunmen threatening their lives, with a storm of madness raging all about them, her own mind threw out words that were all to do with affection and love. She had long thought about a time when she might be able to use the word 'love', not in a jokey or even a friendly way, but in the deep and truly awesome way when it was like some kind of confessing or longing or trusting. It seemed easy enough as an idea. She'd seen and heard people use the word hundreds of times on TV. You even read about it in books. But she was too frightened to use it, to let it come out of her mouth. It would be better to wait until they weren't fearing for their lives.

The cutting was not much wider than a single motorway lane, but it seemed to both Sam and Gwynedd that it was far too wide, far too open to the elements, and offered far too easy a target to any gunman still after them. Sam kept thinking about the single shot, the last sound they'd heard from the cliff-top. It was too much to hope that the gunmen had fallen out, that one gunman had shot the other. But, even if he and Gwynedd had been that lucky, that still meant that at least one gunman was after them. Two gunmen suggested there was a gang at work here. God knows how many more might still be after them.

They were near the bottom of the track.

"Wait here," he whispered.

"Where are you going?"

"To check out where the track ends. If there's no one there, we should be all right."

"I'm coming with you," she said.

"I knew you'd say that. We've had fantastic luck. I don't know how it is that we're still alive. Do what I tell you to do. *Wait here!*"

"But if it isn't safe, you'll get killed. And if you get killed, I want to get killed with you."

"Have you been doing *Romeo and Juliet* this term?"

"Yeah," she said.

"Thought so. What did you think of it?"

He was trying to take both their minds off the mess they were in. Gwynedd knew what he was doing. It was the sort of nice, soft, dopey thing that he did, and that she liked about him.

"I thought it was sad," she said. "Other people messed them about. I told Vinnie about how Romeo and Juliet spent a night together. He said he bet Romeo killed himself because the sex wasn't good enough."

"They were younger than we are. Juliet was only thirteen, and her mother was in her late twenties. They showed us a film at school, but Juliet's mum looked about ninety in it."

Sam's plan had worked. Gwynedd began thinking how strange it would have been if she and Sam had got married in Year 8.

They huddled together near the bottom of the railway cutting, with their backs pressed against the rock. Sam was trying to breathe normally, to control the pain in his arm. Once or twice he winced. Gwynedd knew he was in pain, and that the pain was growing. The trouble was, they couldn't stay where they were. And if they could summon up the strength to move, where could they go?

He never knew how he did it, but somehow Sam dragged up one last bit of strength. He nudged Gwynedd, and pointed down the track. The station building at the bottom of the track was only a few metres away. Creeping silently down, moving sideways on the steep slope, wouldn't take longer than a minute or two. But suppose there was a gunman waiting…

Gwynedd risked a whisper. "What do we do?"

Sam shook his head. She took it as a sign that she should shut up.

They waited. Nothing happened.

"We've got to do something."

Sam cupped his hand over her mouth. She licked it. Nothing else happened. He whispered in her ear. "We have to stay here until we know it's safe to go home."

They sat in silence for a while. Then Gwynedd said: "If we do ever get back home, I bet we'll find Martin's still there."

Sam gave a groan that sounded like an animal in pain.

They huddled closer together.

*

Kyle stood at the end of the fence with the wind battering his body as though it was trying to push him away from the cliff edge to the comparative safety of where he was now. Somehow, that black girl must have worked her way round from the other side of the fence, the side where the cliff ended. If she could do it, so could he. There was danger in it, but only a puny coward stepped back from the chance of grabbing a fortune, and there was a million pounds lying there in that bloody bag.

In all his years as a soldier and a mercenary, Kyle had learnt the importance of making a plan before you set out on any dangerous mission. He made one now. All he had to do was worm his way round the last post of the fence, and then use his elbows and his feet to move forwards on his belly towards the tussock of grass where the bag lay, waiting for him. That would be the dangerous bit. He'd be on the very edge of the cliff for some of that but, once he reached the tussock all would be well. He could take a firm grip on the tough grass with one hand, and grab the bag with the other. Then he could use both hands to drag the bag over the tussock, and worm his way backwards to the end of the fence.

He listened to the sounds around him. There were no more explosions, only the whistling of the wind, the rustling of trees, the occasional splutter of a firework that didn't go off properly, and the rattling of pieces of wood in the debris of what had been the cabin, where Coleson's body lay. There was no sound of any human being. Kyle was alone.

He dropped on to his hands and knees, then down on to his belly. He lay on his left side, with his back to the edge of the cliff. With his right hand firmly grasping the last post of the metal fence, he reached forward with his left hand. At the same time, he dug in with his feet. He slid forward, slowly. He was a quarter-way round the post... half-way... Two more kicks and he was round the post.

This was good. Now it was time to use his toes and his elbows to drag himself nearer the tussock. God be praised for the wind. It was punching his body away from the cliff edge and into the fence, keeping him safe.

Kyle reached the tussock of grass.

There was the bag. The greed that had led him through life was telling him to snatch it, but he kept to his plan, holding on to the grass firmly with his left hand, and slowly reaching out with his right. He couldn't yet feel the handle of the bag. He needed one more push with his feet. There... his hand closed on the bag's handle.

He was out of training, out of condition. Ten years ago he could have balanced himself on a knife edge without difficulty, but this was different. In the storm that was raging round him, it would be madness to stand up. And this crawling and squirming about had built up a pressure on his lungs. He was out of breath, exhausted by the battering from the wind, and he felt he couldn't trust his muscles to do what was needed of them. But he was buoyed up by the excitement of at last getting his hands on a million. He tested the weight of the bag. Yes, it was heavy. Maybe not as heavy as a whole million, but certainly half a million. Now for the tricky bit, and his muscles would have to do what was demanded of them.

He used both hands to take hold of the handle. Still lying on his belly, he lifted the bag off the ground. His stomach muscles protested at the strain he was putting on them, but did their bit. He got the bag onto the top of the little hill of grass.

Greed took over. Nothing in the world could stop him taking a peek at the money.

Kyle saw that the zip on the bag was still padlocked. But the Scumbag Kid had used some of the money. So how had he got that out of the bag? Running his hands over the sides of the bag, Kyle found the slit that Azim had cut in the canvas. That was how the little bastard had done it. Kyle was greatly relieved. The edge of a cliff, battered by a gale, was no place to be struggling to break into a thick canvas bag. He slid his hand through the slit.

He had expected to feel small packets of banknotes. Instead, he felt what seemed like large cardboard boxes. There was a smell of grease and old cheese. There was something wrong. Kyle plunged his hand in further and took hold of one of the cardboard boxes. He yanked at it to pull it out. The box was soggy and tore apart. When Kyle withdrew his hand, it was holding only a corner of a cardboard box, with a piece of stale pizza flopping out of it.

He threw the bits of pizza and cardboard box over the cliff.

So, where was the money? It must be underneath. This layer of pizza boxes was just for cover. All the money would be under that. Maybe not half a million. Maybe only 250k. It didn't matter.

He pulled another handful of cardboard from the bag… and another… and another…

Where the hell was the money?

With much care, Kyle raised his upper body so that he was kneeling on the cliff-top. He told himself that you didn't give up in this game until you'd explored every detail. There was a side pocket to the canvas bag, and it was open. Perhaps the key to the padlock was inside. Then he could open the bag properly, search it thoroughly. Holding on to the bag with his left hand, he shoved his right hand into the pocket, and closed it on the shard of glass that Azim had kept there for his own protection.

Kyle felt the sharp edge of the shard of glass slice through the skin on his fingers. He jerked his hand out of the side pocket, and saw the blood. Instinctively, he pulled back from the bag. As he did so, the wind suddenly dropped, no longer pinning him to the fence. His body swayed outwards. His left hand dropped the bag and grabbed the tussock. The bag began to slide over the edge of the cliff. No, no! It mustn't go over. He tried to fasten his right hand on the tussock of grass, but the blood from his wound made his hand slippery and he lost his grip. The bag was going over the edge. He had to stop that.

Kyle's left hand lunged for the handle of the bag at the very moment when his body started to slide over the edge of the cliff. There was a split second when he might have been able to save himself, if he had let go of the bag. But the moment was gone and his hand still grasped the bag.

Nobody heard his scream as he fell. Mercifully, he was unconscious before his body hit the rocks. The bag had come to the end of its journey.

*

The storm had done its worst. The critical moment, when the whole seafront and beyond had been threatened by high tide, had passed. Though waves were still flinging their stinging mixture of spray and pebbles onto the promenade, life was returning to the town. Chinese and Indian take-away outlets were removing the temporary shutters they'd placed over their windows and re-opening. Pubs and bars were switching on their lights and taking in customers. People were back on the streets. Word had gone round that there was some sort of firework display after all, up on Constitution Hill. Groups of students and some hardy families were even struggling up the footpath that led to the cliff-top, eager to get as close as possible to what was left of the weird and unexpected celebration.

At the bottom of the railway track, Sam and Gwynedd heard voices as groups of young people went by. There was relief and some comfort in hearing ordinary conversation, people calling to each other, joking and teasing. Laughter made even the wind seem warmer. But Sam signalled to Gwynedd that they should stay where they were.

"Not safe yet," he whispered. "I guess it's easier to kill someone in a crowd and get away with it."

"Like, how do you know? Done a lot of killing in Bristol, have you?"

"I watch a lot of TV in my bedroom."

"You've got your own set in your own room?"

"Everyone has."

"I must look for mine then," she said. "I've never noticed it up to now."

"Come on," he said. "We have to keep going."

They emerged from the railway cutting, back on the streets of Aberystwyth, on the edge of the town. Gwynedd helped Sam through the crowds. Her mind was still trying to digest what she had witnessed on the cliff-top. Everything was a mess. She had no idea what had happened to Saqui and Azim; whether or not they had got safely away. And there was Vinnie. In his barmy way, he had played a big part in rescuing everyone from the gunmen. Was he safe? Were she and Sam safe? Had the man called Kyle given up, or was he still hunting them? She wanted to go home, back to Rhayader – though she knew she could never again be safe there. Kyle and the other gunman knew that was where she lived. They could turn up any time.

Now that the immediate panic was probably over, she could see that Sam was exhausted and in considerable pain. He was nursing his arm and flinching whenever it was jogged by someone passing. She had to get him home, too, away from all trace of this nightmare, back to the Dream Cottage in Rhayader. The bright idea as to how this could be done came to her immediately.

She helped him through the back streets, away from the wind, the spray, and the crowds.

"Where are you taking us?"

"To the station," she said. "To get a cab. We can afford it."

"No," he said. "Don't be stupid. We have to go to the police."

Sam looked at Gwynedd expecting to see signs of disagreement. She was shaking her head.

"We don't go to the police. We go to a hospital. We're safe now, and you have to get your arm looked at."

"We go to the police first."

She could tell by his voice that trying to make him change his mind and listen to reason would take longer than giving in and going to the police and then going to a hospital.

"But we don't say anything to them about Azim or the money, or the gunmen. Right?"

"Of course we tell the police all about that. Somebody could have been killed out there. Especially you. You could have been killed more than once."

"But if we tell them all about that, they'll start a manhunt for the gunmen, and another manhunt for Azim. They'll set up road blocks and start combing the mountains for him, and that'll all be a waste of time. And like Vinnie said back there, the police get mad when that happens."

"It's because of 'back there' that we *have* to tell them."

"But if we go to the police, we'll have to tell them about Azim. They'll lock him up." She had made up her mind. She wouldn't say anything to the police about the money she had, the money that couldn't fit into the pizza delivery box on the back of Saqui's scooter. And if Sam was going to call her stupid, she wouldn't do what he said. "And they'll ask questions all night. And by then, your poor arm will probably have fallen off."

 "The gunmen are still out there. Supposing they haven't shot anyone yet, but they shoot someone before the police get to them. How would you feel then?"

"Suppose going to the police first meant that your arm was unrepairable?"

"Irreparable."

He couldn't stop himself correcting her. He expected her to thump him or at least shout at him. But she said nothing. He could see that she was crying and that she was trying to hide her tears. He thought he had made her cry because he'd spoken as though he was a teacher. It wasn't until an hour later, when they were in the police station, that he realised she hadn't cried because of that, or because she hadn't got her way over where they should go first, or because – like him – she was physically and mentally exhausted, but because she cared about him. And it wasn't until several days later that he realised what a massive thing this was. He'd always known that Mum cared about him and loved him, but mums had to do that. Gwynedd had chosen to care about him. And it wasn't until later still that he realised that maybe she hadn't chosen to care about him, but that it had simply happened.

"Please, please, let's go to a hospital first."

Gwynedd had never liked begging for anything, but she was begging harder now than she had ever done in her life.

He knew he mustn't give in to her begging.

"We could have been killed up there. So could Azim. So could Saqui. And Vinnie." Sam peered at her. "Aren't you frightened?"

"No," she lied.

"Then you must be nuts. We're still in danger."

She could see that his hands were trembling.

"We'll go to the police on the promenade, where they closed the roads."

Gwynedd gave in. Sam was right. Of course they should go to the police. They couldn't blame her for anything. None of this had been her doing in the first place. She and Sam had been taken hostage. She'd lost count of the number of times in the last few hours when she'd thought she and Sam were about to die, and now thinking of that made her shake uncontrollably.

"Come on, then," she said. "Let's give ourselves up."

There were only two police officers at the barricade, both of them cold and wet, and both in the mood to lecture a couple of kids for being on the seafront in these conditions.

Sam held up his good arm. "Wait," he said. "Please wait. We've got something important to tell you."

It wasn't how Gwynedd would have put it, but at least he made the police listen. They were sceptical at first. One kept warning Sam that wasting police time was an offence. The other repeatedly asked if Sam had any evidence that what he was saying was true.

"Do you think we're, like, making all this up?" said Gwynedd. "Do we look as though we're having a laugh?"

She burst into tears. She didn't know why. She couldn't stop herself.

The two policemen recognised the symptoms of shock. They led Sam and Gwynedd to their patrol car and drove them to the police station.

For the entire afternoon and evening they had been living under the threat of violence, possibly death. They had fled through streets in howling wind, pelting rain and drenching seawater. Out on the clifftops, they had crawled over sodden earth and grass, and slid down the steep paths that had led them back to the town. They had dodged bullets and feared for their lives. For the last couple of hours, all this had taken place in almost total darkness. Inside the well-lit police station they saw each other for the first time since their journey to this nightmare in the gunmen's car.

They made a sorry-looking pair. Their clothes were soaking wet and caked with mud. They looked as though they had been living rough for a month.

The police sergeant at the desk listened to the patrolmen's brief report. She told them to get blankets and two mugs of tea, then turned to Sam and Gwynedd.

"We've been hoping you'd turn up," she said.

She took them to a room with a door labelled 'INTERVIEW 1'.

"You'll find your friends inside."

They did. Sitting at a table with another woman officer were a very anxious Saqui and a very frightened Azim. In a hurried and jumbled conversation, Saqui gabbled the story of how they had been stopped by the police almost as soon as they reached the road on the other side of the golf course. A member of the Golf Club, out walking his Labrador now that the rain had stopped, had called the police, complaining about hooligans riding a motor cycle over the fairways. The police had asked Saqui and Azim to dismount, and had then asked them a series of questions. Who were they? Where had they come from? Where were they going? What was inside the delivery box?

"It was when we opened the box to show them the money that everything changed," said Saqui. "That was why they brought us here, and the scooter, and the box."

There would be such a lot of explaining to do, thought Sam. About Azim, the kidnapping, the gunmen, the fireworks, the shooting, and the bag full of money. His arm didn't feel good but he didn't want to complain about it because it might send Gwynedd off, and the police might start to make a fuss.

Instead, for the second time in three weeks, he passed out.

Night

Dave climbed into the police car, almost tripping over his stick as he did so.

"They got you, too?" he said.

Becky made room for him on the back seat.

Becky was frightened and exhausted. She had spent the entire afternoon and evening trying to get rid of Martin, and trying to stop Ben biting him. The arrival of the police car had been the last straw. Martin had started one of his 'I told you so' lectures about Sam's irresponsibility.

"What's happened to your Sam?"

"All they say is that it's his arm, and that he's in hospital in Aberystwyth." Becky spoke very quietly. She didn't want the police officers in the front of the car to think that she was complaining.

"Speak up, girl," said Dave. "I can't hear one word."

When they reached Aberystwyth, one officer took Dave into the police station, the other drove Becky to the hospital. The medics had already reset and re-plastered Sam's arm, and placed it in a brand new sling. The young doctor who handed him over to Becky offered to fit a padlock on the sling, but Becky was too near meltdown to see the joke. She asked the hospital to call a taxi.

"I have to go with my son to the police station."

Sam pulled a face.

"You make it sound like I'm a criminal," he said.

With Sam and Gwynedd's help, the police began to make rough sense of what they knew about Azim's short life in Rhayader. Added to Saqui's guarded statement were earlier reports from the woman who sold Azim the pair of boots, from the elderly proprietor of the café where Azim spent his first £50 note, and from the woman who ran the shop across the road from Devil's Bridge station. Gwynedd had also told them about the shot fired at the room above the Chippie, and had given a truthful though confused account of the kidnapping, the escape from the gunmen's car, the flight through the streets of Aberystwyth, and what she labelled 'The Shoot-Out on Constitution Hill'. But she hadn't told the whole truth. There was one snippet of information that she kept to herself.

Becky and Dave pointed out that 'the children' were exhausted. Becky said they needed to go home and get some sleep, and that keeping them here was preposterous. Gwynedd made a mental note that Becky was the source of Sam's posh words. It was agreed that detectives would come to Rhayader in the morning to continue their questioning. They would interview Sam and Gwynedd in their own homes. Few words were exchanged in the police cars that took Dave and Gwynedd back to the bungalow, and Becky and Sam back to Lavender Cottage.

Left with only Ben for company at Lavender Cottage, Martin decided to leave immediately for Bristol. The weather was still foul, which matched his mood, and he arrived at his house with bitterness in his heart. He poured himself a large whisky and sat in his favourite chair in his lonely house. He was through with Becky's bloody son and her bloody son's friends and her bloody son's dog. The whisky quickened his temper. He drank another, and came to the conclusion that he was also through with bloody Becky. He was reaching a third time for the whisky bottle when he had a better idea, and thirty minutes later, he was back on the road to Bristol.

*

The police dropped Sam and Becky at Lavender Cottage. The place was in total darkness. There was no moonlight, and there were no lights on in the cottage. All that could be heard was the muffled barking of Ben. Becky prayed that Martin was gone. All she wanted was to see Sam safely to his bed, and then get some rest herself. She unlocked the front door, went in and switched on the downstairs light.

There was no sign of the dog. The barking was still muffled, as though Ben was far away.

"Martin?"

Becky's prayers were answered. There was no reply.

"Ben?"

The barking increased. It was coming from one of the bedrooms. Sam dashed upstairs. He found Ben in the cupboard of Becky's bedroom. Ben's delight on release almost knocked Sam over. He called down to Becky.

"It's OK, Mum. Ben's up here."

But it wasn't OK. The dog had clearly been shut in the cupboard for some time. The inside of the cupboard door was badly scratched and there was a strong stink of dog pee. Sam quickly shut the cupboard. There was no way he could keep this from Becky, but she might feel better if she'd had a sit down and a drink. For the moment, it was best to get Ben downstairs.

Ben greeted Becky with his usual enthusiasm, but then behaved oddly. He held his nose at the gap between the bottom of the front door and the floor, sniffing hard, and grunting and growling.

"He probably needs to go out," said Becky.

Sam doubted this, but there might be something left in Ben's tank, so Sam opened the front door. The light from inside illuminated the tiny garden. Ben shot out and raced to and fro, sniffing at what looked like emaciated corpses.

"Something's wrong," said Becky.

"I'll handle it," said Sam.

He went over to one of the dead bodies, and recognised Mum's best coat. He and Ben moved to another heap – more of Mum's clothes, and some of his. The garden was covered with piles of shoes, books, DVDs, sports equipment – as much stuff as Martin had been able to cram into his precious car. There was no note, but the message was clear. He had turned them out. There was no longer a place for them in Bristol. Though the rain had stopped, everything was wet. They had only three hands and three arms to move their belongings into the Cottage. It took them over an hour.

SATURDAY

When the detectives arrived in the morning, they reported that a corpse had been found, washed ashore on the beach at Borth, two miles up the coast from Aberystwyth. Injuries to the body suggested that the cause of death was almost certainly a fall, but they had found a gun in the pocket of the black leather jacket worn by the corpse. The gun had been fired, more than once. Ballistic tests were being carried out to see if the same gun had fired the bullet that had killed the male whose charred body had been found on Constitution Hill.

Sam and Gwynedd repeated their story. Their memories of what had happened the previous day had become more confused. Some of it seemed so unreal now. Were there really times when they heard bullets zing past them? Had the man called Kyle really held the muzzle of his gun against Sam's head? Had Gwynedd leapt the fence and almost fallen over the cliff edge? Had they handled thousands and thousands of pounds, filling Saqui's pizza delivery box to the brim?

The Detective told them that, because he had no fixed address, Azim had been kept overnight in the police station in Aberyswyth. Through an interpreter, Azim had tried to explain to the police all about the Farm and the Chief. But he had no idea where the Farm was, and could give no description of it other than that it had big fields and lots of trees and one road that led from it to another road. He told the police about the truck driver: "A big man who drove a big truck with many wheels and a big fuel tank". The police were not hopeful of identifying the truck or of finding its driver, or the Farm, or the Chief. As for the money, that was almost certainly the proceeds of crime, probably something to do with drugs. Every attempt would be made to find out where the money came from, but the police reckoned it would be impossible to discover whose money it was. All the police would say about the money was that it would be submitted to 'the usual process'. On top of that, there were the two bodies that had been found. As a result, the police were now starting an investigation into two suspicious deaths and the theft of what seemed a very large sum of money.

It was going to take a long time for life to return to normal.

SUNDAY

Becky managed to persuade the owners of Lavender Cottage to let her and Sam stay there for another two weeks. She didn't tell them why this was necessary. However, it was the owners' policy never to allow pets in the Cottage, so Ben continued to live with Gwynedd and Dave in the bungalow. Many years before, Dave had sworn he'd never have a dog again, but it hadn't taken long for Ben to wag his way into the old man's affections. Sam's arm began to heal, again. Half term ended and Gwynedd went back to school. She had a tale to tell, but she was reluctant to tell it. There was still the one small detail that she had withheld from the police.

MONDAY

Gwynedd had promised Sam that she would call at the Cottage every day after school, though he had seen it as more of a threat than a promise. On only the second visit, she brought up the subject of what would happen to Azim's money. She was not satisfied with the official attitude and statements: that persons were 'helping with inquiries', that 'others were involved' and, most of all that 'the matter would follow the usual process'. She wanted to know exactly what would happen to the money.

"Bet the police keep it," she said.

Sam said he didn't think they were allowed to.

"So, does Azim get it back?"

"It's not his money."

"He was the one that looked after it, him and Saqui."

"Azim stole the money in the first place," said Sam. "It's not his."

"It ought to be. Some of it at least. It's like Treasure Trove. He should keep half of it."

Sam didn't think it worked that way. "If I still had my phone, we could look up online what happens to money that's been recovered from a crime."

"OK," she said. "Let's leave it for the moment."

Sam was surprised that Gwynedd should suddenly give up like that. He wondered if she knew something about the money that he didn't. If he hadn't still been so tired, he would have challenged her on it. But, right now, he hadn't enough energy.

*

When she got back to the bungalow, Gwynedd sat at her dressing table. She stared at herself in the mirror. Now you got to decide, she told herself. There's that packet of money you took when there weren't no more room in Saqui's delivery box, and you've, like, hidden it in the bottom drawer here and not looked at it. No one knows how much was in that packet when you took it. No one knows how much is in it now. No one knows it exists. Go on, girl, count it. Just to see how much is there.

She took the packet from the bottom drawer. She stacked the few 50 notes in one pile, the 20 notes in another. As she did so, she thought of Azim.

"Yes, please, for me," she said, and for a moment she thought she was going to cry. She pulled herself together and began to count the notes.

She counted them once, and couldn't believe how much money she had. She counted them again.

There were eight £50 notes and forty-two £20 notes.

She had one thousand two hundred and forty pounds.

TUESDAY

The next day, with an envelope containing the eight £50 notes and five of the £20 notes stuck to her waist with duct tape, Gwynedd spent six and a half tense hours at Llandrindod High School. It was not a PE day so she didn't have to change her clothes. Even so, there was often a physicality attached to her days at school that was ill-suited to hiding a near fortune on her person.

Immediately school was over, she hurried out. She had arranged for Saqui to do her a favour. He was to take her to Builth Wells on the back of his scooter. There he was, waiting for her in the road outside the school. She waved and rushed over to him. He gave her the spare helmet, and they set off.

The journey to Builth took only twenty minutes. In that time, Gwynedd hung on to Saqui while she wrestled with her conscience. It wasn't really her money. Even the fact that she was about to spend a great deal of it on someone else didn't make it legally hers. But if she bought a new smartphone for Sam, to replace the one that he'd lost in the back of Kyle's car, her hope was that it would make Sam realise how much she loved him. It was an enormous sum of money – the equivalent of fifty or so nights' work at the Chippie, two hundred hours of cooking, cleaning, mopping floors, fetching and carrying. And there were so many other things she could do with the money. Buy Dave a decent TV for one thing. Buy a new cooker for the bungalow. Buy some new clothes – outfits that would dazzle Sam. Maybe even have a shower installed in the bathroom at the bungalow. And save all the rest of the money for when she and Sam lived together.

They reached the shop. Gwynedd told Saqui to wait outside.

Her feet took her into the shop. Her hand reached out for the printed piece of paper giving the details of the model she thought Sam would like. Her feet took her to the counter, and her shaking hand held out the little piece of paper.

The man behind the counter smiled as he took the piece of paper. He unlocked a glass cabinet and took out what seemed too small a box to hold five hundred pounds worth of anything. He opened the box, took out the smartphone, caressed it, and praised it.

*

Dave was used to her being late, but not with her being more than an hour late. It was his first afternoon looking after Ben. He and the dog had got on well together, but Dave wasn't going to admit that to Gwynedd.

"The bloody dog's been scratching at the door all afternoon."

"Why didn't you take him out then? Give him a walk?"

"I was waiting for you. Waiting to make sure you weren't being kidnapped again."

"No," she said. "No one was interested this afternoon."

He aimed a blow at her with his stick. It wouldn't have hit her anyway, but Ben grabbed it in his mouth and pulled it out of Dave's hands.

"See," he said. "Everyone's on your side. No one's on mine."

He sounded like a child.

"I'm on your side," she said. "Haven't really got much choice. Tell you what, I'll get you a cup of tea, and a piece of cake. Then I'm off to see Sam."

"You takin' Ben with you?"

"Not this time."

"Special walk, is it? Not one suitable for dogs?"

"I don't know," she said. "And I might not tell you when I come back."

She wanted to make clear that she might be gone for some time.

Dave understood. "Take your time, love. Don't mind me or Ben. We'll be fine."

She kissed the top of his head.

*

She and Sam walked by the river, past the derelict buildings and the ruins of the castle. It seemed an age ago that they had broken into the house and found the £50 note. They were different versions of themselves then. That was what growing up was all about; finding a new version of yourself, one that fitted more comfortably than the one that you had grown out of.

Gwynedd was carrying a small bag. She was nervous about what Sam might say when she showed him what was inside, and what he might say when, if, she told him that she loved him. Sam didn't ask what was in the bag. She waited until they were settled on the big rock they called the Throne before she opened the bag. He felt inside it with his good hand and pulled out a handful of notes.

"What the hell is this?" he said.

"It's what was left of the money. The notes that wouldn't fit into Saqui's pizza delivery box that night on the cliffs. I kept it."

She knew what he was going to say.

"You must give it to the police," he said.

She longed to tell him how she had battled with her conscience in the mobile phone shop in Builth. How she had so wanted to buy him the smartphone because of how she felt for him, but her conscience had defeated her. She had lost the battle, and tears of defeat had trickled down her cheeks. But she knew she mustn't tell him any of that. She must show Sam that she was honest and responsible. But, though she did so wish she could tell him how much she had wanted to spend £500 on a present for him, she knew that would be cheating – trying to have your moral cake and eat it.

"Come on, then," he said.

"Where are we going?"

275

"To the police station."

He was looking at her in a strange way. She thought it was because he didn't trust her to hand over the money, and that thought hurt. She was surprised when he gave a little laugh.

"What's funny?"

"I just remembered how we found that first £50 note down here, immediately after we'd kissed and you said we should go on kissing all night..."

"And in the morning we'd be millionaires." She finished the sentence for him.

"Not too late to give it a try," he said.

"So long as I mind your arm."

ONE MONTH LATER

It was called an Immigration Remand Centre, three words that didn't make much sense to Azim even when one of the other inmates translated them for him. It was not a bad place. The grown-ups didn't beat you or kick you. The food was good, by Azim's standards. You didn't have to work like a slave. Azim spent his mornings learning English and his afternoons playing football. Learning English was hard. Playing football was great. Azim had a natural ability, and a pushy determination. He always played striker. In every game, his excited voice could be heard, calling for the ball: 'Yes, please, for me!'

He didn't know where the Centre was. Clearly, it was a long way from the Welsh mountains that he had crossed on foot, and from Saqui and all his other friends. He was getting used to the idea that he would never see any of them again. Saqui had already sent him a food parcel, with a letter that said Azim's enemies were dead and there was nothing more to worry about. Saqui wanted Azim to come back to Rhayader, but the staff at this place called a Centre told Azim that this was impossible. As Azim didn't know how to write, Saqui never received a reply and assumed that his food parcel had never arrived. Saqui sent no more.

The staff had asked Azim a great many questions when he first arrived. They wanted to know about his Uncle – where he lived, what he did, the names of the people he'd paid to transport Azim to UK. Azim didn't know the answers to any of these questions. All he could tell his questioners was that Uncle lived in a large house, across the street from a coffee shop, and near where the school had been before the Taliban bombed it.

He had a certain prestige among the other young inmates. The story had got around that, once upon a time, Azim had possessed the wealth of fables – hundreds and hundreds of thousands of pounds. The story grew and grew. Two killers wanted to get their hands on the fortune. They had chased Azim all over UK. No, there had been four killers. No, it had been an entire gang of murderers, guns blazing, and Azim had escaped from them by pinning himself under a truck… by stealing a motorbike… hijacking a Mercedes… by diving off a cliff into a stormy sea…

At first, Azim denied all these ridiculous claims, but after a couple of weeks he gave up. Let the others lads in the Centre believe what they wanted. He was OK. Life in the Centre was cool.

But, oh, how he missed his goats.

AND AFTERWARDS

Sunil woke up, hoping it had all been a bad dream. But no, this was real. He was still in this bad place they called 'The Farm', and still a slave to these bad men.

It was dark. It was cold. He pulled the rough blanket tight up under his chin. He was frightened. The whole Farm was run on fear. Yesterday the man they called the Chief had made all the kids who worked in the kitchen parade before him. He had shouted at them. Sunil didn't understand a word, but he knew the Chief was threatening them. Later, one of the older boys told Sunil it was all to do with a kid who'd escaped only ten days ago with a whole lot of the Chief's money… it was said to be millions of pounds…

How long had he been here? Others had been here before him, and they had cut deep scratches in the wall. Jo figured they had made one scratch for each day they'd been here. The scratches were in blocks of five, and Sunil had done the same. He reached out from the grimy mattress and counted with a finger the deep scratches he'd made in the wall with a small knife he'd stolen from the kitchen. One scratch for each day. Ten days. He tried to work out how many days it was since he'd left his home thousands of miles away…

If you want to read of the earlier frightening adventures of
Sam and Gwynedd, then read *A Dog's Life*

It s a Dog's Life:
Introduction

The tyres hissed and bumped on the wet road as the vehicle sped up the valley into the Green Desert of Wales. Thanks to power steering, the driver needed only one hand on the wheel to guide the vehicle through the twists and turns of a road that skirted boulders, clung to the high ground where it crossed the marshy plateau, and stroked its way round the massive curves of the mountains themselves. The rain didn't bother him. He knew this road well. Though he was driving with only sidelights that barely lit the road for more than a metre or two, he made good speed.

There were other vehicles on the road, other drivers taking care not to draw attention to themselves, though only the Devil knew who'd be on the lookout for anything odd in this wilderness, at this hour.

'Bit of a crowd tonight,' said the driver.

His mate, sitting beside him, laughed. 'It's a growing sport.'

'But you don't get this on TV Saturday afternoon, do you,' said the driver. 'Not even on Sky Sports.'

'That'll be the day.'

The driver muttered a curse at a sheep that had wandered into the road. 'You packed everything?' he asked.

'Everything. Netting…buckets and sponges'

'Sawdust?'

'Sawdust…first-aid box…After all, we don't want any *unnecessary* suffering, do we?' They both laughed.

'Lanterns?'

'…and the scales. And the shotties.'

They laughed again.

'Gotta have the shotties. And we've got the contestants nice and cosy in their crates.'

'Ready and waiting. Warm-ups and main attractions.' The driver changed gear as they came to a steep bend, then accelerated along a rare straight stretch of road. They were in a hurry to reach the destination and set up the arena. It would be a long and busy night – with risks attached. But, if all went as planned, there'd be plenty of cash to take home in the early hours of the morning – a fair exchange for a corpse or two dropped down a disused mineshaft…

It s a Dog's Life: Extract

Gwynedd and Sam blunder into the world of illegal dog fights run by the weird and sinister Len and Mags. Sam's pet dog Ben is stolen by the villains who plan to feed the dog, alive, to raise the bloodlust in their own savage killer dogs. Gwynedd and Sam take desperate steps to rescue Ben, but are pursued by the villains across the mountains of central Wales. Just when Sam and Gwynedd think they're safe…

A voice ordered them to stay where they were. It was an unnecessary command, for they were both incapable of movement. For what seemed a long time there was no sound save the rushing of the river and the unsettled snuffling of the sheep. Then they heard the voice again, from behind the light, not as loud this time, but more sinister.

'All right, Len. We've got them. Now… what the hell do we do with them?'

'We don't do anything. Beauty'll see to them.'

'No, Len.'

'Every dog must have his day, Mags, and this is Beauty's day.'

It was the end. Both Gwynedd and Sam knew that. Even if they had had any strength left, there was no way for them to turn. The road, the river, the little grove of trees... this was their entire world. This was all they had. This was where it would end.

'Let's get the business done and get the hell out.' Len bent down to unfasten Beauty's chain.

'God Almighty! You can't let the dog do it!'

The dog was already over-excited. Len's fingers were cold, and he was having difficulty unfastening the chain round Beauty's neck. He swore as he worked at the clip, and muttered to himself.

'All me and Beauty are after is satisfaction... Stand still!... And a clear conscience. You can't shoot kids and get away with it... What's the matter with this bloody clip... Still, damn you!... That's why we're not having any shooting, Mags...'

Mags pulled at his arm. 'Please, Len. Let the kids go!'

'You read about it all the time in the papers. Kid killed by savage dog... Do you hear me?... Don't you bloody *move*!...'

There was no way of telling from his snarling voice if the man was talking to his dog or his wife. All three were losing control.

'But with Beauty here... Still, I said!!!!...'

The more he swore, the more he tugged at the chain, the more both Mangles screamed and shouted at each other, the wilder the dog became. The shivering children could still see little of what was happening, but they heard the rattle of the dog's chain and the snarling of the dog. They also heard, dimly, the uneasy snuffling and bleating of nearby sheep. The sheep had sensed the presence of dog for some time. Now, the roaring and shouting and Beauty's growling made them take fright. They started moving in clumsy panic along the wire fence that separated their field from the road.

Sam felt Gwynedd's cold hand reach into his. He grasped it tightly.

At last Len had managed to release the catch. 'Go get 'em, Beauty!'

There was a cry of horror from Mags. The light snapped off, and Sam and Gwynedd were blinded by the darkness.